My Best Friend's Dad

COURTNEY ROBERTS

Copyright © 2024 by Courtney Roberts

All rights reserved.

No part of this publication may be reproduced, distributed, or transmitted in any form or by any means, including photocopying, recording, or other electronic or mechanical methods, without the prior written permission of the publisher, except as permitted by U.S. copyright law. For permission requests, contact the publisher at courtneyrobertsauthor@gmail.com.

The story, all names, characters, and incidents portrayed in this production are fictitious. No identification with actual persons (living or deceased), places, buildings, and products is intended or should be inferred.

ISBN: 9798884336216

First Edition: 2024

Contents

1. Callie — 1
2. Callie — 5
3. Callie — 11
4. Callie — 17
5. Alex — 30
6. Callie — 35
7. Callie — 43
8. Alex — 55
9. Callie — 64
10. Alex — 74
11. Alex — 84
12. Callie — 90

13.	Alex	100
14.	Callie	111
15.	Alex	118
16.	Callie	128
17.	Callie	133
18.	Alex	145
19.	Callie	150
20.	Callie	161
21.	Alex	165
22.	Alex	172
23.	Alex	180
24.	Callie	186
25.	Alex	197
26.	Callie	210
27.	Callie	223
28.	Alex	233
29.	Callie	243
30.	Alex	255
31.	Callie	263
32.	Alex	275

33. Alex	286
34. Alex	301
35. Callie	312
36. Callie	319
37. Callie	329
38. Callie	332
Epilogue	342
Thank You	350
About the Author	351

Chapter One

Callie

I've never been skiing in all my life. So why the hell I agreed to this trip is beyond me. Most days, I'm lucky to make it through a full twenty-four hours without tripping over my two left feet or walking into a wall. It's for sure killing myself on two wooden sticks in the mountains of Montana wasn't my idea of celebrating the breakup of a lifetime, but my bestie insisted this was the getaway I needed. So, I caved.

She better be right.

"Are you having fun yet?" Jade shoved my arm, her puffer jacket swishing as she walked to the front door of our cabin, ready for take off.

"I'm still not seeing what's so sweet about Sugar Slope Lodge. I imagined something a lot more like Candy Land." I winked, pulling my chocolate waves into a bun.

"Oh Callie, get out and enjoy the fresh air! It's exhilarating!"

"Flying down a snow covered mountain with no brakes?" I winced. "Don't worry about retrieving my remains. Just leave me."

"Always the pessimist." Jade's hand disappeared into a green glove.

"Can you blame me?" I scoffed, the wound of my fiance's betrayal crushing my heart. It was barely beating anymore.

"Travis put you through hell, Callie. Leave his ass there where it belongs," Jade encouraged, her bright auburn locks glowing under a pink headband.

"I know. You're right." A burning sob seized my throat, wanting out, but I wouldn't let it. "It's just hard to pretend that I'm happy, Jade. I want to have fun. I do. But my heart is broken."

"I know, Cals. I know." Jade wrapped her arms around me, bringing me back to reality. "And we can go home right now if you want."

"Really?"

"Mm-hm." She pulled away with a smirk. "We can take the next flight to North Carolina on what would have been your wedding weekend, stare at all of the dying flowers and stale wedding cake, and cry."

I rolled my eyes, getting her point.

"Or," she went on, handing me a coat. "We can totally forget that son of a bitch and give this weekend a facelift."

I nodded, tearing up a little, but not because of Travis. Because I had the absolute best friend on the freaking planet. I didn't deserve her.

"So, what's it gonna be?" Jade curled her lips and popped a ruddy brow, already suspecting my answer.

I slid my arms into the winter coat, blinking rapidly to keep the tears at bay. "A facelift sounds nice."

Jade cracked up and cheered, putting on her ski boots and skis. I slowly followed suit, trying to remember everything the instructor told us when we arrived yesterday during our first lesson, not that Jade needed it. But I desperately did.

Grabbing our ski poles, we counted down from five to one like a couple of silly school girls and let the mountain take us away, thankfully not too fast down her slope.

I copied my bestie, keeping my knees bent with a slight forward lean as we picked up a little speed, aiming my skis in the direction we wanted to go. Luckily, the ski lift was straight ahead, and I remembered the snowplough technique to stop, drawing the tips of my skis together while my heels spread obnoxiously apart.

"You look great!" Jade called out, and I belly laughed, closing my eyes as an icy gust flew past me, causing me to lose my balance and face plant into the cold white stuff, coming out looking like a damn snowman.

"Oh my God! You asshole!" Jade pointed her ski pole and screamed at the top of her lungs, offering her hand. "Are you okay, Cals? That guy didn't even see you!"

"Yeah," I spit out some ice, tasting a little blood. Still, despite the painfully embarrassing fall, I was able to laugh it off and take Jade's hand, not at all meaning to drag her down with me, but nevertheless, that's what happened.

"Oh shit!" Jade fell forward, and there was no stopping it. She crashed hard next to me and squealed, passersby gawking at a couple of goofballs who were laughing so hard no sound came out.

"Timberrr!" I whacked Jade with my glove and somehow managed to sit up, the two of us wheezing in hysterics.

"How about some cocoa and a hot tub?" Jade asked with snow packed in her goggles. I cracked up harder than ever and wiped her lenses clean, my stomach stinging from the cold and laughter.

"Yes," I barely muttered. "That sounds nice."

Chapter Two

Callie

The smile on my face was as frozen as the icicles drooping from the windows of Polar Pub, Jade's retelling of our catastrophic skiing adventure just as hilarious as the event itself. I cradled my steamy mug of hot chocolate and sipped as she cackled, snuggling in the warmth of my kelly green turtleneck sweater, praying no one in the restaurant saw.

"I think that was a sign from the universe." I set the chunky mug down on the glossy tabletop. "Skiing is not for me."

"Oh Callie, you were doing great before that douchebag knocked you on your ass! You'll get it next time!"

I tilted my head, squinting. "Easy for you to say, ice queen. Since your dad bought the lodge, you've become a pro."

Jade shook her strawberry bun, swallowing a spoonful of soup. "A pro? Hardly!"

"I guess you've taught me that it's never too late to learn something new. Although, thirty is pushing it."

"Thirty is when the fun begins, Cals. Trust me," Jade insisted, eyeing a group of men at a nearby booth. "Trust. Me."

I curled my lips, savoring the last drop of cocoa. "In that case, I'm going to have to take your word for it."

"You never know, you just might have a date for your Valentine's birthday this year."

I snickered, "Cupid will have to work overtime to make that miracle happen, I'm afraid."

Jade raised one eyebrow, pointing her spoon. "A lot can happen in a month."

I pushed the negativity away momentarily, deciding to think of the good that could happen instead. "I suppose you're right."

I reached for my wallet when Jade waved her hand over the table. "No. Do not pay. I told you. This trip is on me."

"How much is your dad charging you, anyway?" I teased, noticing a bumblebee puffer jacket through the glass doors of the pub, Jade finishing her last bite of tomato bisque.

"Not a damn cent." She clapped, and I snickered as the sunflower shade pulled my gaze again, the form-fitted coat practically painted across the chest of one of the tallest men in the pub, his entire head covered with a black ski mask, however.

"Oh, my God! I think that's the asshole who knocked you down!" Jade whispered and dabbed her lips with a napkin.

"Shhh! We don't know that!" I hissed back.

"You deserve an apology."

"Jade Ellen Harrington," I begged. "Please! For the love of God, don't say a word."

"Callie Jo Harper." My bestie crossed her arms and studied the man from afar as he ordered coffee, scrunching her lips to the side. "I'm not promising that."

"I was in the way. It wasn't his fault."

Jade's eyeballs popped, and she tossed her napkin down. "Oh, I'm definitely saying something now."

"No!" I exclaimed under my breath as she turned in her seat with her arm in the air like we were back in fifth grade asking permission to use the restroom.

"Excuse me!"

"Jade, I swear to God—"

The man's head spun in our direction as he received the coffee cup from the barista, and he tugged the bottom portion of the mask down, walking our way. I sank into my chair, mortified with every step he took closer, about to crawl under the damn table.

"Hey! I think you ran into my friend!" Jade called, her hand forming a C at her mouth. "Your mama not teach you any manners or what?"

"Dammit Jade." I covered my face, looking down, feeling a towering presence suddenly over me.

Jade's tone instantly changed, laughter on the tip of her tongue as I slammed my lashes closed, my brown waves wilting as she asked in a loud voice, "Dad!?"

"And just what are you accusing me of?" a deep, raspy voice returned her question with a question, and I slowly slid my hand down, peering up as Mr. Harrington pulled the top of his mask off, choppy silver hair matching the stubble on his cold, red cheeks.

"You made Callie fall! Didn't you even see what you did?" Jade gestured toward me, and my lips parted, stunned.

"No way. Are you kidding me?" Mr. Harrington set his coffee cup down and removed his gloves, offering his giant hand. "Callie, I am so sorry. Forgive me."

I was redder than Jade's soup and reached for his hand, my tiny fingers disappearing into his hot grasp. "No worries. It was bound to happen sooner or later."

"No, girlfriend. It wasn't," Jade interrogated her dad some more. "She was doing great until someone flew by and knocked her on her ass."

I slid my hand away and offered a half grin, wanting to disappear. "You are making a bigger deal of this than it was."

"Not to mention, I fell in the process too." Jade drummed her fingertips on the table, showing no mercy.

"Like a couple of dominoes." I tried laughing it off and met Mr. Harrington's icy blues, noticing the tiniest dimples form around his mouth as his lashes creased, his jawline looking like it was sculpted by Michelangelo himself.

"Callie, I cannot say how sorry I am. Truly. When I'm skiing, sometimes I completely zone out." He raked through his damp locks, his bicep flexing under the coat. "I had no idea I caused such a disaster. I'm—"

"Ashamed of yourself?" Jade pressed, and I felt the heat in my cheeks sizzle.

"Very," he admitted. "It's not every day my daughter and her best friend get to have a girls weekend like this. I hope I didn't put a damper on your trip."

"Of course not. It's a beautiful resort. I'm excited to be here since," I stopped myself, not wanting to mention Travis's name.

"Since her life has taken a dramatic positive turn." Jade winked, and I fiddled with my fingers, the crackling fireplace mimicking the nerves popping up my spine.

"Well, cheers." Mr. Harrington picked up his cup and sipped. "I hope you'll enjoy the rest of your stay with us,

Callie. If there's anything I can do to make your visit more comfortable, please let me know."

Jade stood from the table and gave her father a side hug, his arm folding around her shoulder as she said, "Thanks, Dad. Believe me. We will let you know."

"Oh, I don't doubt it," he laughed. "Bye girls."

"Bye," I barely breathed, watching him leave, more embarrassed than the fall that I couldn't seem to look away.

Chapter Three

Callie

Evening came, and we followed through with our hot tub plans, the jets rumbling against our backs under the starry night sky. My glass of strawberry merlot warmed me on the inside as the steamy bath thawed my muscles, the little ball lights draped around our cabin deck like twinkling stars themselves.

"Mmm," Jade swallowed. "This is heaven."

I clinked my glass to hers, the coffee wisps around my face curling from the steam. "Now, that is something I will agree to."

Jade closed her eyes and tilted her head back, letting out the most pleasant sigh, "I'm so happy you're here, Cals."

"Me too." I let the bubbly water run over both shoulders and met my best friend's warm gaze, the wine relaxing me all the more.

We studied the diamond sky as the moon beamed in all its glory, taking in the splendor of the heavens. I couldn't help but feel like a speck in the universe at that moment and wondered if my life would ever shine as bright, ashamed at the time I wasted on Travis.

"Not that I want to bring up his name again, but have you heard from Travis at all?" Jade winced, practically reading my mind.

I didn't want to admit the truth, but couldn't hide anything from her. "Unfortunately, yes. He's texted quite a bit."

"I thought you blocked him."

"Believe me, I will. I just want to make sure I get all my things back. I haven't been back to the house since—"

"Since you found that no good, sorry excuse for a man getting his toothpick gobbled by his assistant in *your* bedroom? Not to mention on Thanksgiving." Jade smacked her lips.

"That would be correct," I huffed, the image of my fiance leaning against the wall with his coworker on her knees sucking him off forever burned in my brain. For a hot minute, they never even noticed I was watching, her blonde mane bobbing so hard and fast I wondered how she was breathing.

"Mmm. I would have killed a bitch," Jade snarled. "Then beat *her* ass next."

I met her amusing stare and cracked up, clinking my glass to hers again in agreement. "It was a sight to behold. One thing that helps me sleep at night is knowing how disappointed Tracy must have been when she saw his dick for the first time. More than the size, what it's capable of."

"Yes girl. Keep going." Jade poured another glass. "This is the trash talk I live for."

"All I can say is she better invest in some vibrators because that man couldn't get a woman off if his life depended on it," I scoffed, thinking of my underwear drawer.

Jade stared at me wide-eyed. "Never?"

"Never."

Jade blew a loud *shewww* and dipped her shoulders under the water. "I should have pinged him for a loser in high school. Sorry, sis."

I shook my head, taking a deep breath, contemplating it all. "No, he really wasn't that bad in high school. A little cocky but at least back then he seemed to care."

Jade frowned, letting me ramble on.

"Things really took a turn after college, I think. He landed his dream job of being a financial advisor and month by month I watched him slip away. He became so wrapped up in material things, I hardly recognized him anymore."

"Oh, Cals."

"Financial stability is one thing, but it was like he was never satisfied, always comparing himself with the wealthiest clients." I shook my head. "You know, it's pathetic thinking about now, but when Travis got his promotion last June, I was so proud despite all of the bullshit I was swimming in with him. His company was hosting a party in his honor, so I went all out. I spent a stupid amount of money on a new dress and just as much on nails and hair." I gulped, tears stinging my lids. "I wanted him to be just as proud of me too."

"Callie," Jade comforted with a soft brush on my arm.

"His face said it all when he got home from work to pick me up for the party. He was disappointed." I flicked a lone tear off my cheek. "I spent the rest of the night at a lonely table while Travis gave an earth-shattering speech and mingled. Even then, I noticed Tracy. She was obnoxiously close to him that night. And likely had been for a while."

Jade set her glass aside and wrapped her arm around me, resting her head on my shoulder. "She can have him, Cals."

"I thought the same thing," I scoffed under my breath. "But clearly there must be trouble in paradise for him to be texting me. I guess he found out the grass wasn't greener."

"He'll regret it for the rest of his life, Callie." Jade sat up, steam curling between us. "Any man would be honored to have you on their arm. He blew it."

"Yes. He did." I took a breath. "Thankfully, I was able to walk away without any ties. No kids. No pets. The house is in his name."

"Check, check, check." Jade smiled.

"I do have to go back sometime though to pack the rest of my stuff."

"Girl, I'd burn that place to the ground first."

I couldn't help but laugh, my life's walking cliche only giving me two options. Face it with humor or drown myself in tears. "Well, I could do that, I guess. But it would be hard to teach the kiddos from prison."

"You're right. They would miss the hell out of you." Jade reached for her wine. "Not worth it."

I nodded, finishing my glass.

"Are you still working remote?"

"Yeah. I love it. It just works, you know. I can pre-record my lessons and have set times for live streams. I'm not tied anywhere, really. And that is so freeing right now with everything going on."

"Are you really thinking about leaving North Carolina?" Jade curled her lip under.

"No, of course not. Although, my mother is driving me insane. I really need to get my own place."

"Hey, I have a spare room with your name on it."

I knew my bestie would let me stay with her for as long as I wanted, but our lives were very different. Her bubbly personality thrived on entertaining and socializing while I longed for quiet nights with a movie playing or getting lost in a book.

"Aw, you are the sweetest. I actually have my eye on a couple of places. You know me." I shrugged.

"Yes, I do. You need your downtime. I get it," Jade acknowledged with a soft grin. "But still, the offer stands."

"I appreciate that more than you know. Thank you." I mustered a smile through a quivering lip. "For this trip. For being my friend. For everything."

Jade wrapped her arms around me, squeezing me tight. "This is going to be the best year of your life, Cals. I just know it."

"Yeah?" I whispered over her shoulder. "I sure hope so. I've wasted so many years on Travis. Twelve. Twelve fucking years."

"I know. But not this one," Jade encouraged, her sparkling green eyes full of hope. "I'm so excited for you, Callie."

A bright shooting star sailed over our heads, a sign from the universe if I had ever seen one. Thankfully, we spotted it before it disappeared and gazed up in absolute awe and wonder, Jade's sweet nod and big smile bringing my emotions to the surface, hope rising in the pit of my despair, the silver lining a little clearer now.

Chapter Four

Callie

Once our fingers and toes looked like prunes, Jade and I changed into pajamas and hopped into bed. She was snoring in no time, the wine and hot tub lulling her into a deep sleep. And while I desperately tried to do the same, I only ended up tossing and turning as the hours passed, dreamland nowhere in sight.

As if that wasn't awful enough, my phone lit up on the nightstand, the harsh light blinding me as I squinted to read that it was shortly after midnight. Someone else apparently wasn't sleeping either.

Travis

> Baby? Are you up?

> ...

Don't do it, Cals, Jade's voice shouted in my mind. Ugh. Dammit.

> I am now...and I'm not your baby.

Okay, maybe I lied a little.

Travis
> Fuck, Callie. I miss you.

> I can't do this right now, Travis.

Travis
> I'm staring at our engagement photos. I can't stop thinking about tomorrow.

> What about it?

Travis
> It wasn't supposed to be this way. We were supposed to be getting married.

> Well, I'm not the one who fucked that up, am I?

Travis
> ...

Unbelievable.

Travis
> I know I messed up, baby. Please. Where are you? Can we talk?

> That's none of your business anymore. I don't want to talk. I'll be in touch at some point to get the rest of my things.

Travis
> I love you, Callie. I'm so sorry.

I groaned under my breath and clicked the phone off, any hope of falling asleep completely gone. By this point, the alcohol had long worn off, and my stomach was gurgling in hunger, the only options at the cabin being a pack of peanut butter crackers or a bag of gummies.

Now, I knew it was late. And beyond freezing outside. But I needed to burn off some steam and grab a quick bite. Especially if I wanted to get any sleep.

Jade was still snoozing under her quilt, so I tiptoed out of the bedroom toward the front door, slipping on my boots and coat and peeping my head into the winter air, the sign to Polar Pub glowing almost as bright as the moon.

It was a short walk, but my nipples were practically slicing my shirt open by the time I made it inside, only a few guests sitting here and there. The bar was wide open, so I sat myself down, keeping my coat zipped, and waited to be served, reading over the menu covered in igloo drawings.

Mmm.

Snowbank burger and fries.

Don't mind if I do.

I glanced all around for a waiter or bartender and came up empty, wondering what was going on while my phone continued to vibrate in my pocket relentlessly.

> **Travis**
> I need you. Please forgive me. You're the only one I want.

I raked through my messy waves, feeling like a damn fool for ever falling for this man, let alone agreeing to marry him. After a few more pathetic texts, I tossed the phone down on the bar, mad as hell and all the more starving.

"Callie?"

His voice pulled my head up from the black screen, the most pleasant but unexpected surprise of the night thus far. "Mr. Harrington? What in the world are you doing here?"

He was beautifully dressed in a black long-sleeve sweater, thin but cutting right at his waist. The glint of a gold chain popped around his neckline, the same sparkle in his gaze as he looked at me and dried the inside of a glass, lips curving. "Well, I had a few employees call in, so here I am. The show must go on."

"Right." I relaxed on the stool, scanning the menu. "Is it too late to order? I can—"

"Order whatever you want," he insisted. "Please."

Heat painted my cheeks bright pink, and I pretended to study the menu some more, already knowing what I wanted. "How about the snowbank burger?"

"That's our most popular item. Good choice." He flashed a straight line of white teeth, short silver hair catching the light above him.

"Great," I breathed as my phone buzzed on the bartop. "I'll have that."

He rushed to the back and quickly returned with my meal, even going as far as to bring a glass of cold cider, setting each item carefully before me.

"Wow, this looks amazing, Mr. Harrington. Thank you so much."

He handed me a white paper straw. "Alex, please."

My belly fluttered, and I echoed, "Alex."

I watched him step away from the bar to check out the last remaining customers, sneaking glances as he counted cash back, ashamed at how long my eyes lingered on his fingers as they sifted through the bills, one in particular brushing his tongue when a couple of ones stuck together.

Dammit.

What in the fuck is wrong with me?

He's nearly fifty, for God's sake. Old enough to be my father. Screw the fact that he's drop-dead gorgeous with a kind heart and warm personality. None of that matters. This is wrong. So wrong. He's my best friend's dad. I'm guilty as sin for looking at him in any other way.

I forced my conflicting feelings down with the burger and fries, savoring every bite. The meal was scrumptious, but soon, I realized I was the only customer left in the pub as Alex moved toward the door and locked it, shutting off the sign. I quickly read my phone and realized the obvious. It was closing time.

"Shit, I'm so sorry." I stuffed a fry in my mouth and downed the last of the spicy cider, about to bolt when Alex moved closer, gliding behind the bar with ease.

"Take your time. Don't rush. I'll be here awhile," his voice was like sizzling butter, hot and smooth.

"I don't want to keep you." I pushed my plate to the side, and he set another tall glass of cider in front of me.

"Callie," he said my name, urging me to stay. "It's okay."

It's okay.

That's what I had told myself repeatedly for months since Travis and I broke up. It's okay. Everything is going to be okay. Some days, I truly believed it. Others, well, not so much.

I offered the smallest smile and sipped the refreshing drink as my phone went off again, only this time it was a call, not a text. Long vibrations rattled my device, and I quickly turned the screen over as Travis's name appeared, noticing that Alex saw it.

He pushed up his sleeves and wiped the bar as another chime went off. Voicemail. I shook my head and let out a frustrated sigh, deciding to turn the damn thing off for the night. Something I should have done hours ago.

"Are you alright?" Alex tossed a white towel over his shoulder, bright blues piercing right through me.

I wanted to make up an elaborate story about how I was perfectly fine and handling everything like a queen. That I didn't cry myself to sleep most nights or snoop on Travis's social media pages to see all the women who followed him. To proclaim that this was just a little bump in the road and that I was indeed *alright*.

But I wasn't.

I really wasn't.

"No," a jagged whisper split my mouth open, tears spilling over the brim of my lids without warning.

I covered my eyes in embarrassment, feeling like the damn room was on fire as heat soared into my face, my heart hammering so fast I should have died.

I heard soft footsteps and the subtle squeak of the leather stool next to me, a warm presence at my right, silent but immensely strong. Peering through the gaps in my fingers, I noticed his large hands on the bar top, loosely laced with bulging veins spidering through them, another choppy breath leaving me.

He never said a word.

Mustering up what little bit of dignity I had, I pulled my hands down and met his understanding eye, his half grin and dimple holding me hostage as he slid a napkin to me, the scent of cherry smoke captivating me just as much.

"Thank you." I dabbed my nose, salty slime running down the back of my throat. "I'm so sorry. I never meant to—"

A gentle rumble vibrated from his chest, and he locked his gaze on me harder, blue flecks dancing all over my face before he said, "That's the second time you've apologized to me tonight."

"I'm sorry." I realized what I said and laughed at myself, Alex cracking up a little too.

"You do not owe anyone an apology, Callie. You have every right to express what you are feeling." Alex sat taller. "You've been through hell. And rarely do we make it out of hell without shedding a few tears."

I stared at this man.

This beautiful fucking man.

"Jade told you, huh?" I was thankful for it, not having an ounce of energy to rehash the mortification.

Alex's jaw rippled, and he looked away a moment before back into my eyes. "Not the details. But yes. She said you needed this getaway because of your, um—"

"Cheating fiance?"

He cleared his throat, "Well, Jade used a few more expletives to describe him."

I laughed, drying the dew at the corners of my lashes. "Jade would be accurate."

"Was that him?" he asked, glancing at my phone.

"Yes." I nodded, tucking a chunk of hair behind my ear. "Tomorrow was supposed to be our wedding day."

Alex's chest swelled with air. "Oh."

"I guess Travis is regretting his life's choices." That damn picture popped into my brain again, the one where my soon-to-be husband was getting head from another woman.

"He'll regret it for the rest of his life, Callie." Alex's words mirrored Jade's and, like a shooting star, illuminated the darkness, a twinkle of light in the blackest of nights.

I absorbed what he said, blurting a little more than I planned. "You know, I'm surprised he's still reaching out to get back together. For so long, I was just a shadow in his world, something that always followed him around but never shined."

Alex swallowed, a shade of pain falling over his face. "Shame on him for never seeing what he had."

The air left my chest, and I shivered, barely breathing, "And what's that?"

He rose from his seat, and I felt his tall stature from behind, his words like a cloud of smoke all around me. "The sun."

I was too afraid to look into his eyes after that, too terrified to look at the man who had my stomach pummeling to the ground, my body quivering in response. Soon, I heard the purr of his zipper and panicked, feeling like a fool once I found the courage to look at him again, realizing he was putting on his coat.

"Let me walk you back." He slid on two gloves next, then a hat.

"No, I've troubled you enough for one night." I hopped off the stool and shoved my phone in my pocket. "It's a short walk."

"I know, but animals can still roam around at night. Please. I insist." Alex unlocked the door and propped it open with his foot, peering outside.

My legs were like gelatin on the way out, threatening to drop me with every step. I barely brushed past Alex as the winter air whipped against my cheeks, cooling the redness.

Soon, we were strolling toward my cabin under a blanket of stars, our boots crunching upon the snow in the stillness of the night. I stole another glance as we moved closer, a white cloud leaving Alex's lips into the chilly atmosphere as he looked up with the lightest dusting of snow sprinkling from the skies.

A white dot landed on Alex's cheek, and I instantly became jealous of that damn snowflake, wishing I could touch his skin and melt into it. God! No! What in the fucking hell, Callie? Shut up, brain. Shut the fuck up.

I suppose breakups really do fuck with your head and your heart. I was just hurting and vulnerable, right? That's all it was.

He brushed the wet spot from the gray stubble as we made it to the front door of the cabin, waiting like a gentleman for me to slip inside. It's for sure I was thanking God above that he couldn't hear my thoughts. I would have thrown myself off this damn mountain or let a hungry grizzly devour me whole if that were true.

"Thank you, Alex." I unlocked the door. "For everything."

"My pleasure, Callie." He stood with his hands in his pockets, wearing the sweetest smile.

"Oh, shit!" I realized I hadn't paid for my food and reached for some cash before handing it over. "I'm so sorry. My mind is a little aloof these days."

"Stop apologizing," he laughed, refusing my payment. "And you are Jade's guest. Absolutely not. Put your money away."

I did as he requested and took one step inside the toasty foyer, turning one last time. "If you say so."

He chuckled, nodding. "Goodnight, Callie. Sleep well."

"Goodnight, Alex." I offered a wave and closed the wooden door, praying Jade was still asleep.

Her snoring eased my fears.

Like a damn stalker, I stared through the front window as Alex walked back to the pub, my nosy ass not being able to stop gawking at his tight cheeks flexing with each step, wondering all the while what his thighs must look like, his waist, his...

Fuck.

I took off my coat and boots before jumping into bed, feeling beyond ashamed of myself. This was not okay. Not even a little okay. There was no way Alex was thinking anything like this about me. He was a gentleman, full of old-school chivalry and honor. Of course, there was nothing more than a platonic friendliness between us. And that was only because I was Jade's BFF.

He probably had a girlfriend or at least a special someone in his life. Someone his own age, for fuck's sake. God, I was such a gutter rat. A nasty, despicable woman and not to mention friend.

Dammit to hell.

Fuck you, Travis.

Fuck you for ruining me.

Chapter Five

Alex

It had been years since I last saw Callie, my daughter's twenty-first birthday party coming to mind. I was recently divorced and working non-stop to pay for Jade's college since her mother and I split. As happy as Jade was that night, I couldn't seem to pull myself out of the hole I was in, feeling as though I had lost my family...my everything.

Adultery never leaves you the same, no matter what people say. Sure, some couples work through it and become stronger than before. But you can't tell me that those suspicions ever go away once that trust is broken and betrayal slithers its ugly head into your life like a poisonous serpent, leaving you permanently scarred or dead.

That was me.

That was my marriage.

That was my life.

I remember the first time I caught my ex-wife, Marcy, cheating. Jade was a senior in high school, and we were supposed to meet at the house one particular evening to watch a play she was in. By the grace of God, I was able to cut out of work an hour earlier than usual and rushed home, excited that I would have time to shower and dress up to celebrate Jade's leading role in Romeo and Juliet.

The shower was taken, however.

By my wife.

And her dipshit boss.

That was most definitely the beginning of the end, as they say. However, the process of getting there took a lot longer for me. For years after the fact, I tried to be better, to be perfect for her. I worked my fingers to the bone and then some to make more money, to give her all she wanted. I set aside time every week for dates or romantic getaways to show her how important our marriage was. After work, I would stay up late doing laundry, dishes, or meal prepping to take the weight off. And still, with every effort I made to show my loyalty despite her infidelity, she wanted someone else.

What a relief when I realized it wasn't my fault that Marcy cheated. It wasn't because I was this awful husband or father that she chose to be unfaithful and *remain* unfaithful not only to me but to the family we made together. There was something very broken in Marcy that had nothing to do with me. I know that now. And while we aren't together anymore, I hope one day she will heal that wound within herself.

Sitting in bed, I reached for my laptop and opened the lid, the harsh light making me squint. I swiped my readers off the nightstand and slid them on as I typed Callie's name in the search engine.

C-a-l-l-i-e

H-a-r-p-e-r

Her social media page popped right up, and I scrolled through her photos, the most recent one being the most beautiful selfie, alone and without Travis. But the further back I went, the more countless photos of them I saw. Fuck. Callie had the most dazzling blue eyes I had ever seen. So radiant with the most subtle flecks of green woven in them. And while she smiled in every photo with Travis, her eyes told another story. One of loneliness and deep despair.

Oh, I've been there too.

I went back to the beginning, having seen quite enough of Travis's cocky smirk and dead gaze. Callie stared back at me now, wearing the same green sweater she had on tonight, red nails holding a coffee mug as her post wished all of her friends and family a very merry Christmas.

God, she was so loving even while drowning in her own misery.

I went to her *about* section and beamed when I read she was an online teacher for children, laughing a little at the quote she wrote about herself. *Being awkward is my superpower.* I spotted her birthdate and gushed all the more, never realizing it until now.

Valentine's Day.

I couldn't think of a more perfect day for her to come into this world.

Fuck.

What the hell was wrong with me?

She was Jade's best friend for God's sake. A lifelong friend. And here I was lusting after her, a woman younger than my daughter.

I sank into the pillows and threw an arm over my eyes, Callie's gorgeous face lighting up my brain. Her rich waves. The pouty cupid bow below her nose. Fuck. Her voice. That smile.

My dick swelled under the flannel sheets, wanting something it could never have. To ease the throbbing, I shucked my underwear and grabbed my cock, stroking slowly at first as the tip glistened.

"Fuck," I muttered, cursing myself as I imagined Callie riding me, hoping this quick fantasy was enough to get it out of my head for good.

I gradually picked up speed, moaning in my empty bedroom as I felt the familiar build that would inevitably launch me into euphoria. I imagined kissing her, holding her, pleasing her, and ultimately hearing my name roll off her tongue as she came with me.

"Fuck!" I groaned, ropes of come firing into my hand before I could fetch a towel. "Son of a bitch."

I collected myself the best I could and walked into the bathroom, deciding to grab a quick shower before bed. Hot beads of water sprayed over me and I contemplated drawing a bath and drowning myself at what had just happened. I thought rubbing one out would take the edge off of wanting Callie, but it only ignited my desire, making me want her more.

Chapter Six

Callie

The morning sun stirred me awake as metal clinking tugged my ear, Jade's voice following soon after, "Cals! You up yet?"

"I am now!" I yelled back, a smile on the tail end of my words.

"Good, bitch! We have an appointment!"

"We do? What do you mean?" I wandered into the kitchen and saw my bestie stirring hot tea, her smile making me feel guilty as fuck for imagining her dad as *daddy*.

"We are going to the spa!" Jade clapped, and my mouth fell open, completely surprised.

"Wait a minute. I thought we were just hanging out at the cabin today." I raised a brow, Jade smiling so hard her eyes wrinkled.

"I had to surprise you!" she laughed. "Don't worry, it's not far from the cabin. The resort has its own spa."

"Jade." I shook my head, feeling so undeserving of her kindness.

She approached me with open arms, and I fell into her hug, deciding right then and there to never think about Alex, er, Mr. Harrington, in a naughty way ever again.

"I love you, Cals."

"I love you too, Jade."

We ate a quick breakfast and ventured straight to the spa, the fresh scent of citrus hitting me as soon as we stepped through the glass doors. Instantly, we were swept away into dimly lit rooms and snuggled into warm beds as massage therapists entered and began their magic, almost putting me asleep again.

I savored every moment the kind woman spent on me, not realizing how much tension was living in my muscles until this experience. A breathy sigh slipped through my lips as more and more stress left my body, and ultimately I gave in to the sweetest surrender—relaxation.

For so long, I had neglected myself this way, never taking the time to do anything self-care related. And after Travis's fling, I spiraled into an even darker place where it took everything just to get out of bed some days.

This was the wake-up call I needed.

I deserved to be taken care of.

I was worthy of being pampered.

I didn't have to do a thing to earn it.

I was enough.

Once the massage was over, I sat straight up as tears rolled over my cheeks, Jade noticing right away and coming to my shoulder. "Cals? Are you okay?"

"Yes." I blotted my lashes. "That was wonderful, Jade. You don't know how much I needed that. Something released."

"It's powerful, isn't it?"

"Yes." I sniffled. "Thank you so much."

"You're welcome. I wanted to do something extra special today before our flight back home. Something that would leave you refreshed and rejuvenated."

"It did that and more." I slid out of bed, wearing nothing but a towel wrap.

Jade flashed a bright smile and gathered her clothes before pointing at the door. "I'm going to use the bathroom and change. I'll be right back."

"Yeah, sounds great." I waited for her to leave before dropping my towel, my breasts prickling as the air kissed them.

Quickly, I dressed and grabbed my phone, remembering I hadn't listened to Travis's voicemail.

Delete.

Damn, that felt good.

Jade was itching for some fried food, so back to the Polar Pub we went, absolutely no sign of her father anywhere. I wrestled with a wave of relief crossed with a shadow of disappointment and ultimately came to terms that maybe it was for the best.

"I know we have to leave in just a bit to make it to the airport, but I really want to say goodbye to my dad. I'm not sure when I'll get to make it back to Montana. Business is booming."

"Well, you are *the* greatest event planner of all time." I winked. "Of course. Take your time. I'm going to go pack."

"Thanks, love." Jade suspected nothing whatsoever. "I'll see you back at the cabin in a half hour!"

I watched my bestie slip out of the restaurant and veer right, curiosity getting the better of me as I observed a little closer, noticing her knocking on a quaint cabin for one. One glance at Alex's silver wisps in the open frame was all it took, and I made a beeline toward the exit, marching in the opposite direction.

God, this was so stupid.

Right?

Was I a coward for not telling him goodbye too?

I'm not sure if *coward* was the right word. I think the harsh reality was that I was fearful. How could I be around Alex and Jade not pick up on the fact that I was crushing on her dad? She knew me too well. Better than I knew myself sometimes.

So, like a turtle ducking in its shell, I disappeared into our cabin and stuffed my clothes into a small carry-on, remembering Alex's words that damn near paralyzed me.

The sun.

My heart catapulted, and my cheeks turned blood-red as Alex's words played over and over again in my head. I analyzed everything. His tone. His mannerisms. Any clue that would lead me to believe that it *wasn't* platonic.

Shit, I really needed to get a grip.

Why was I looking for hope in a hopeless situation? This could never be nor should I want anything else. I needed to get the hell out of here. North Carolina was where I belonged with my mom, *for now*, my students, and my future. Not in Montana. Surely not with Jade's dad.

I was carrying my luggage to the door when Jade twisted the knob from the outside and stomped the snow off her boots before exclaiming, "Dad's taking us to the airport!"

"What?" I noticed Alex's car in the background, his bright coat moving to the trunk where he opened the lid. "I thought we were calling a cab like before."

"Well, Dad offered. Besides, those drivers creep me the hell out." Jade shook her ruddy ponytail and scanned the cabin for anything she left behind as I struggled to scrape my tongue off the floor, Alex's form taking up the empty doorframe seconds later.

"Hey, Callie." He glanced at me and pointed to the bags at my feet. "Those yours?"

"Oh. Yeah." I flushed, about to die.

"I'll get them for you." He scooped them up with one hand and stacked them carefully in the trunk as Jade looped an arm through mine, gazing at the mountains with a curled lip.

"Until we meet again, Montana." She beamed, and I followed her to Alex's car, creeping into the backseat as she took shotgun.

Instantly, I was enveloped with that same smoky smell with the hint of cherries and was transported back to the pub in my mind, inhaling slowly to take it all in. Notes of leather and aftershave also filtered through the vehicle, and I hated the way my body was responding to it, my pulse racing as my stomach tossed and turned.

Alex slipped into the driver's seat and put the car in reverse, his hands grazing over the wheel in smooth circles as he backed up, the other shifting gears.

I stared at this man simply *driving a damn car* and was coming out of my skin, his relaxed stance as his fingers pushed the ball around turning me into a puddle in the seat behind him. Jade was going on and on about something, an upcoming event she was planning, when Alex's eyes lifted into the rearview mirror and locked on mine, holding them a moment before he returned his focus to the road.

Oh, God.

I stared out the window the rest of the way like a little kid on a school bus, trying to keep my shit together. Thankfully, the airport was less than an hour from the resort, and soon enough, we were pulling into a space, the winter air such a relief to breathe in as I practically threw myself out of the car, inhaling as much as my lungs would hold.

"Callie? Are you okay?" Jade asked, studying me close.

"Yeah. I'm fine."

"Car sick?" she pressed.

"You know, that's probably it." I patted my damp forehead. "I haven't been in the backseat of a car in a while."

"Well, that's a shame," Jade joked, and her father barely curled the side of his lip, silver strands shaking as he reached for our bags.

"Funny," I laughed it off and watched Jade wrap her arms around her father's neck, pecking his cheek goodbye. They exchanged several more pleasantries and another hug before Alex brought my bag to me, his eyes screaming so much while saying nothing at all.

"Here you go, Callie." Alex handed me the small carry-on, and that damn dimple formed at the corner of his mouth, making me weak in the knees.

"Thank you again, Mr. Harrington. For everything."

It looked like I slapped him across the face by using the most formal form of his name. I hated to do it but felt there was no other option in this situation. He was off-limits. That was a fact.

He nodded in understanding and stretched his bare hand to me as our hands meshed, the ever-slight brush of his thumb across the top of my hand causing my heart to flatline. I drew my lower lip in between my teeth and let out the faintest gasp, watching his chest swell as I did so.

"Goodbye," he breathed with a gentle nod, sliding his fingers away.

"Goodbye."

Chapter Seven

Callie

Mom greeted me with a big hug once I was home again, offering to unpack my bags at once. I loved my mother more than anything, but her helicopter parenting was smothering me. I really needed to get my own place. Stat.

"Thanks, Mom. But I got it."

"Are you sure? Well, how about something to eat? I made your favorite! Loaded baked potato soup!" Mom exclaimed from the kitchen as I wandered down the hallway to my old bedroom, her gray locks swishing over her shoulders.

"Yes, that sounds amazing!" I called back, plopping on the bed and dropping my bag.

"Well, come on out! It's ready!" Mom urged, and I rolled my eyes with a half grin, joining her at the table as she poured a glass of tea for me.

"Thank you, Mom. You didn't have to go through all this trouble." I dropped several crackers in my bowl and stirred.

"I have to eat too, you know." She took a bite. "It was no trouble at all."

"Still, I appreciate it." I smiled, swallowing a warm bite of cheesy potato bliss.

"So! How was the trip?" Mom's eager eyes popped and fixed on me. It's for damn sure I couldn't say a thing about Alex. Well, at least that there was anything brewing between us. Hell, it was likely all in my imagination anyway.

"You know, it was great. I really needed it."

"That was so kind of Jade. She's a great friend, isn't she?"

Damn me.

"Yes. The best."

Mom squished a pack of crackers into her bowl and ate some more. "Did you get to talk to her father at all?"

"Hm?" I pretended not to hear.

"Did you see Jade's father? You remember Mr. Harrington." Mom tapped her chin. "Although he worked so much when Jade was younger, I suppose you were rarely around him."

"Of course I remember Mr. Harrington," I coughed. "Yes, he was there."

"Oh, I'm so glad he bought that place. The previous owners were terrible managers from what I hear."

"Oh really?" I had no idea.

"Mm-hm." Mom nodded, sipping her tea while spilling the rest. "The cabins were rundown and everything was so unkempt. But by the sound of things, Mr. Harrington turned it all around."

"Wow, in that case, yes. He certainly has." I sat in amazement. "It's a beautiful resort. Truly. Anyone would enjoy it."

"That's fantastic! Good for him." Mom scooted her chair back and went to the cabinet for a few napkins. I pondered a moment, knowing Mom probably had all the scoop I was curious about.

"Mom, can I ask you something?"

She sat at the table in a flash, tapping the napkin stack. "Of course! You can ask me anything."

I hoped I wouldn't regret this.

"Do you know what really happened? Between Mr. and Mrs. Harrington?"

"Oh." Mom drank a long gulp of her tea as her eyes bulged, dabbing her mouth and blowing a sign. "Jade never told you?"

"The only thing she ever said was that her parents tried but couldn't make their marriage work," I revealed, wondering what the real reason was.

"Ah, yes. Well, that only attests to the wonderful man Mr. Harrington is for not telling his daughter. He caught his wife cheating. Multiple times, I'm afraid."

I nearly fell off my chair. "He did?"

Mom nodded, eyes drifting off in thought. "Mrs. Harrington worked at the legal office downtown as a receptionist, and he caught her and her boss in the damn shower during your senior year of high school."

"At his house?" My mouth fell open. "How did you find out?"

"The truth?"

I nodded, on the edge of my seat.

"Mrs. Harrington told me. At your graduation," she confessed, drumming her fingers on the table. "I simply asked where Jade's father was and she said they were having problems, going as far as to reveal the story. She begged me not to breathe a word for Jade's sake."

"Wow. I don't remember Mr. Harrington being there. At graduation, I mean."

"No, he was. He just arrived a little late is all. That was the other part of the story. That poor man was working two and three jobs shortly after the affair. He did everything from construction to sales, trying to provide and make his wife happy." Mom shook her head in disgust. "So the fact that

Mr. Harrington is doing so well for himself is wonderful. He deserves nothing less."

"Al," I corrected myself. "Mr. Harrington is a wonderful man, isn't he?"

"That he is." Mom smiled. "I only wish your father was half the man he is."

"Mom," I cut her off, not wanting to talk about my deadbeat dad who left when I was two years old.

"I know, enough breath wasted on him. Sorry," Mom sighed, finishing her meal.

"It's okay." I brushed it off, and Mom took her dishes to the sink, a thought popping into her brain.

"Oh! I almost forgot! Travis stopped by with some of your things."

"He *what*?"

"I told him you weren't here but he insisted. He said he left you a voicemail and set a box at the door. That was it." Mom scrubbed her bowl. "I set it in your room."

"Oh okay, thanks." I carried my bowl to the sink and started to wash when Mom shooed me away with a smile.

"I've got this. Go on."

"Okay." I grinned and moved back the hallway into my room, noticing a brown cardboard square on the floor filled with familiar items.

Clothing.

Makeup.

Photographs.

Some other odds and ends.

But underneath it all, a velvety box with my engagement ring and a note reading,

> *Hey baby,*
> *I know you gave this back to me. But it's yours. I meant every word when I gave it to you. I want you. Only you. Forever. My hope is that you will wear it again someday.*
> *I love you.*
> *-Travis*

Narcissistic prick.

I chucked it in the box, making a mental note to sell it, and went to my carry-on, taking out my clothes to wash them. My finger bumped against a sharp paper corner at the bottom of the bag, and I rummaged through the few remaining things until a small envelope was exposed, my name in black pen written neatly on the front.

Like a damn loon, I whiffed the white square and caught the faintest blend of smoke and musk, my fingers shaking so hard I could barely open it.

It was a card.

A beautiful mountain range was illustrated on the front with the words, **Thank you for staying at Sugar Slope Lodge. We hope you enjoyed your stay!**

Ah. Okay. Maybe this wasn't as personal as I thought.

I was wrong.

So wrong.

> *Dear Callie,*
>
> *I'm so sorry about the generic card. It was all I could find at the last minute :) I want you to know that it was an honor having you stay at the lodge, and more than anything, I hope you go home feeling better than when you arrived. There's no one more deserving of a relaxing getaway.*
>
> *I only wish your trip wasn't over just yet.*
>
> *I feel there was so much left unsaid between us and I couldn't let you leave without telling you that. More than anything, I want you to be okay, Callie. Seeing you this weekend reminded me of how cruel life can be but also the unexpected light that can be born in the darkness.*
>
> *I'm always here if you need me.*
>
> *Be well, Callie.*
>
> *Always,*
>
> *Alex*
>
> *(P.S. So sorry again for knocking you over. I promise it will never happen again...lol)*

Holy shit!!!

I covered the stupid smile on my face, rereading the note over and over and over until I had it memorized. My stomach lunged into my throat as I noticed the smallest little sun drawn at the bottom of the card with Alex's phone number, a sign from the heavens that this wasn't all in my head.

I pulled out my phone and typed away, a giddy grin still plastered on my face.

> What a surprise. Thank you so much for the card.

He responded almost immediately.

Alex
> You made it back safely?

> Yes! We got back a couple of hours ago.

Alex
> Good. I'm so glad. I've texted Jade with no response. lol

> You know Jade. It might take 5-10 business days for her to reply.

Alex
> LOL! Very true.

> I did have a wonderful time at the lodge.

Okay, that's enough. Don't say anymore, Callie. Not a damn word. Ugh. Fuck it.

> I'm so happy you were there, Alex.

Damn me!

Alex
> Not Mr. Harrington? JK

> Okay, I'm turning red. LOL I'm sorry. I shouldn't have said that.

> Alex
>
> **No, I understand why you did. And if makes you feel any better, you've got this old man turning red too.**

> **Old man? Hardly.**

> Alex
>
> **Are you feeling better? I was worried after the other night at the pub. And with today being, well, you know.**

Holy hell.

My hands were sweating so much I could hardly type.

> **Thank you. Yes. Much better. It's going to be a process for sure. But on the upside, I came home to a box of my things that Travis returned so I won't have to go back to his house.**

> Alex
>
> **Wow. That's great, Callie.**

> Yes. I know it sounds silly but I feel like the future can finally begin.

Alex
> Not silly at all. I understand completely.

> Maybe 30 won't be so bad after all ;)

Alex
> Ha! Are you kidding me? This is going to be the best year of your life!

> That's what Jade said too :)

Alex
> Enjoy it, Callie. You deserve nothing but happiness.

Okay, Callie.

Say goodbye and end the damn text before things get out of hand!

> **Are you happy, Alex?**

Chapter Eight

Alex

I nearly fell on the damn floor, staring point-blank at my phone without having the slightest clue on how to respond. Sweat lined my brow, and I peeled off my shirt, the roaring fireplace in my cabin suffocating me. The gold around my neck heated up against my clammy skin, and I started to type so Callie wouldn't think I was ignoring her.

> I'm getting there.

Holy shit. Well, on one hand, I was fucking relieved that Callie didn't seem to think I was an absolute creep for stuffing that card in her bag. I almost didn't do it, fearing that she would think the worst of me. But her doe eyes on the ride to the airport. Fuck. I had to. I couldn't help myself.

> Callie
> **I'm right there with you, Alex.**

Dammit! My heart was dissolving under a nest of gray chest hair, a painful reminder of our age difference. Callie was so young and in her prime while I was nearly over the fucking hill. God, most people would say this was some midlife crisis. But I couldn't get Callie out of my head. More than that, I didn't want to.

> Callie
> **I'll be happier when I'm out of my mom's house. LOL. But I have some prospects in the works. Fingers crossed.**

> **Yeah? I'm not sure where you're thinking, but I still have some connections from when I lived in Asheville. I could make some calls if you're looking to rent.**

> **Callie**
> **OMG! Are you serious?**

I let out a soft laugh, hearing her voice in my head. Fuck. Her voice. So airy and warm.

> **Absolutely.**

> **Callie**
> **Well, I would appreciate that more than you know. You have no idea.**

> **I'll get right on it :)**

> **Callie**
> **Thank you, Alex. You've made my day. Again :)**

> **I'm so happy to hear that, Callie. I'll be in touch soon.**

> Callie
> **Ok!**

A deep sigh rumbled through my chest as I set the phone down, my heart yearning for more but stopping myself. This was a dangerous game we were playing, walking along this tightrope of emotions, both of us one step away from falling.

Fuck, Jade would never speak to me again if she discovered any of this. Not the fact that I was helping Callie find a place but everything else that was bubbling like water in a teakettle, ready to explode.

Ugh. Son of a bitch.

Deciding to push that thought aside, I showered and dressed before heading into the office, surprising my employees. Typically, I worked remotely on the weekends unless there was a major issue, which thankfully, was rare. But I needed to get out of the cabin and clear my head before making a few calls, hoping clarity would come about what the fuck I was doing with my daughter's best friend.

"Hey, boss! What brings you in?" Nick, one of my best customer service reps, greeted from his desk, pointing my way.

"Oh, I have some calls to make. How are things going?" I asked, genuinely interested.

"So far so good. Smooth sailing for a Saturday," he laughed. "Although, I've had a lot of people ask about when the lodge is closing for the season. Are you still set on April? Or did you want to push it out a little?"

April.

That's three months from now.

God, so much could be going on in three months.

Would Callie and I be...?

Shit.

"Yes, April for sure. So technically the last day of March would be it. Business slows down after that. There are too many expenses to consider staying open longer," I instructed, and Nick typed away before answering another call, nodding.

"Thanks, Nick."

He gave a thumbs-up and continued speaking with a guest as I moved into my office and shut the door, slowly sitting down and turning on my computer. I waited for the browser to boot and typed the construction company I used to work for, happy to see Chuck was still running that ship.

I picked up the phone and dialed, his familiar raspy voice answering right away, "Hello?"

"Chuck? Chuck Daniels?"

"Speaking! How can I help ya?"

I smiled. "It's Alex. Alex Harrington."

Chuck cracked up, wheezing something God awful. "Well, how in the hell are ya, ya son of a bitch?"

"Better than you, asshole. You still smoking?"

"Oh, I've cut back," he coughed, laughing.

"Yeah? One pack or two?"

"I don't have to tell you shit!" he teased. "One most days."

I shook my head, chuckling right along with him. "Well, I can't say much. I still enjoy the pipe every now and then."

"No judgment here," Chuck cackled, and I quickly looked up the area I had in mind for Callie, near her mom's but not too close.

"Hey, the reason I'm calling is I have a friend in need of a place to rent and I was curious if you had any information about that old house we flipped on Cedar?" I tapped my pen as he hummed in thought.

"Cedar, you said? Shit, that was at least ten years ago, Al."

"Yeah, I know. I remember some rich guy bought it strictly to rent. Nothing is coming up online about the status. I was just curious." I scrolled, reaching for a spare set of readers in my desk and gliding them on.

"Hang on, Al. Let me ask one of the guys."

I listened as Chuck put the phone down, his voice so loud I could hear every word. A warm smile appeared on my lips once I found some online photos of the house, a beautiful historic home that was completely renovated by our team but still held its classic charm. Callie would love it.

"Hey, Al?" Chuck called.

"Yeah, bud. I'm still here."

"Ya gotta pen?"

I flashed a smile, reaching for a slip of paper. "Yes, sir. Fire away."

"Name's Davidson. Robert Davidson. He owns the property. No idea what the status is but here's his number."

I scribbled the digits and read them back, my stomach knotting a little, thrilled and terrified. "Thanks, Chuck. You're a life savor."

"Anytime, Al. Take care."

"You too."

I hung up and took a deep cleansing breath, soon dialing Mr. Davidson with all the hope in the world. Somehow, I felt this was my way of showing Callie how much she meant to me. To be able to do this for her even from afar. I couldn't disappoint her. Her text sounded so excited.

"Robert Davidson," the man answered using his name, and I cleared my throat.

"Yes, hello! Mr. Davidson. My name is Alex Harrington. I have just a couple of questions for you about your property."

"Which one?" he gloated, and I rolled my eyes.

"Um. The colonial, sir. On Cedar."

"Oh hell. You and everyone else. Look, I'll tell you like I've told the rest, it's not—"

"Sir, I was part of the team that helped restore it. I know how valuable it is."

Silence.

"You were?" he paused. "What'd you say your name was again?"

"Alex Harrington."

"You work for Chuck?"

"Yes. I mean I used to. Years ago. I own a ski lodge now in Montana, but I have a friend who could really use a place."

"A friend, hm?"

I flushed, feeling my collar was choking me. "Yes, sir."

"Well, Mr. Harrington, I'll be frank," he sighed. "I've got a waiting list out the ass for that place."

"You do?" I gripped the phone, my palm sweaty.

"Mm-hm," he huffed. "My current tenants are moving out by the end of the month. Which is a damn shame because they were the best renters I could ask for. They respected the property, no nonsense."

"I know the perfect person to take their place, sir."

A short chuckle sounded in my ear. "You are persistent, Mr. Harrington."

"How much is rent? If I may ask."

My eyeballs popped, and I had to ask Mr. Davidson to repeat it, all the while pretending not to be shocked. "Alright. Sir, I will pay February, March, and April's rent right now, if she can have it."

"She?"

"Yes. My friend."

"Ah, right." Mr. Davidson let out a long and dramatic breath. "You're going to have to give me some more information about her, though. She's not some wishy-washy, irresponsible—"

"She's almost thirty. No children. No pets. A teacher."

"No kids?"

Not yet.

Dammit! What the fuck is wrong with me?

"No kids, sir."

"And you have the money? Right now?"

I beamed, so happy I could do this for her. "Right now."

"Well, in that case, Mr. Harrington, you've got yourself a deal. We'll reassess in April. Hang tight. Let me transfer you to my assistant. She will go over all the details with you."

"Thank you, Mr. Davidson. I can't thank you enough."

He laughed, "Pleasure doing business with you."

Chapter Nine

Callie

"Alex! This place is fantastic!" I moved around the open house on video chat, charmed by the modern twist on such a classic historic structure. The Carolina mountains were visible from the back windows, a stunning backdrop to an already breathtaking home. But they weren't nearly as beautiful as the mountains I left behind, however. They were missing Alex's beauty.

"Woah! Slow down! You're giving me whiplash!" Alex teased, and I moved into the living room, captivated by the fireplace and built-in bookshelves.

"Oh my God, these are beautiful." I traced the glossy edges, imagining all the spines that would fit inside.

"That was my favorite part of the project. Painting them." Alex curled the side of his lip, and I admired him from afar, speechless.

"Alex, I...I don't know what to say."

"Say you'll move in." He raked through his silver hair, bicep flexing on camera.

"What's the catch, huh? A place like this rarely becomes available."

"No, catch, Callie." Alex flashed a bright smile. "Like I said, you'll be doing the owner a favor. His tenants had to move quicker than expected. Rent is covered until April."

I teared up, blotting the corners. "Alex."

"You deserve it, Callie. Make it yours."

I had to sit down to process it all, the little ledge by the fireplace catching my ass on the way down. Alex and I had been texting and calling ever since the day I came home to North Carolina, the tension rising more and more after each one. And now he had found me a home. More than anything, I wanted him here. To hug him. Touch him. Thank him for whatever strings he pulled.

"I can't," I struggled. "I can't thank you enough, Alex. You don't know what this means."

"Callie," he began, but I kept going.

"No, for so long I felt like a roommate, Alex, taking up space in someone else's house. It never felt like mine even though it should have. This is like something out of a fairy tale, and I don't know how to accept it."

Alex's jaw ticked, and he looked down, words rough and husky coming through the phone. "Callie, fuck. I'm so sorry he made you feel that way."

"It's okay."

"No, it's not okay. Not even a little okay," Alex encouraged. "Hey, look at me, Callie."

I pulled my gaze from the knotty wood floor into his blue eyes, tears spilling. "Yes?"

He rubbed his lips and sighed, "You deserve this. You deserve to be taken care of. And he failed you. Miserably."

"My heart knows that," I stammered. "It's my head that needs to catch up sometimes."

"Take your time, Callie. Enjoy every minute," Alex cleared his throat, grinning ear to ear. "I'm so happy you are happy."

I moved into the kitchen, covering my lips at the stunning blue cabinets and white walls. Instantly, I pictured Alex at the table, eating his breakfast as I cooked him more on the stove, soon feeling his strong arms around me, his lips on my cheek.

"I wish you were here," a breath hitched in my throat, making my words so faint I'm not sure if he heard them.

I could tell Alex wanted to say something but held back, rubbing his mouth as his cheeks lit up. "Me too, Callie."

I swatted my lashes, feeling like I couldn't breathe. "Jade is going to flip when she sees this. Although rustic was never really her style."

"Jade will love it for you."

"Modern is more her thing. New and on the up and up." I diverted, feeling like I was going to cry again.

"Callie," Alex tried pulling me out of it, but I was completely torn, wanting to celebrate this with him but fearing the worst.

"What should I tell Jade, Alex? I don't want to come between you and your daughter."

"Callie," Alex said again, our eyes locking as I clutched the phone, wishing it was him instead. He assured, "I know we're walking in uncharted territory here. I'm scared too."

"You are?"

"Yes." He nodded. "Let's just take it one day at a time, okay? In the meantime, it's totally fine to tell Jade about the house. It was an old connection that worked out in your favor."

"Really?"

"Yes." He cheesed. "And if it makes you feel any better, I helped Jade get the house she owns now, too. So..."

I dabbed my forehead, the room spinning. "Eh, not really."

"Sorry." Alex offered a painful smile, fingers laced on his desk. "But I meant what I said, Callie. I want nothing more for you to enjoy it. Promise me you will."

How can I enjoy it without you?

"I will. I promise."

Alex's phone started ringing in his office, and he grumbled, popping his brow. "Ugh, I have to take this. But I'll call you soon. Tonight okay?"

"Yes. I can't wait. I'll talk to you then."

"Bye, Callie."

"Bye, Alex."

I barely hung up when the front door pounded, my throat closing in as I carefully investigated. Holy shit! Jade!?

"Cals! I just stopped by your mom's and she said you had found a place!? What the hell? Open up!"

I flung the door open, and my best friend stood wearing a sophisticated skirt and blazer with bright pink heels. Her red hair was in the neatest bun, and she hugged me before examining every nook and cranny.

"How old is this place?"

I brushed my nose, following her around. "Oh, around two hundred years."

"Geez, Callie. What if it's haunted?"

"As long as the ghosts are quiet and let me read at night, I don't mind." I moved into the bedroom, thinking of Alex's nude body under the sheets. Fucking hell. "It's a really big house, but I couldn't pass up the opportunity."

"Really? How did it come about?"

"Honestly?" I held my breath. "Mr. Davidson is the owner and somehow had connections to the company your father worked for years ago. I think they may have renovated it."

"Oh my God! Yes! I remember Dad talking about this place!" Jade crossed her arms, studying the shiplap in the bathroom. "What a small world. I hope he's not charging you an arm and a leg."

"No, it's surprisingly cheap," I fudged. "Something happened with his last tenants and I don't know. The stars aligned."

Jade looked out the bathroom window, hand on her hip. "Well, antique typically is not my thing. But this house has you written all over it, girl. Congratulations!"

"Thanks!" I could breathe again. "I'm thrilled."

Jade put her arm around me and reached into her jacket pocket, placing a tiny red box in my hands. "I know your thirtieth birthday is technically thirteen days away. But as you know, I have that ridiculously extravagant wedding in South Carolina to organize."

"Right. How's that coming along?"

"It's coming." She shrugged, not at all worried. "So, since I'll be out of town, I wanted to give you this in person."

"Jade, you've done so much for me already. You didn't have to get me anything." I gulped, guilt gnawing my insides.

"Callie, you only turn thirty once! Open it!" She clapped.

I peeled the shiny paper away and met Jade's excited gaze, feeling hot all of a sudden. She waited patiently as I exposed a little white box, opening the lid to find the prettiest golden necklace in the world, a heart with an amethyst stone inside.

"Jade." I grazed the jewelry, words failing me.

"Happy birthday, girl. Lift those waves for me!" She took the necklace out, and I gathered my hair as she fed the claw through the loop, the pendant landing in the center of my chest.

"It's perfect, Jade."

She eyed it. "Yes. It sure is."

We cracked up and moved toward the foyer, our footsteps echoing in the space. Jade read her buzzing smartwatch and cursed, head shaking.

"Duty calls?" I asked.

"Unfortunately. I have to take this. Ugh!" She hugged me and grabbed her purse. "Happy early birthday, Cals. And this house, holy shit. What did I tell you, huh? Best year ever!"

"You called it," I sighed with a smile.

"We will celebrate soon. I promise." She waved and rushed out the door, but not before hugging me goodbye, a mountain of worry taking her place that everything good in my life would crumble and bury me alive.

Hours passed since Jade left, and evening had replaced the afternoon sun, nine o'clock shining brightly on my phone as a video call came through, Alex right on schedule.

"Hey!" I greeted, wearing my floral pajama tank trimmed in a lace.

"Hey, beautiful." Alex was nestled in his bed like I was, only this time wearing a thin white tank with the same gold chain I noticed in Montana. He had never called me *beautiful* before, and I felt the blood rush to my head, turning every shade of berry imaginable.

"I don't know about that." I sat taller in bed. "I seem to deteriorate throughout the day."

He let out a giant, *ha!*

"What?"

"That is the biggest lie I've ever heard." His eyes lingered on mine and fell lower for a split second. "Wow, that's lovely."

I realized I was still wearing the necklace Jade gave me and clutched it, peeking down to admire it some more. "Well, you have good taste. Jade gave it to me. An early birthday gift."

He nodded with a grin. "I love it."

I ruffled my waves, the warm candles creating a soft glow around me. "I noticed your necklace back at the lodge. Does it have a special meaning?"

Alex curled the side of his lip, offering a smolder that made me ache between the legs. Shit! If he could do this to me thousands of miles away through a screen, what in the hell could he do to me in real life?

He tugged the gold out of his tank top, a tiny compass dangling at the bottom as he brought it to the camera for a closer look. "I've had it since high school. My father gave it to me."

"Wow," I squinted, studying the tiny lines etched in the gold, N, S, E, and W circling its face. "It's gorgeous."

"Thank you, Callie." He peered at it himself. "I lost my father not long after he gave this to me, so yes. It has all the meaning in the world."

"Oh, Alex. I'm so sorry. I didn't know."

"No reason to be sorry." He winked. "I love talking about him. Although it's an odd feeling. I'm so much older than my father was when he passed. It's surreal, you know?"

I blinked tears. "I can only imagine."

He kissed the charm around his neck and let it fall, watching me with those dazzling eyes of his. You could get lost in them for hours. Beautiful shades of sky and sea, both about to swallow me whole. And I welcomed it.

"What's on your mind, Callie?"

I tilted my head, unable to hide my concerns for another second. "Oh, Alex."

"Yes?"

"Is it wrong?" I looked away. "What we're doing?"

"Callie, I don't want to make you uncomfortable." Alex swallowed. "Just say the word and—"

"No," I begged, quite embarrassingly. "Alex, that's what I'm trying to say. I want more. And I feel awful about it."

"Oh, Callie." He watched me cry. "Oh, I wish I could hold you right now."

"I'd let you, Alex. I'd crawl in your arms and never leave."

"Cal," he shortened my name, and I met his gaze, a sloppy weeping mess.

"How can I want you and still be Jade's best friend?"

He lowered his head, staring off. "How can I want you and still be a good father to Jade?"

I breathed his name, drying my face. "I guess we can't, can we?"

"Callie, please," he pleaded.

"I'm so sorry. I have to go."

Chapter Ten

Alex

I nearly threw up after Callie ended the phone call, barely sleeping a wink, thus mindlessly scrolling at work the following morning. Maybe she was right. Maybe this was an impossible web of deceit we were weaving around ourselves, my daughter inevitably about to be stuck in it, never to return to life the way it was.

But my heart still throbbed for her.

For Callie.

It wasn't simply a physical attraction for me. But every fucking thing about this woman brought me to my knees. Everything. What she saw as flaws, I saw as priceless treasures that I wanted to keep close and never let go. How could I close the door on something so precious?

"Hey boss!" Nick popped his head in my office as I stroked my temple, a migraine brewing, no doubt.

"Hey, Nick. What can I do for you?"

"This just arrived for you." He passed a brown shipping box over, and my heart tore to shreds all the more, feeling like a damn fool.

"Thanks, Nick. I appreciate it."

"Sure thing."

I carefully sliced through the tape and popped the flaps open, moving packing paper until I spotted it. Callie's birthday gift. Fuck. This was stupid. So fucking stupid. Again, what the hell was I thinking? I guess when it came to Callie, all logic and reasoning went out the damn window. Case in point staring back at me.

Dammit.

I set the box on the floor and plopped in my computer chair, holding my head in misery. After Callie hung up, I decided to give her space. No calls. No texts. If she ever wanted to talk to me again, I would be here. If not, well, I had to accept that no matter how bad it hurt.

Callie

It was nice sinking back into my routine. Early mornings. Quiet coffee time. Recording my classes. Lunch. Livestreams. Grading. And Evenings filled with books and soft candlelight, not because I couldn't pay the electric bill but because I craved the ambiance.

Still, nothing could keep my mind off of him.

I tried getting lost in life to forget the way I thought about my best friend's father. *Jade's* father. It was like a mantra in my mind. This man does not belong to me. He belongs to *her*. Not in a romantic way, of course. But Alex belongs to Jade. That is a boundary never to be crossed. I would never have another friend in the world like Jade. Why risk it?

It sounded logical, reasonable.

Tell that fucking shit to my heart.

Clearly, Alex was giving me space. That was a sure thing. God, he was so perfect. A gentleman. Even without talking, I felt his heart calling mine, and still I refrained from picking up the phone to call or text. I was afraid to. I had convinced myself that if I reached out, I wouldn't be able to stop myself from revealing everything I had been thinking and feeling since our eyes first locked in Montana. But maybe that wouldn't be the worst thing in the world.

> **Jade**
> **Happy 30th birthday!!! MUAH! Love you so much :) Cannot wait to get back home and PARTAY!**

> **You are the best friend in the world. Love you too! Hope everything is going good in SC!**

> **Jade**
> **OMG. The DRAMA. This bride is totally unhinged. I can't even.**

> **LOL! Please give me all the details.**

> **Jade**
> **Believe me. I'm taking notes. You won't even believe half of it.**

> **Wow. I'm sorry! They better pay you well for your pain and suffering.**

Jade
> **Yes. I'm itemizing this shit on their invoice. Ridiculous!**

> **So sorry girl. Hang in there. If anyone can handle it, you can!**

Jade
> **Thx! Gotta run. I hope you are treating yourself to something amazing tonight for your birthday. No staying in! Go out! Get some peen!**

> **JADEEEEE**

I died laughing when she texted a string of eggplant emojis followed by water squirts, peaches, lips, mushrooms. Hell, anything that resembled a penis or a vagina. I texted her back that I would think about it when a big skull came through, making me laugh all over again.

Knock knock.

I glanced at the time and popped a brow, curious as to who would be visiting so late in the day. It was still light out but hazy, quite the perfect time for me to cozy up with a good murder mystery.

"Travis?" I opened the door, utterly and completely shocked. He was wearing his suit from the office, I assumed, his dark hair messy in the front and a bouquet of roses in his hand.

"Callie. Happy birthday."

I scoffed, crossing my arms, mad as hell. "What in the hell are you doing here?"

"I miss you." He stretched the flowers forward, and I froze, shaking inside.

"Travis, there's nothing left to say. It's over. Please leave."

"But it's your birthday, Callie. Come on. Let's go out. Have some dinner. Just as friends."

I blinked at rapid speed, stunned at his arrogance. "Why in the fuck would you think that I want to be friends? God, you act like you weren't the reason why we broke up! Why our wedding was called off! Are you that dense?"

"Please, Callie. Please talk to me."

"Wait a minute." I held up my hand. "How did you even find out where I lived?"

"Callie, come on." He shook his head, patronizing me. "People talk. It didn't take me long to figure it out."

I stared him down, beyond pissed. "Still, you're not welcome. Get the fuck out of here."

"Damn, you callous bitch! I was trying to do something nice for you and this is how you treat me?"

"Yeah. You're right. I'm such a bitch, right? For absolutely no reason!"

"Fuck you, Callie," he spat. "God, I wasted so much time with you."

"One thing we agree on."

He took one step down, body turned to face me. "My only saving grace is that I had my share of good pussy over the years besides your starfish ass. God help the next man who falls for you."

My lip wrinkled in humiliation and I looked at my feet, for the first time really believing that something was wrong with me. That I caused him to cheat. I wiped my snotty lip and shook from head to toe, looking up to see Alex storming up my porch and punching the ever-living shit out of Travis, in a tuxedo no less.

"Who the fuck are you?" Travis stumbled, nose busted with blood.

"How dare you speak to her that way?" Alex seethed, veins protruding from his hands as he squeezed Travis's collar. "You piece of shit."

"Looks like someone wandered away from the nursing home," Travis laughed, teeth bloody as hell. "Callie, why don't you call 911? Someone will come get him."

I covered my mouth in horror, stunned that Alex was here and mortified by my ex's behavior. I couldn't stop shivering, slinking back against my door, tears running on their own will.

"If you ever come here again, I'll fucking kill you. Do you understand me?" Alex yanked Travis's jaw, and I heard a popping sound, slamming my lashes closed.

"Whatever. She's a lousy fuck anyways." Travis glared at me and Alex scoffed in wild rage, tossing my ex off the porch like a sack of potatoes as he rolled all the way down each step. I will admit it was satisfying seeing him crawl on all fours across the yard like the dog he was. But once Travis was completely gone, I broke all the more as Alex rushed forward and took me in his arms, holding me as we shuffled through the door, Alex's fancy shoe closing it.

I clung to the back of his jacket for dear life, burrowing against his chest with heavy sobs. He held me so tight, not letting up for even a second, his words making me cry all the more, "I'm here. Fuck, baby. I'm here."

"I'm so happy you are," I cried, looking up into his face and stroking his smooth cheeks. "I missed you so much."

"You don't know how happy I am to hear that. I thought..."

"I was miserable all week, Alex. Absolutely miserable without you." I hiccupped and he grabbed the side of my face, eyes piercing mine.

"I want you to be sure, Callie," he growled. "If you don't want me to kiss you, tell me now. Tell me now and I'll walk out that door and you'll never see me again."

I whimpered like a damn puppy, shaking my head no.

"Because if you don't and I taste you, you're mine, Callie." His sweet smoky breath tickled my nose. "There isn't a person on the face of this earth that can stop me from wanting you. No one. Not even my daughter."

"Alex." My head fell back.

"Tell me now, Callie," he implored. "I'm begging you, baby. Tell me to get the fuck out of here. That you don't want my lips on yours. That you don't want me to touch you. To fuck you."

"Alex," a throaty whine escaped, and I stretched high on my tippy toes, closing the small gap that existed between us, our lips barely touching at first as though we were both waiting for the world to come crashing down if it happened.

And when it didn't, when we felt the sinful softness of each other's longing lips, we caved, our mouths pushing and pulling as I drowned in a sensorial symphony of sweet smoke, musk, and mint all buried under Alex's guttural moan, yearning for more.

"Baby, you taste like heaven," he sucked my lower lip, his mouth finding my cheek, then neck. "Oh, God."

Our lungs competed for air as we embraced again, not being able to get close enough. He inhaled my scalp and kissed the top of my head before rubbing my arms as I slid my hands into his jacket, feeling his sides. We fisted the fabrics on each other's clothes, silently tugging and touching as the intensity of the situation fell to a sweet calm. And once I could breathe again, I took a step back, holding my heart, and stared at him, almost as if to convince myself that it wasn't all a dream.

Chapter Eleven

Alex

I talked myself out of flying to North Carolina about a hundred times, trying to convince myself that Callie wanted nothing to do with me. But before I completely let her go, I had to see her in person. To look her in the eye to see if that beautiful spark was still there, the light that came on only in my presence.

Travis was indeed a rusty wrench in my plan to surprise Callie on her thirtieth Valentine's birthday. Fuck, I wish I could hit him all over again. What a cocky son of a bitch.

Callie had kissed me. I was still high from it. But the way her body trembled in her adorable powder blue sweatsuit frightened me. Did she regret it? Did she regret me?

She took several slow breaths and sank into her sofa, drawing her legs into her chest. I removed my jacket and sat with her, meeting her eye before I touched her knee.

"Baby, you're shaking."

She grabbed my hand, and dammit if I didn't see stars, her two tiny hands stroking one of mine, holding on with everything she had. God, she was so scared. I had to find out, though. Was it because of me? Or Travis?

"Baby, did he ever hurt you?"

She covered her eyes, still holding my hand with one of hers. "Physically? No. Emotionally? Yes. Every day."

I gritted my teeth, scooching closer. "That's over, Callie. He will never hurt you again."

"I know." She rested her head on my shoulder, and fuck, I melted inside.

"I wish I would have hit him harder."

A broken laugh slipped through Callie's lips, and she looked up at me, eyes still weepy, but at least she was smiling. "You definitely gave him a good ol' southern ass beating."

I rubbed my knuckles. "I don't know if you could call that an ass beating, but—"

"Thank you, Alex," she stopped me, eyes rounded in adoration.

I tucked her hair away, on the brink myself, gazing into her beautiful face, lost at how any man could hurt her. "Callie, you don't have to thank me."

"I do." She nudged me with the cutest half grin.

"Well," I stammered, wanting to kiss her all over again. "I would do it all over again, Callie. To defend you."

She bit her lip, trying to keep it together, and traced my red tie from the knot to the V-shaped hem, staring up in the most stunning curiosity. "I have to ask. Why are you wearing a tux?"

Shit.

Her gift.

It had to be in the yard after all the ruckus.

"Hang tight." I took her hand and kissed it, slipping outside and seeing my carry-on waiting in the grass like an Easter egg. I swiped it and quickly went back inside, joining Callie on the sofa as she tried to steal a peek when I unzipped the tote.

I had to explain first.

"Callie, when we last spoke, I had already ordered this because I wanted to make your birthday special."

"Alex," she breathed, touching her lips.

"And I know I should have consulted you first, but honestly, I thought that after our last conversation you might not ever speak to me again."

Fuck, my heart about stopped just imagining it.

"I'm so sorry." She shuddered.

"Baby," I assured. "It's okay. I understand it. All of it. But I had to see you today. Not through a glass screen. To really see you."

She fell into my palm that found her cheek, closing her eyes as though my words were a prayer.

"I had to see for myself if this was really over, this small but thriving bud poking its head through the soil begging for sun." Fuck, I couldn't help myself. I smashed my lips on her forehead, hearing her soft gasp.

"Alex," she echoed. "It's not over."

It was a bold move, but I went in for another kiss, relieved that she welcomed me, puffy lips tasting so sweet with the hint of salt. I tested the waters a little and opened my mouth when she offered her tongue, mine brushing hers, unable to stop the grunt that broke from my chest.

"Fuck," I gasped, panting.

"So," she teased with the cutest eyebrow pop. "What did you get me?"

A rumble slipped out of my mouth next, and I rummaged through the bag, squinting in her direction, appearing overly confident but truly wondering if she would like it. Callie watched closer once I retrieved a square package wrapped in pink and turned red, her little hands opening as I placed it into her palms.

She stared at me and stripped the paper from the white box underneath, slipping off the lid as the tissue paper crinkled. I started sweating, no doubt, fearing this was the dumbest thing I had ever done, when she completely lit up, pulling out a dress, the color of bright shamrocks, the same shade as the sweater she wore in Montana.

"Alex," she cooed, holding it up. "Oh my God."

I wiped my brow, tugging at my tie to loosen it. "Do you like it?"

"No."

I froze.

"I love it!" she laughed out loud and wrapped her arms around my neck, kissing me softly at first, then hungry. "Where did you find this?"

Fuck.

My dick jerked, and I tried moving my legs to disguise it. Thankfully, she didn't notice. Or at least, I don't think she did.

"I spotted it at a shop in Montana. It was in the window as I drove by." I loved how she admired the dress, its long lacy sleeves and sweetheart neckline under her traveling fingertips.

"And you thought—"

"I *knew* it had to be yours." I blushed. "Although you should have seen me trying to describe your size to the saleswoman. God, you would have lost it. She took a guess, ordered it, and I prayed."

Callie cracked up, taking a look at the tag. "Well, your descriptions must have been immaculate because you are spot on, Mr. Harrington."

Another jolt to my cock.

I took her hand, seeing the hunger in her eyes, the fire that tells a man a woman is pleased. I had seen it very few times in my life. Callie's eyes screamed it louder than anyone ever before.

"I wanted to take you on a date tonight, Callie. A real date," I revealed. "To a ridiculously expensive restaurant where the portions are way too small but the atmosphere makes you feel like a star because that's what you are to me, Callie."

"A star?" she breathed.

"Yes."

"What about the sun?" She curled her lips, and I fucking died all over again.

"Yes. That too," I choked, not believing I was sitting here in person with this woman. That she had kissed me. And was flirting with me. "You are everything bright, Callie. A light I've never had in my life."

"Never?" She stroked my cheek before her lips kissed it.

"Never."

She held the dress for another brief moment and stood from the sofa with the most sultry grin on her face. "In that case, I better go put this on."

Chapter Twelve

Callie

My body was still shaking from the whirlwind of events that had taken place in less than an hour. Jade. Travis. And now Alex.

How was this all happening? At such a rapid speed, no less. I was terrified of the acceleration but longed for it, my heart ultimately more fearful of it not happening altogether.

I was naked in my room, Alex still sitting downstairs on the sofa. The old house creaked a lot, so I would have noticed his big footsteps had he followed me up the stairs. But he didn't. God, he was such a gentleman.

I wondered what Alex would think of my body, as stupid as that sounds. Had I known the likelihood of us having sex was this high, I would have waxed. There was absolutely no time for that, my dark mound catching my eye from the mirror above the vanity.

Oh well.

I found a thong that I rarely wore and stepped into it, then the dress. It glided on with buttery ease, the long trumpet-style gown hugging every curve. What in the hell did Alex pay for this? It was breathtaking.

The zipper was at the top of my ass, and I couldn't seem to get a firm hold on it, much less pull it up on my own. I took one last glance in the mirror and walked down the stairs with no shoes on, Alex twisting his head around, his lip falling open.

"Cal," he barely whispered.

I felt my cheeks heat up and peered over the gown. "Could you help me zip it up?"

He jumped off the sofa, and I sheepishly turned around, closing my eyes as the fabric around my body squeezed tighter with Alex dragging the zipper over my spine. His fingers lingered at the back of my neck, causing chills to explode from head to toe, his arms coming around me just like they did in my fantasy.

"Maybe I shouldn't have bought you this dress," he huffed in my ear.

"And why is that?" I gripped his forearms, closing my lashes.

He sucked in a stream of air, words heavy in return, "Because baby, I'm barely standing right now. One more look at you and I'll be on the floor."

I smirked, leaning into him harder and feeling his hard cock, the ache between my legs burning. "Then how will we ever get through dinner?"

He carefully turned me around, eyes sweeping over my body as his dimples popped. "I don't fucking know."

I gulped, mustering the courage to say, "Well, it is February 14th. Can the birthday girl make a request?"

His chest swelled with so much air as he locked his blues on me, urging, "Anything."

I stepped closer, our chests dusting, and leaned in, my words falling on his mouth. "Let's stay in."

Finally, the air left him, a deep raspy exhale that allowed him to take my mouth into his, starving sucks that made me weak. We stumbled into the stairway with our lips sealed, breathing each other's names and yanking each other's clothing.

By the time we made it into my bedroom, my dress was unzipped and hanging off one shoulder, a breast about to fall. His tie was somewhere on the stairs, a button open at his collar where his gold rested. I had left my necklace on too, almost feeling guilty about it, but not guilty enough apparently. That would come later.

"Cal," he begged, squeezing my hair at the back of my head, peppering my neck with kisses. "Fuck, baby."

My nipples prickled against the satin liner of my gown, needing his touch more. I nearly shed the beautiful garment when Travis's harsh voice blared in my mind, his degrading insults that I was lousy in bed screaming louder than Alex's gentle tones.

"Baby, what's wrong?" He touched my arms as I stiffened.

I collected myself, my breath falling into a normal rhythm. Still, my pussy was on fire. Fuck you, Travis.

"I think there's something wrong with me, Alex," I blurted, embarrassed as hell.

"Not possible."

"No," I insisted. "You don't understand. There is something really wrong with me. I can't—"

He scrunched his brow, sparkling blues locked in.

"I mean I *can*. But not when," I stuttered. "Shit."

"You never came with Travis." He read my mind, and I fumbled for words, shocked that he guessed it.

"Yeah." I plopped down on the bed, ashamed. "It's true what he said about me. I'm not good at sex."

Alex hung his head before eyeing me with the softest sway of his salt and pepper hair. "Baby, there's nothing wrong with you."

"No, you're not hearing me," I began.

"Oh, I hear you. Loud and clear." Alex sat down and put his hand on my knee. "But I need you to hear something too."

I swallowed, watching him watching me.

"Most men have no idea what they are doing."

I laughed out loud, my belly buzzing in anticipation. "Well, in that case, I had the cream of the crop in that department."

"Was Travis the only man you were ever intimate with?"

Shit.

More embarrassment.

Let's just unload it all while we're at it.

"Yes," I confirmed, about to puke. "Pathetic, isn't it?"

"No, Callie. Not pathetic. Not at all," he encouraged. "But I think the toxic relationship you had with him has polluted the way you see yourself."

My head drooped, torn. "You think?"

"Let me correct myself." He flashed the most gorgeous smile, taking my hand. "I know."

There was a thrilling confidence about Alex that always left me wanting more. Yet he radiated it with such grace. Not arrogance.

I nodded, trying to take it all in, and met his longing eye, my entire body on fire. My finger traced Alex's long white sleeve, stopping at the slope of his shoulder before moving over to unbutton more of his shirt.

"Cal, it's okay. We don't have to."

I clamped my lower lip, needing him. "Tell me you don't want me, and I'll stop."

"Callie," he begged as I straddled him.

"Tell me now," I whispered in his ear. "Tell me to stop, Alex."

He swallowed a deep moan, palms gripping my hips. "Baby, that's the last thing I'm going to say."

He flipped me over, suspended on top of me in all his beauty. I lost all the air in my lungs as his palm coasted from my ankle to my thigh, the green lace the only barrier between us. Somewhere, I gathered enough courage to tug the top down, exposing both breasts. Alex's eyes darkened, and his lips fell on mine at once, his strong grip ripping the dress off the rest of the way.

"Do you have any idea how stunning you are, Callie? How fucking beautiful?" He panted in between words, studying my bare breasts, belly, and the cotton triangle barely covering me.

"You keep saying that. I want to see you too," I pleaded, sitting up in only a panty to unbutton his shirt completely, amazed at the hardness of his chest and arms.

"I hope you like what you see."

"Alex." I felt him all over, wanting to see more. "You're gorgeous."

"Not an old man?" He rubbed the gray hairs between his nipples.

"Hell no." I smiled, glancing at his belt. "May I?"

"Yes."

My fingers trembled as I unfastened the black leather around his waist, feeling the hardness of his cock through the dress pants. I popped the button open and glided the zipper down, shucking the pants and smiling at his red briefs.

"How festive." I winked.

"It *is* Valentine's Day." He cheesed, kissing me some more. I fell backward and throbbed between my legs, rubbing my thighs together to ease the ache. Alex sat up, and his eyes barely flickered to my pussy, the wet spot on my underwear driving him feral.

"Fuck," he roared and took my mouth, tongues batting, almost fighting with each other. I squeaked under him and tugged at his underwear, freeing him before stealing a glance and aching all the more.

"Alex." I marveled at the size of him, so long and wide as he pulsed, a short patch of silver hair above him with dark hairs speckled throughout. "Oh, Alex."

My knees fell apart as he slid the tiny thong away from my hips, all fears about my own pubic hair going out the window as he worshipped her, damn near crying at the sight of me. And that alone nearly sent me into euphoria, tinged with the sad reality that I had missed out on this type of treatment for so many years of my adult life.

"Cal." Alex admired my pussy then stared into my eyes. "Oh, Callie."

"I can't wait much longer, Alex."

"No, baby." He reached for his pants and pulled out a foil packet, tearing off the top and sliding it on himself. "No more waiting."

I nodded, so wet but scared.

"May I touch you, baby?"

"Please."

Alex's warm fingers skimmed through my lips, hot glossy wetness begging for more. He swirled around my opening and went higher, not directly touching my clit but drawing soft circles on the side of it, creating a new sensation I had never experienced.

"Tell me how it feels, baby."

"Oh God," I was panicking but trying to surrender.

"Too much? I can slow down."

"No, I'm just...surprised."

A little burst of laughter came through, and his voice fell to my ear. "Right now, I don't want you to think about anything else other than the pleasure you are feeling. Not even about me. Just you."

I nodded, choking on choppy air. "I'll try."

He moved to the other side of my clit, drawing little circles next to it. I was more sensitive on that side and jerked, causing him to pull back and return to the other side.

"Note taken, baby."

"Shit," I cursed, squirming.

"Your pussy is so beautiful," he glorified, moving his finger around and around, gradually picking up a little speed, adding the perfect amount of pressure.

I moaned out loud, not meaning to, and looked down, watching him touch me. That alone was beyond erotic. My head fell back into the pillows, and the build climbed higher and higher, shocking the hell out of me. I had never finished without a toy or the occasional bathtub faucet. I would take that to the grave.

Although.

Alex was changing things for me.

Fast.

"Ah!" I bucked into his hand, and he didn't stop, using my cues to go on. He didn't tell me to come or pressure me in any way but simply continued doing what felt good to me. So fucking good.

"I think I'm," I felt the need to explain, but he paid no mind, tracing my opening a little before returning to his clit circle play. God Almighty. I was almost there. So close.

He was smiling so big, biting his lip as he slipped one finger in, then two. His thumb began doing the work around my clit, the change of temperature and pressure making my belly clench, tingles soaring all throughout my body not even five seconds later, a weak cry falling out of me as he held my quivering pussy, the juices of my orgasm falling into his palm.

Chapter Thirteen

Alex

Our chests were like two sails on an open sea rippling against harsh, tattered wind as Callie came down from the high, the sight and feel of her orgasm sending me there with her. I glanced down at the condom filled with semen on my cock and took another deep breath, still cupping her jerking pussy.

Once the fluttering stopped, I carefully pulled away, in awe of the magnificent creature she was, and slid off the bed, but not before kissing her forehead. "I'll be right back."

She barely nodded and closed her eyes, pulling a blanket over herself, cheeks bright pink. Holy God. Holy shit.

I remembered the bathroom being in the hallway and walked toward it, noticing Callie stare at my bare ass on the way out. I grinned at her and kept moving until I was at the toilet, removing the condom and tossing it in her trashcan.

I went to the sink next, my palms and fingers shining with Callie's come. I lost my breath at the sight of it and turned the sink on, washing my hands before splashing a little cool water on my face.

The man in the mirror was not someone I recognized. He was proud, happy, satisfied, and falling harder and faster than he ever had before. God help me. I can't lose her.

I raked my hair back with the dampness of my hands, smoothing out the messy gray strands, and returned to the bedroom where Callie was under the covers, her little hand reaching for mine, making me weak.

"Hey, baby." I crawled under with her, and she latched on to my side, fitting perfectly against me.

For the longest time, I held her there, and she didn't say anything. I was beginning to worry if she regretted what had happened. Soon, her tears on my skin convinced me she was sorry about it all. And that about killed me.

"Cal? What's wrong?"

She sniffed and peered up at me from below, her shiny necklace dangling between both perky breasts. "Nothing is wrong. I just hate that I believed Travis for so long. That I was broken or something."

"It's alright." I squeezed her tighter. "Oh, baby. It's alright."

"I wasted so many years," she cried.

"But we're here together now." I came to the realization that had one thing happened differently in my marriage or her relationship with Travis, the odds of us being in this bed together would be quite slim.

"God, you're right. I'm sorry, Alex."

I smooched her brow, not letting her go. "Don't apologize."

She snuggled into me harder, the feel of her nipples and tuft between her legs making me hard again. I took a deep breath and tried adjusting myself when she propped herself up on an elbow, her delicate voice stopping my heart.

"May I ask you a question?"

I sat up a little more, bringing the blanket to cover myself. "Anything."

She flushed and looked away, biting her lip with the sweetest smile. "Where did you learn how to do that?"

I blushed too, running a hand through my hair. "Honestly?"

"Yes."

A sigh vibrated my chest. "When my wife cheated all those years ago, I convinced myself that it was because I was a bad lover. That I was the problem."

"You did?" Her eyes popped.

"Mm-hm."

"That sounds a lot like me," she divulged, and I had to hold the tears back, already thinking this too.

"I know, baby. I was in that place. Trying to figure out what I was doing wrong. I got every book I could find on the subject and devoured them all." I crossed my arms.

"On female anatomy?" She inched closer.

"Anatomy, arousal, pleasure zones, orgasms." I raised a brow into my hairline, smirking.

Callie softly laughed into my bicep, the feel of her lips pecking my arm taking every thought out of my head. Thank God she spoke up. I forgot what the hell we were even talking about.

"So you educated yourself." She beamed.

I shrugged. "I thought so. But Marcy didn't want me in that way anymore. No matter how hard I tried to make things better. Soon, I realized that it *wasn't* me."

"You did?"

"And it wasn't you either, Callie." I swiped a brown wave from her eye, longing to see her better. "Don't ever think that."

"I can't believe she walked away from you," Callie whispered, blue eyes sparkling.

"It hurt like hell at the time. Like your heart has been ripped out of your chest and stomped on."

Callie nodded, looking down a moment.

"But as life is teaching me, my heart never belonged to her like I thought it did. And knowing that is so freeing."

"Oh, Alex," she whispered, running her fingers through my mop as chills danced on my scalp.

"The same is true for you, baby."

She kissed my arm and sat tall, her breasts catching my attention. I focused on her face despite the temptation, her words breaking my heart.

"I know that's true." She offered a painful grin, pulling the sheet over her chest. "It's just that we were in a relationship for twelve years. How do I not hate myself at the time I'll never get back? The family I'll never have."

"Family?" My stomach zapped.

"I always wanted to have a baby. It was my dream." She touched the blanket over us. "Travis never did."

I gulped, taking her hand as she continued.

"You know, I think that's why I became a teacher." She brushed her nose, on the brink. "And I know becoming a homemaker and having children is considered old fashioned or—"

"Not to me," I uttered, not being able to help myself.

Callie's shoulders softened, curling forward a little. "I was a fool for thinking I could change him."

I cupped her arms, rubbing up and down before kissing her lips. "Look at me, Callie."

Her gaze lifted, beautiful blue stones drowning in water.

"You deserve to experience everything that your heart desires in this life. I want you to know that."

She blinked, and a drop fell as my thumb caught it, her famished kiss surprising me next, a muffled groan escaping as I held her cheeks. Fuck. This woman. Would she pack her things and disappear forever if I told her I could picture it? Her belly swollen with my child. Fuck, it sounded crazy in my own head. I was old enough to be a damn grandfather, not to mention Jade's best friend would be the mother of her half-sibling.

Jesus Lord.

"I want you," she pleaded, her ivory skin warming up, my cock rock solid.

"So soon? Baby, are you sure? I don't want to hurt you."

"Please, Alex. Please." She threw the blankets off, panting.

I reached below for another condom and tore the top off, rolling it on and hovering above my queen, her legs parting so beautifully for me, the wetness of her marking the sheets.

"Fuck, Cal." I dove into her open mouth, delivering kiss after kiss as she reached for my shaft and brought it to heaven's entrance, the tip barely tasting the paradise inside that awaited me.

"Alex," she moaned. "Fuck, you're so big."

"No, I'm not," I laughed, secretly reveling that she said that.

"The hell you're not."

"I don't want to hurt you, baby."

"But I want you."

I pecked her nose, my chest swelling with breath. "Let's go slow, then."

"Okay," she breathed, kissing me slowly as I pulled myself out and traced around her opening until she was dripping, my tip going in much easier.

"Shit," Callie moaned, and I thought the worst.

"Are you okay?"

"Yes. That feels good."

"Ah." I held her thigh with a smile. "A good *shit*, then?"

She laughed, "Yes. Very good."

I gave her a little more and waited, her smile encouraging me to keep going. And once I was fully inside, I never slid out again, which at first confused her, the look on her face asking me what the hell I was doing.

"Hang on, baby." I slid my arm under her waist and pulled her down so I was just a little more forward than her in bed, dropping my pelvis and grinding upward, her enchanting yell nearly making me come right there.

"What are you...I mean, how did you do that?" She gently tugged at my chest hair, grazing the gold chain.

I inhaled through my nose, concentrating on her, reading her. "Enjoy every second, Callie."

She rolled her beautiful head to the side, cocoa waves splayed in every direction as I carefully rubbed against her, giving her all I could in soft strokes.

"Alex," she called, my heart surging.

"That's it," I encouraged, watching her climb higher. "That's it, baby."

God, to be inside of her, filling her, taking root in her. I never wanted her to let me go. If only this pleasure could heal her wounds, those deep wounds within herself that no one sees or knows about. It's for sure the raw edges of mine were coming together under the power of Callie Jo Harper, her satin flower caressing every part of my soul, restoring all that was lost.

Callie arched her back with a yelp and wrapped her legs around my waist, driving me harder into her. Fuck. I was holding on, holding back, needing her to come first, wanting nothing more.

Fuck the man who denied her this, who used her body for his own gratification while she was left wanting. She would never experience that again if I had anything to do with it.

I continued to rub into Callie's clit, studying her harder. She scrunched her face, eyes wandering, her thoughts racing just as much.

I knew how much my ex took from me, how mentally exhausting it was recovering from the bullshit she put me through. But to see the same thing playing out on Callie was almost too much to bear, her broken whimper and lost gaze gutting me.

"Callie?" My voice pulled her back, worry still rising to the top of her eyes like oil in a glass of water. "Baby, we can stop. It's okay."

"No. Please don't stop," she begged. "I need you. I'm just—"

I knew what was happening. Travis's fucking garbage he used to spew was still overwhelming her, polluting her mind. I desperately wanted to get Callie out of her own head, to bring her back to the present so she could let go.

"Breathe with me, baby," I panted, still inside of her.

She lifted her long lashes, sapphires glued to mine, waiting.

"That's it, baby. Keep your eyes on me." I smiled, rubbing the side of her bare thigh and inhaling through my nose as Callie followed my lead.

She exhaled with me through a quivering lip, her soft chin bobbing up and down.

"All the bullshit he put you through, baby. Every fucking lie he told you about yourself." I ground into her pink pearl, summoning a gentle moan from her body. "Let it all go."

She squeezed her lashes closed as two big drops seeped from them, aiming her chin high as her legs parted wider. She cried out a little more, soon locking her gaze on me again. Fuck yes.

I couldn't contain the smile on my face, the dimples around my lips forming, no doubt. Taking another breath, I relished that she was letting me guide her in this moment, taking control a little so she didn't have to think about anything.

"Keep breathing with me, Cal." I scooped her bare ass cheeks and lifted them a tad, venturing a smidge deeper inside of her. "You're so fucking perfect, you know that?" I praised.

"Alex," she stifled another moan, swallowing it, her belly tightening right before my eyes.

I had to keep going. To keep encouraging her. Glorifying her. And while what was running through my mind was risky to say out loud, I couldn't deny Callie, my only mission being to get her there.

"You take me so beautifully, baby," I spoke nice and slow in her ear, staying tucked inside of her pussy, her tiny clit pulsing against me. "You're going to come for me, aren't you?"

"Shit," she cursed, legs starting to shake. "Yes."

"That's my girl." I sucked her neck with a tiny nibble, growling deeper as chills popped along her shoulder just under my lips. "Let me take you there, Cal."

Callie's back arched off the mattress as she screamed, clinging to me, her sweet mouth hitting the nest between my nipples, and instantly I felt her pussy flutter as her eyes rolled back.

I drank her in, coming with her so fucking hard into the condom. "Oh, baby. God."

She pulled back, her body trembling, and gazed up at me before planting a ravenous kiss on my mouth. I savored her taste, the pleasure she was experiencing melting into my lips through squeaky breaths. I could hardly breathe myself, unraveling at the sight of this rarity as she slowly released me, the glint in her eye speaking to my heart just as much.

And with one more soft peck, she slid out of bed and walked down the hall, the sound of water shooting out of the clawfoot tub filling my ears seconds later. I stared at the sheets, still smelling her, smelling us, and knew beyond a shadow of a doubt that what I had been feeling this entire time wasn't lust or a fantasy.

I was fucking in love.

With my daughter's best friend.

Chapter Fourteen

Callie

After turning the faucet on full blast, I sat on the toilet to pee, staring at the tile floor and hating myself. Not because I felt guilty about sleeping with Jade's father. But because I *didn't*.

I felt good. So fucking good. Literally and figuratively. But how did Alex do it? I was still recovering from the magic of his body, the power of his words, the unwavering passion of his soul.

When my thoughts started to spiral, he carried me there, to that otherworldly place of blinding euphoria, only joining me when I arrived first. Not only once, but fucking twice. How was this possible? I was still reeling from it all.

I unrolled several squares of toilet paper, legs quivering, my heart jolting even harder. Quickly, I flushed, washed up, and grabbed a robe just as Alex walked into the bathroom, a sheepish grin forming on his mouth, those dimples shining in all their glory. He stood at the toilet and removed the condom before tossing it, then approached the sink, staring at me in the mirror, still smiling.

Holy hell.

He looked like a god. One of those mythical beings out of a damn book that you only dream of. I studied his biceps as he washed his hands, the muscles in his back flexing just as much. And God, that ass. So round and tight. I couldn't help but stare and drool as he lathered his hands and drenched them under the faucet when he turned around, his massive cock taking my breath once again.

"Get a bath, baby. Enjoy." He pecked my cheek, about to leave the room, when I laughed out loud, not believing he said that.

"And just where do you think you are going?"

"Hm?"

"Join me," I requested. "Please."

"Yeah?"

I leaned closer, our lips almost touching. "I insist."

He held my cheeks, giving a soft smooch and bright smile. "Anything for the birthday girl."

Still in my white robe, I went to the tub and pulled over a stool before feeling the water, gesturing with my head for Alex to get in. He looked puzzled, his little dimples forming as he scrutinized the bath, then me.

"You're not getting in?" he asked.

"Not yet. Please. Sit down."

He stepped one foot in, then two, all the while staring with a half smirk. Soon, his luscious rump hit the tub floor, and I scooched the stool closer and sat down, leaning over the porcelain lip. "May I wash your hair?"

"What?" He was stunned.

I flushed. "Nevermind. It was stupid. I shouldn't have said anything."

"No, Callie. I would love that. No one's ever asked me that before."

I relaxed a little, my belly tossing and turning. "Okay. Lean back."

He bent both knees and inched forward, resting his head on the back wall of the tub, closing his eyes. I reached for a nearby bottle of shampoo and opened my robe, allowing it to fall off my shoulders as I sat topless behind him, biting my lip in anticipation.

I scooped some water with my hand and drizzled it over his scalp, beautiful shades of gray turning darker as I saturated them more and more. And with a dab of shampoo, I massaged the fruity cleanser into his hair, bubbles foaming, making the fluffiest squishy sounds.

"Mmmm," he moaned. "This is totally unfair, Callie. It's your birthday. Not mine."

I giggled, wondering when or if he would notice my nipples. "When *is* your birthday?"

"I'll give you a hint." He smiled, eyes still sealed. "It's a holiday too."

"No way." I stopped scrubbing. "Really?"

"It is." Alex flashed a bright smile. "It's a very lucky day, lassie."

"March seventeenth? You were born on St. Patrick's Day?"

"Yes," he chuckled, finally popping his baby blues open and seeing me. "Woah! Have you been sitting like that this whole time?"

"Took you long enough to notice," I teased, rubbing his soapy head as he stared wide-eyed, beaming.

"Oh, I noticed long before today. Believe me."

I took a cup and rinsed the suds. "Me too, Alex."

He sat up once I was finished and scooted all the way back, gesturing for me to come here with his finger. "Your turn, birthday girl."

I lost the robe and stepped in front of him, sitting down in between his legs. He gathered my hair and swiped a scrunchie I had hanging on the faucet before tying it high on my head, dunking a bar of soap next in the water, and rolling it over my back.

"Mmm," I moaned, melting under his soothing touch. "Alex."

Once my back and arms were lathered, he rubbed in firm but gentle strokes, almost putting me asleep between the heat of the water and the relaxing massage.

"Feel good?"

I laughed, "I haven't felt this good in quite a long time. Honestly, ever."

"You deserve it, Callie. Not just on your birthday. All year long."

"Still, this is a birthday I'll remember forever. You've given me the best birthday gift I could ever ask for."

He rubbed my shoulders, his hot hands softening my muscles. "The dress?"

I leaned against his chest as his arms came around me, water sloshing. How could I even express what he had given me? It was hard to put into words.

"The dress was beautiful, but no, I'm talking about something else."

He held me tighter, giving me all the time I needed.

"You've shown me what I've been missing, Alex. What I think I've always longed for. And that it's possible, you know?"

"I know. I know exactly what you are talking about."

He scooped some water and poured it over my back until the soap was rinsed, pecking the back of my neck and hugging me again. I kissed his hairy arm, not wanting him to ever let me go.

"Normally, I would call Jade and tell her everything about a night like this. But I can't. And as much as that kills me, I don't want this to end."

Alex stood with fluid ease and stepped out of the tub, reaching for a towel and wrapping it around his waist. He stooped low so we were eye to eye and took one of my hands, water dripping along his hairline.

"I don't want this to end either, Callie. The thought of that makes me sick."

"Sicker than if Jade discovered what we were doing?"

Alex pumped my hand, eyes on fire now. "Yes."

"Oh, Alex."

"We will tell her, Cal. When the time is right."

I stared into the murky water, the soap creating a white film on top. Soon, Alex's finger brushed under my chin, lifting it until I was looking at him again, the sight of him taking my breath away. "I can't lose you, Callie. I can't. I've never felt so alive with another woman in all my life."

"But Jade..."

"Jade is my daughter. My child," he blew a sigh. "But she's grown now. An adult with a life of her own. I've always respected her boundaries and privacy in that regard. And she has done the same."

"But we've never had those boundaries, Alex. Best friends don't keep secrets like this. God, she will hate me for eternity and beyond, won't she?"

Alex swallowed a husky moan, helping me stand out of the tub. He grabbed my robe and wrapped it around me, bringing me to his chest next. "I don't know what the future looks like, Callie. I can stand here and tell you that everything is going to be perfect, but that would be a lie."

I glanced away until he spoke again.

"But," he began. "I know my daughter. She is a spitfire and speaks her mind without skipping a beat."

"Yes," I agreed with a smile.

"But she loves even harder. And that gives me hope, Callie. For us. For our situation."

I hugged Alex with everything I had, our bare chests colliding. "Oh, I hope so, Alex. Because I can't imagine my life without you...or her."

Chapter Fifteen

Alex

We ordered dinner for the night and ate quietly together at Callie's table, the soft flames of the candles licking the air symbolizing so much of what was going on inside of me. The burn I had for this woman, the light she brought out of me, the warmth of her heart most of all that revealed just how cold and lonely my life had been without her.

I watched her take a bite of her pasta, noticing that she covered her mouth when she chewed, just like the night she ate at the pub in Montana. Fuck. She was so beautiful. Even in her powder blue sweats and messy bun. I preferred this look over the dress, to be honest. Her natural beauty taking my fucking breath every time I looked at her.

"Mmm," she sighed. "So good. How's yours?"

"Perfect." I set my napkin down, drinking her in as much as the red wine.

"Are you disappointed that we didn't go out?"

"Are you kidding me?" I reached across the table to take her hand. "I would choose this every time."

She squeezed my hand with a smile and let go, taking one more bite of alfredo before pushing the bowl forward, unable to eat another thing. "I'm stuffed."

I drank the last of my wine, feeling the same way. "Me too."

She gazed at me from her chair, her eyes lingering on mine before asking, "How soon do you have to fly back to Montana?"

Ugh.

A fucking jab to the gut.

"Early, baby. Very early tomorrow morning."

"Oh," her voice trailed, breaking my heart.

I didn't want to leave her. That's the last fucking thing I wanted. But I couldn't ignore my responsibilities at the lodge. Beyond that, simply being in North Carolina was a risk. I wondered if anyone saw me hit the fuck out of Travis. Or worse, that Jade would find out a single detail before I had the opportunity to talk to her.

"I'm going to stay here as long as I can, Cal." I stood and collected our dishes before leaning down to kiss her, assuring her the best I could.

"In that case, we have no time to waste." She helped clear the table and went into the living room, fingers brushing over what appeared to be DVDs. "What movie do you want to watch?"

I joined her, amazed at her collection. "You are the only person I know who still owns these."

"I'm not giving them up." She shook her head, and I laughed out loud, noticing an array of romcoms and older films.

"Nor should you." I read more titles. "However, it is still your birthday. So, it would only be right if you picked the movie. What's your favorite?"

"Oh, I'm not telling you that."

"What? Why not?"

"It's too personal."

I cackled out loud, thinking of just how *personal* Callie and I had become over the last several hours. "Too personal?"

"You'll think I'm stupid," she sighed.

"Not possible," I insisted with a gentle nudge against her. "Come on. Which one?"

She pulled the sleeves of her sweatshirt down, covering her hands before selecting the movie she was so nervous to tell me about. I scanned the title and understood why she felt a little reluctant. Although she never had to hide anything. Not with me.

"She's Having a Baby," I read out loud. "Callie, this is a classic."

"So, you've seen it?"

"Many times."

She turned bright red and stared at the cover. "Then you know it's not just about the baby but about falling in love and all of the choices that come with it. It's about discovering what is really important in life. The simple things that you find out are really big things. The people you could never live without."

I was fucking speechless.

"I guess that's why I love it so much." She took it back and was about to put it away when I reached for it and dove under her legs, carrying her up the old wooden staircase as she squealed with every step.

I lowered her to the bed and noticed the DVD player on her dresser where her TV rested. I popped the disc out and waved it around. "Oh, we're watching this. Every second."

She laughed and looked away, the opening credits beginning in no time as I crawled into bed with her, loving the way she fit beside me. Fuck, I could go to bed every night like this for the rest of my life.

The hours passed like minutes, time flying by too fast around Callie. Soon, the movie was ending, and Callie's eyes were wet by the final scene, a happily ever after if I had ever seen one.

She wanted that for herself.

Hell, don't we all?

It killed me that Travis had access to her body and mind for so many years, making her feel like shit daily when she only longed to love and be loved in return. To enjoy the priceless simplicities of life, love, and family. I wanted to give her that now. But was afraid of scaring her away.

"I'm going to miss you so much, Alex," she breathed. "I'm aching now just imagining you not here."

Fuck.

Maybe she did feel the same way I did.

"Baby, come here." I opened my arms to bring her closer, her body burrowing into mine.

"I know you can't stay. But I really don't want you to leave."

"I don't want to leave either, baby."

Callie straddled me, resting her sweet ass on my thighs as she peeled her sweatshirt off, revealing her breasts and belly. I traced the area just under her belly button, loving that it wasn't flat but so soft with the prettiest round shape. Fuck. I wanted to shoot my come inside of her, fill her with every drop and make the baby she wanted. The family she wanted.

No.

That's fucking crazy.

She tugged at my clothes until I was only in briefs, so hard and ready for her. I had one condom left and fumbled for the damn thing, trying to not kill the mood but protect us. For now.

"I want to taste you," she begged before I tore the foil packet and traced her tongue around my rim, moaning into my dick.

Holy shit!

"You taste so good, Alex."

"Take your pants off, baby. Put your ass up here," I ordered, and she chewed her lip before taking them off, her glossy slit making my mouth water all the more.

I slid down for her and turned on my side, my dick throbbing so hard for more. She was nervous and started breathing heavier, unsure of what to do next. I smiled, reassuring her.

"I want to taste you too. Put your leg over my shoulder."

She parted her legs, and I nearly came, her beautiful pussy so pink and wet. I lapped once around her clit, and she yelped, my balls about to bust at the sound alone.

"Mmm," I moaned into her sex. "Fuck, baby. You taste good too."

Callie took more of my cock than I was expecting, using her palm to glide down the shaft as she sucked. Fuck. I was closer than I wanted to admit. But didn't want her to swallow if she was uncomfortable with that.

"Callie, baby," I gasped, about to explode. "I'm about to come."

"Well, that *is* the idea," she laughed, sending more vibrations to my head.

"You don't have to—"

"Please, Alex. Come in my mouth."

Fuck!

I shuddered and couldn't stop the orgasm if I wanted to, milky strings spraying down Callie's throat as she moaned, only intensifying the pleasure. I swear to God I saw fucking stars after that, not wasting another second before diving back into her pussy, needing to hear her cry my name, needing to take that memory and sound back to Montana in just a few short hours.

I moaned into her shell, lapping harder and faster, damn near going feral. With every suck, I imagined drawing the venom of Travis's words out of her body and swallowing them, taking them from Callie so they could die inside of me, the man truly meant for her.

Her legs shook around my face, and I only ate more of her, Callie's screams of pleasure filling the bedroom as I barely grazed my teeth against her swollen bud. How the fuck I was already hard again was beyond me. My dick had surpassed the quota of my lifetime.

I had to have her.

One more time before I left.

I reached for the foil square and rolled it on with haste, her begging and calling my name driving me wild. Soon, I was inside of her, performing as I had before, keeping my dick inside and caressing her clit.

She cried out to God, to me, and was about to climb the walls, wailing and writhing under my body, tears streaming down both cheeks.

I wanted to tell her what I was feeling. That I was fucking in love with her. That I wanted to take her back to Montana and give her everything she wanted. To make love to her endlessly in the coziest cabin or under the stars.

But I couldn't.

I couldn't tell her that.

As much as I wanted to.

Fuck.

I didn't want to scare her away, her heart so torn already between Jade and me. I was torn too. So fucking torn. The last thing on the face of the earth I would ever want to do is crush my daughter's heart.

But what about my heart?

"Are you okay?" I choked as Callie rubbed her eyes. She opened her mouth to say something but stopped herself, and for a split second, I believed she wanted to tell me the same thing. That gave me comfort. But also an indescribable pain.

"Yes," was all she could summon from her heart. "Please. Don't stop."

"I've got you, baby." I smiled and rolled my hips over her, the gold heart between her breasts forcing my eyes closed. Dammit.

She folded her legs around my waist and squeezed, guiding me under her symphony of moans. I wanted to surrender to her for the rest of my life, to give her this over and over again, this moment we were living in.

Callie's hands came up and tangled with the gold at my neck, a blend of sweat and old cologne painting her fingers. Her thighs vibrated, and she gagged for air under me, clawing my chest with soft scratches, about to fucking combust.

I didn't want to hurt her, but fuck I couldn't help but buck into her pussy like a damn animal in the mountains, yanking her ass into my palm and lifting her to go deeper, the unmistakable flutters inside of her body taking flight seconds later.

A primal growl melted through my clenched teeth as she finished, come shooting out of me so fucking hard I thought I would pass out. I could only hold the woman I loved as she trembled violently under me, her cries of pleasure filling the room. There was another sound buried under her ecstasy, a tinge of fear of what we were embarking on. I heard it. I know I did. But despite the trepidation of what would fall later, nothing could stop us from chasing the love we were discovering. Not even ourselves.

Chapter Sixteen

Callie

I awoke to the sweetest smell of cherry smoke, the room pitch black except for a small glimmer of light from the balcony outside my bedroom, Alex's tall form catching my eye next.

"Ow," I hissed as I swung my legs off the side of the mattress, so tender between my thighs. Soon, the stinging subsided, and I made my way to the man who had caused such sensual pain, smoke rolling out of his smiling lips once he saw me.

"Baby, it's freezing. Go back inside."

"What are you doing out here?" I crossed my arms, shivering already.

Alex took one last puff of his pipe and set it down, blowing a heavenly whirlwind into the night air. He was fully dressed in vintage Levi's and a worn flannel, the stubble along his jaws catching the moonlight.

"I didn't want to wake you. You were sleeping so soundly." He hugged me, and I trembled all the more, following his lead back inside the toasty room.

"I guess it's about that time, isn't it?" My heart broke. "Your flight?"

He nodded and smooched my forehead, a sliver of pain behind his gaze. "Come with me, Callie. Pack a bag and come back to Montana."

I nearly wept with joy, but reality smacked me upside the head just as fast. "Oh, Alex. I would love nothing more."

"But?"

"But I can't. Not yet."

"Is it work? You can have all the space you need. I'll see to it." His pleading tone stabbed me in the heart, paralyzing me.

"Alex, no. It's not that," I blubbered. "I mean, I do have work, but Jade wants to celebrate my birthday and the house and—"

"Shit. Of course. What the hell was I thinking?" He turned all sorts of pink, even the tips of his ears.

"I just—"

"No, baby, I know. We can't let the cat out of the bag yet." He winked, and I laughed, otherwise I would have cried all over again. His chest vibrated as he wrapped his arms around me with a loving sigh, a sound of longing and understanding, a deep melody of patience and hope.

"Thank you, Alex."

He pulled back and watched me limp across the floor before sitting on the bed, wincing. "Speaking of cats, my dear. How is yours doing?"

I cracked the hell up, needing that comic relief. "Honestly? She's going to be in her crate for a while."

He busted into laughter himself, kneeling before me like a knight before a princess. "I'm so sorry."

"I'm not."

He rubbed one of my knees, blue diamonds open and sparkling. "Do you need anything? I can run to the drugstore before I head to the airport."

My shoulders sank at his thoughtfulness. "That is so sweet, but no. This is nothing a warm bath won't cure. Although I may be in bed most of the day to recover."

He stroked my cheek, eyes holding so much behind them it was hard to sort through it all. He didn't want to leave me. That rose above everything else we were experiencing, the future so unknown.

"I'll call you the minute I land, baby." He kissed me with fire, drawing a throaty whine out.

"Please do. As soon as you can."

"I will." He nodded and kissed the top of my head, staring at me as long as he could until his big shoes clicked down the steps and the old door squeaked shut.

A cab was already waiting for him outside in the darkness as he put his bag inside the backseat, the sight of him driving away creating more pain than I ever imagined feeling. The warmth of my house suddenly went cold. A blazing fire suddenly doused with water. And as embarrassing as this is to admit, I crawled into bed and caught the faintest whiff of his skin and broke down, knowing I had experienced love for the first time with a man I wasn't supposed to have it with.

Alex

I fucking cried all the way to the airport, not giving a damn. The driver every now and then would glance in his rearview mirror to catch a glimpse of a grown-ass, nearly fifty-year-old man drying tears off his cheeks throughout the drive. But he didn't say a word. Nor did I.

The sun was barely popping over the horizon when we made it, and I went through the motions of checking in and boarding, soon fumbling into a seat and staring out the window, wishing to God I could rewind the last twenty-four hours and relive them all again.

I must have dozed off at some point. The gentleman next to me patted my arm as the passengers filed down the aisle, a wad of drool collected at the corner of my lip. Ugh. Gross.

"Thank you." I nodded and stood to reach for my carry-on before following the crowd off the plane into a mob of people like ants all coming and going, their paths making my head spin.

I hopped in my vehicle and began the drive back to the lodge, thoughts running a million miles an hour despite the traffic slowing me down. I couldn't wait another second. I had to call Callie.

"Hey!" she answered after the first ring. "I was just thinking about you."

"Hey baby." I swallowed a burning lump. "You have no idea."

We chatted until I was back at Sugar Slope, my insides twisting when it came time to say goodbye. I didn't want to get back to the real world. Not with my world back in North Carolina.

Flashes of her body filled my head, her sweet voice calling my name, and fuck if I didn't start smiling like an idiot walking into my cabin, a new call coming in at the same time.

Only it wasn't Callie.

It was my daughter.

Chapter Seventeen

Callie

After talking to Alex, I slept most of the afternoon and evening away, arising the following morning bright and early to prepare for my classes. I tried to concentrate, but every time my eyes wandered from the computer screen, I saw him in my mind, so strong and powerful over me, creating more pleasure than I had ever experienced with a man.

Travis never cared about what made me feel good. What got me *there*. He always climbed on top of me in bed and pumped for a solid thirty seconds before rolling over. I was foolish to believe that it would get better as time went on. Eventually, I accepted it for what it was, never knowing what was really out there waiting for me.

I guess I should say *who*.

My phone vibrated against the wooden table, scaring the shit out of me. Jade's bright face lit up the screen, and I took a full breath before answering her video call, noticing she was shopping.

"How does it feel!?" she asked, over the moon excited.

I crossed my legs, guilt creeping back up again. "How does what feel?"

"Thirty!"

"Right!" I beamed. "It feels...fucking good."

"Ah! Well, you are absolutely glowing."

Shit.

"Really?"

"Yes! Did you get that peen after all?"

My mouth fell open, eyes about to fall out of my perverted brain. "What?"

"Let me guess. You popped in She's Having a Baby, didn't you?"

I blushed. "You know me well."

"Well, if you are free tonight, I would love to take you out! Dinner and talking trash. I've got some goss to share!"

"That sounds perfect," I chuckled. "Pick me up at seven?"

"It's a date!"

Frantically, I finished lesson planning and uploaded a new video for my students before doing a short livestream. I went through the entire house and cleaned, making sure to take out the damn trash filled with condoms. God help me.

Everything was in order. No sign of Alex anywhere. Fuck. My phone! I went through and deleted all of the incriminating text messages and went as far as to change his name to Andrew on the slim chance Jade saw anything. I even sent a text to Alex saying I would be with his daughter for the evening and to wait for me to call.

God.

I'm such a cunt.

An evil, twisted cunt.

It truly felt like I was the one cheating now. Only it was my best friend I was betraying. Shit. This was worse than an unfaithful fiance. This was fucking treason.

Knock knock!

I clipped Jade's necklace on and admired my black top and dark denim for the night, a camel cardigan with matching booties my outfit of choice. I rushed to the door, heels echoing in the empty space, and found my bestie waiting in her own chic attire of dressy wide legs and a fitted pink top, a long plaid coat hitting her thighs.

"Cals!" She hugged me as I returned her embrace.

"Hey Jade." I squeezed.

"Are you ready? I found the perfect little place to eat." She waved and marched to her fancy sports car as I followed, soon taking off to an unknown location, a sign reading, The Glassy Lounge catching my eye.

"Oh, this looks nice." I unbuckled my seatbelt.

"Isn't it cute? It's brand new." Jade pointed. "They have private seating areas upstairs. I reserved a room just for us!"

"You are a gem." I followed Jade inside, and we were immediately seated on the second floor, a cozy but elegant space filled with soft lighting.

"Mmm." Jade eyed our host from afar over her menu. "He was fine."

I never noticed.

"You think?"

"I'll get his number by the end of the night. Unless you want him, of course."

"No." I sipped my water. "He's all yours."

Jade laughed under her breath, and soon we were rattling off our orders to the waiter, my bestie hardly able to wait until he was gone before she started spilling the tea.

"Cals, I do not even know where to start." She tucked a long red strand behind an ear.

"Uh oh." I leaned over the table. "Should I be scared?"

"Well," she trailed off.

I gulped, wondering what the hell she was talking about.

"No! It's nothing bad. Just *interesting*." She drummed her fingers and pursed her bright red lips. "I stopped at the gas station in town to fill up before driving to your house and you'll never guess who I ran into."

"Who?"

"The toothpick gobbler."

"Tracy? Oh my God."

"That's not all. Travis was waiting in her car like a lost puppy. He made eye contact and holy shit, girl. Someone beat the hell out of him."

I dabbed the dew on my brow, feeling like the room was on fire. "Well, it sounds like he pissed off the wrong one this time."

"Damn straight. I wonder if it was Tracy's husband?"

"Honestly?" I sucked in some air through my teeth. "I get the feeling that he and Tracy aren't monogamous. But I suppose anything is possible."

"Jealousy is a raging bitch. But my God is it hot when a man takes care of business the good ol' fashioned way."

I took off my cardigan, flashes of Alex beating the shit out of Travis flooding my thoughts. God, I wanted to tell Jade everything. Every earth-shattering detail. But I couldn't. And that about killed me.

"Has Travis been bothering you anymore?"

"Nope," I lied.

"Good. Worthless prick."

"Amen to that." I grinned, and our food arrived piping hot, a beautiful array of chicken, mashed potatoes, and roasted carrots. I was starving, but my belly hurt so much from it all I wondered if I could stomach a morsel.

"Okay, aside from the Travis drama, there's more."

I covered my lips and chewed, not sure if I was ready for it.

"I think my mom and dad might be seeing each other or something." She aimed her fork at me, contemplating the clues in her head. I dropped my damn knife on the floor and cracked my head on the table as I retrieved it.

"Fuck," I hissed.

"Oh no! Are you okay?"

"Yeah," I lied again. "Sorry."

"No problem! So, anyway, I got this weird text the other day, and at first, I thought it was spam so I ignored it. But once I checked it later, it was a notification thanking me for booking my flight to Asheville."

"Oh, I get those spam messages all the time," I shoveled in more food, about to pass out.

"True, but I had to investigate. So I clicked on it and that pulled up the airline website Dad used to pay for our tickets to Montana. I must have been signed in to his information still because it took me right to his purchase history. Same credit card. Under the name Alexander Harrington."

My heart stopped.

Still, I tried to cover.

"Why did it text you, though?"

"Because Dad changed the number to my cell phone so I would have all the ticket info before our getaway," she laughed. "I guess he forgot to change it back!"

"Wow." I set my fork down, about to puke.

"So, being the little detective that I am, I called Dad yesterday just to check in, and he had the cheesiest ass grin on his face in the entire world, right? So, I'm snooping like I always do and notice his travel bag in the background."

"You did?" Dammit to hell.

"Mm-hm." She took a bite. "I didn't come right out and say that I knew about the flight but asked how his Valentine's Day was. He said he was alone in the mountains."

"Maybe he really was."

"Eh, I dunno. He had that look, you know?"

"What?" I held my breath.

"Like a little kid keeping a secret."

I scratched the back of my neck, nearly drawing blood. "But why do you think he was seeing your mom? He could have come to North Carolina to see anyone, right?"

"I can't think of anyone else Dad would book a flight to see in Asheville. On Valentine's Day of all days." Jade sipped her sparkling water. "You know what's also ironic? My mom has really been going down memory lane lately. Saying that she misses Dad and what life used to be like."

"But I thought your mom—" Holy shit. I stopped myself at once, remembering that my mother said Alex shielded Jade from what truly happened.

"Hm?"

Shit.

Think fast.

"I just meant I thought your mom was dating."

"She's *always* dating someone. But she never remarried. Not since Dad." Jade shook her head. "I guess I got excited thinking they had maybe rekindled things."

I wilted inside, unable to say a damn word until she spoke up again.

"Can I be honest with you about something?"

Jade, you are killing me.

"Absolutely."

"I know how devastated you were when Travis cheated. I wouldn't wish what you experienced on my worst enemy. But a small part of me was relieved that you weren't getting married. It felt like I got my best friend back."

"Jade," I sighed, trying not to break down.

"It's childish, I know. And unbelievably selfish." She stared at her plate.

"No, it's not selfish, Jade. I was in a really bad place. For a really long time. You weren't the only one who lost me. I lost myself too."

Until your dad.

"And now you are the queen of your castle, open to a world of endless possibilities with any handsome king you want." Jade swirled her glass, popping a ruddy brow.

"Any king I want, hm?"

Oh, Jade.

If you only knew.

"Any king you want. With your best friend's approval, of course." She winked, and I wanted to throw myself into oncoming traffic.

I curled a weak little smirk.

Pathetic.

"Oh, shit! I almost forgot! Speaking of *kings*, Dad is turning fifty next month, and I want to throw him a surprise party! What do you think?"

My belly flipped. "Yeah? That sounds nice. Where?"

"Well, I would love to do something here in Asheville. Maybe invite some old friends and coworkers? I was thinking my condo, but it's a little small for something like that. I'd love to rent out a banquet room at a fancy hotel. Lots of black decorations!"

"That sounds amazing, Jade."

"Getting him here is going to be tricky, though. I'll have to come up with a really good excuse. Or maybe Mom could help! Especially if they are meeting up like I think they are."

"March seventeenth will be here before we know it," I blurted without thinking.

"Hey, how did you know?"

"Hm?" *Dammit.*

"Oh, I must have said something at some point, I guess. It's sad, but I don't ever remember having parties for Dad when I was younger. Birthdays I mean."

"You're right." I thought back. "I always remember him working."

"Yeah, he worked a shit ton. I barely saw him myself."

"I'm sorry, Jade." That wasn't a lie.

"Hey, it's all good. Things are finally on the up and up." She beamed. "For everyone."

"Yes." I blinked, my throat burning and collapsing in on itself.

"You have to promise not to tell him. Not that you would have any reason to call my dad, but just in case, keep those lips sealed."

I choked on my water, debating on drinking more and just drowning myself right here right now.

"Damn, Cals. You okay?"

I gasped, coughing. "I...I think so."

Jade cracked up and paid for our meals before we drove back to my house. Quickly, she parked in the driveway and asked, "Can I use your bathroom before I go?"

"Of course! The upstairs one is bigger."

"Thank you." She formed two praying hands and rushed inside as I followed her up the stairs, her red head swiveling behind as she whiffed. "Are you burning a candle or something? Incense?"

"No." I looked around. "It is a really old house, though. Weird smells, maybe?"

"Hm." Jade shrugged and closed the bathroom door behind her as I wandered into my bedroom, Alex's brown pipe catching my eye from the balcony door, my eyes screaming in silence.

I heard the toilet flush and sprinted outside, snatching the pipe and throwing it under the bed. The bathroom door squeaked open not even a minute later, the scent of fruity smoke consuming me.

"All better?" I asked and led Jade down the stairs, offering her coffee.

"I wish I could stay, but I have to meet a potential client. They messaged late last night. Wedding season is coming. Pray for me."

"You can handle anything, Jade."

"Thanks, girl." She hugged me. "Happy birthday again. I love ya."

"I love you too."

Jade sauntered out the door, calling back one last time before she left. "I'll be in touch really soon about Dad's party!"

"Sounds great!"

Sounds fucking terrifying.

Chapter Eighteen

Alex

I stared at my phone like the desperate man I was, hopelessly waiting to hear Callie's voice on the other end. It was getting late, and all I could think about was if she and Jade were safe, my anxiety evaporating once her name flashed across the glowing screen.

"Cal," I answered immediately. "Baby, I was getting worried."

"I know. I should have called sooner. I got home a couple of hours ago."

Fuck.

That hurt.

"It's okay," I assured, noticing the slight lift in her tone that told me she was overwhelmed. "Everything alright?"

Silence.

"Callie?"

"Alex, Jade knows that you booked a flight to North Carolina. She got the text notification and now she thinks you and Marcy are seeing each other."

I nearly fell off the damn bed. "What a minute. Text?"

"Yes. Jade's number must have been the last contact you had on your account. Did you change it?"

Fuck, I hated technology. She was nice most days. But boy could she be a ruthless tattle-taling bitch.

"Callie, I booked that flight so fast I don't think I did. Fuck. I'm so sorry."

She huffed in my ear, a slight sniffle following. "You know, I'm not even mad that she knows you were here. But when her face lit up at the thought that you and her mother were back together. Shit. I felt like the scum of the earth, Alex."

"Baby, please. Hang up so I can video call you."

She barely breathed the word *okay* and disconnected, my fingers not moving fast enough to call back. Soon, however, her weepy face filled the rectangle in my hands, my broken heart wishing I was holding her instead.

"I'm so sorry, Callie. All of this is my fault."

"No, it's not, Alex. That's not true."

"I never wanted Jade to hate her mother. So I never said anything about what Marcy was doing. And maybe back then that was the right thing to do. But I can see now it's really tainted her view on things."

"You were just trying to protect her heart, Alex."

"Yes. I was." I wrestled with it all. "But keeping the truth for so long, I don't know, maybe that was wrong of me."

The gravity of my words hit us both in the gut, Callie's beautiful face scrunching in sadness. "We're wrong too. Aren't we?"

"Callie, listen to me. This world is not fucking black and white, baby. We cannot paint this one way or another. Right or wrong. Good or bad," I swallowed. "We follow our heart and hope to God it leads us where we're supposed to be. Life is a series of choices, Callie. And fuck, I would choose you all over again. Over and fucking over."

She reached for a tissue and buried her face into it, staring back at me with red, swollen eyes. "I want you more than anything I've ever wanted in my life, Alex."

"Yes, Callie, that's why I think we should—"

She interrupted, "I think we should stop this now before anyone gets hurt."

"Before anyone gets hurt? And by hurt, you mean Jade?"

Callie bawled, "We are going to crush her with this, Alex! It is going to destroy her! I can't have you! I was never supposed to have you."

"No, baby," I wept. "I'm right here. I'm yours, Callie. You are the only woman I want to be with for the rest of my life, however many years that is, baby. God. No. Don't do this."

She set the phone down, and all I could see was a black screen, the sound of her heaving sobs fucking demolishing my heart. I waited until she had collected herself and was looking at me again, cheeks so red and puffy I wanted nothing more than to kiss them and hold her through it. But I couldn't.

We were beyond that now.

"I can't lose my best friend, Alex. As much as I'm already grieving you, the thought of coming in between you and Jade is too much to bear. She would never speak to us again."

I hung my head, devastated. "So we just end this, Callie? Go back to our lonely lives, burning every day for each other until the end of time?"

She shook her beautiful waves, crumbling. "I want you more today than yesterday, Alex. This has nothing to do with what I want."

"We can make this work, baby. I know we can. Sure, it would be a shock at first to Jade. But I know in time she would accept us."

"How do you know that? I have lied so much to Jade that I can barely stand to even look at myself in the mirror. How would she ever forgive me? Forgive you? she scoffed, spiraling.

"Maybe she would. Maybe she wouldn't."

"And you're okay with that? With your one and only daughter hating your guts?"

"For falling in love!? Yes! I'm okay with that!" I roared, terror filling me that Callie would never know how I felt and I would lose her forever.

"What...what did you say?" she hiccupped, tears streaming.

Fuck. I didn't want to tell her this way. She deserved more. But this was our reality. A rollercoaster of highs and lows threatening to drop us from the skies, sending us to our doom.

I broke down, a man begging, not wanting the healed parts of my heart to be ripped open again. "Callie, I love you, baby."

She cried all the more, unable to form a syllable.

"I wish I was holding you now and telling you that," I gulped, tears spilling on their own. "God, I love you."

"I love you too, Alex," she wept, but there was no life in her voice.

Please, baby.

Say something else.

Anything else to let me know we're okay.

But she didn't.

"I can't tell you what that means to hear, Callie," I spoke up first, watching her look away. "Baby?"

"I'm so sorry, Alex. I have to go."

Chapter Nineteen

Callie

I don't think I cried so much in my entire life. My entire body ached from head to toe, not to mention my eyelids felt like someone had set them on fire. I picked up the phone so many times to call Alex and beg him to come back to North Carolina, even just for one more night. Maybe that could be the arrangement. We could meet several times a year at a remote location that no one knew but us. I would gladly give up any sort of fantasy of a husband and children if it meant I didn't have to give him up completely.

But we were so much more than an *arrangement*.

We were in love.

Why, then, wasn't that enough?

They say that love can overcome anything, right? I'm guessing the people who coined that phrase weren't in love with their best friend's father. A relationship that forces you to choose between the best friend of your life or the love of your life.

How the fuck was that fair?

It wasn't.

Life for me had been a cold bitch. And she wasn't letting up anytime soon.

It felt like months had passed when, in reality, it had only been about three weeks. No calls. No texts. Absolutely nothing from Alex. And like a coward, I mailed his pipe back to Montana with a note telling him how sorry I was. As embarrassing as this is to admit, I ended the letter thanking him for showing me what true love looked like and wished him well, hoping he would find happiness. What Alex didn't know was that even the slightest, fleeting thought of him with another woman about sent me into the next universe.

The separation never stopped me from thinking about him. His smile. His beautiful chest. His enormous dick that he knew exactly how to operate. Dammit to fucking hell.

I stared at the cucumbers in the grocery store and bit my lip, moving the hell on. To be honest, I didn't feel like eating a damn thing but needed to. I looked like absolute hell, the dark circles under my eyes and constant state of nausea making me look like I had the plague.

I whizzed past the meat section and caught a glimpse of a giant beef tongue, the sight and smell sending a dry heave up my throat. What in the fuck? I stopped the cart and took a deep breath, which only sent the raw meat aroma even further up my nose, and I knew it was showtime, fight or flight kicking in.

I decided to abandon my cart and raced to the bathroom, holding my mouth, the thought of having to vomit in a public toilet enough to make me puke on its own. However, my choices were limited, and none of them sounded good.

I reached for a paper covering and barely got it on the toilet seat when I upchucked the little bit of orange juice and toast I had for breakfast, the smell of the bathroom making me hurl two more times.

"Shit," I breathed to myself, panting. "Holy shit."

I heard the sink running and waited, soon stepping out to find a pregnant woman washing her hands, a smile of understanding curving on her mouth. "Hit you too, huh? I hate grocery shopping."

"Oh, I think I'm just feeling a little under the weather." I brushed it off, my stomach still convulsing.

"Oh. I'm sorry. I thought you were pregnant too." She smiled. "I still have morning sickness. Normally my husband picks up the groceries, but I needed some last-minute things. I can't walk by the meat section without wanting to gag."

I nearly fainted.

"Here, these are great for when you feel sick. Pregnant or not." She reached into her giant purse and handed me what appeared to be a cough drop. "They have ginger and lemon in them."

I held the little candy and popped it in my mouth, already feeling relief. "Thank you so much. I thought I was going to die out there for a minute."

"You are so welcome. Take care." She waved, and I washed up, taking a paper towel and running it under the faucet as well before dabbing the back of my neck.

Once the wave of sickness passed, I wandered out of the bathroom, not believing I literally took candy from a stranger and ate it. Jade would kill me. My mother would kill me. But whatever the lady offered helped, and I continued to shop, wanting nothing more than to get the hell out of there.

I grabbed a pack of toilet paper and mosied down the aisle, a row of feminine products catching my eye next. I paused, thinking about how many tampons I had left at the house, and threw another box in my cart just to be safe. I should be starting any day now. Add that to the endless list of reasons why I feel like shit.

Finally, after checking out and locking myself in the car, my phone went off, a text from Andrew coming through that made me wrinkle my brow. I realized immediately who it *really* was and quickly changed the name back, on the brink of a damn nervous breakdown.

> **Alex**
> Your package came. Thank you so much for mailing it.

> **I'm so glad. I knew you couldn't go long without your pipe lol**

> **Alex**
> ...

I waited, holding my breath.

> **Alex**
> I can't go much longer without you.

I typed in response, tears welling.

> **I know. I feel like I'm dying.**

Alex
> **Fuck, baby. I can't take this. I can't live without you.**

> **But what other choice do we have, Alex?**

Alex
> **I don't care anymore, Callie. All I want is you.**

> **I want you too, Alex. I'm just scared.**

Alex
> **We can be scared together lol**

I barely smiled, and that damn wave of nausea hit me again, forcing me to open the car door and vomit on the asphalt. Beads of sweat lined my temples, and I threw up the last remnants of whatever was in my stomach, tasting acid and the ginger drop, deciding then and there to face another fear, and went back into the store.

Alex

I waited for Callie to respond, hoping to see the flashing dots or, at best, a call. But she didn't. Maybe I said too much. It was clear she had set a boundary, and I needed to respect that. But fuck, knowing that she loved me, wanted me, missed me. That was too much to ignore.

Callie

> Sorry, I didn't forget you. lol I just got sick.

> What?? Are you ok?

Callie

> Yeah, I just started feeling bad in the grocery store. I'm going home now.

> **Are you okay to drive? I can get a cab for you.**

Callie
> **From Montana? LOL**

> **Phones can be a wonderful thing.**

Callie
> **You are sweet. But I'm okay to drive. Thank you though. I appreciate it :)**

> **Okay. Please let me know that you got home safe.**

Callie
> **Sure will**

Dammit. I should be there taking care of her. Not here. The countdown was fucking on. Once Sugar Slope was closed for the season, I was packing my shit and flying back to her ASAP. But not before talking to Jade. That had to happen first.

My phone lit up, and while I was expecting Callie, my daughter's name flashed on the screen instead, a tinge of guilt stinging me as I answered.

"Jade!"

"Hey, Dad!"

"How's it going?"

"Honestly? My condo is completely flooded. A pipe burst."

"What? Holy shit! Are you alright?"

"Other than standing in water up to my ankles, yeah I'm fine."

"Shit, Jade. That's terrible. What can I do?"

"Well, at the moment everything is under control. But I was hoping you could come and help me move my things?"

"It's that bad, huh?"

"Yeah, I can't stay here. The damage is going to take a while to repair. I hate to call and bother you. I'm just completely overwhelmed."

"No, I'm glad you called. How soon are you thinking? Like tomorrow?"

Jade hummed in thought. "Well, I have a cleaning crew here now and will likely finish tomorrow. In the meantime, I'm staying at a hotel. But I have to be completely moved out by March 17th."

I cracked up, flipping through my desk calendar. "Making me work on my birthday, huh?"

"Sorry, Dad."

"No, it's totally fine. I don't have plans, anyway. But there is something I've been meaning to talk to you about."

"Oh, this sounds juicy! Spill."

I rolled my eyes and covered my lips, praying to God for mercy. "In person, Jade. I want to talk to you in person."

"Alright, I guess that will be acceptable," Jade laughed, and I closed my eyes.

"Okay, so I'll book the flight and will be there as early as I can on St. Patty's Day." I calculated, hoping this all fell in our favor. "Is there anything else I can do?"

"Not a thing. I'll have everything boxed and ready to go. I just need help getting my stuff out and into the new place."

"You've found a new place already?" I was impressed.

"Of course, Dad! I'm making things happen over here!" she cheered, and I chuckled.

"Well, that makes me feel better. Count me in. I'll be there."

We hung up shortly after, thoughts drowning me about the two women in my life that I couldn't bear to hurt. My daughter. And the woman I was madly in love with. Was it possible to have it all? To live in happiness with Callie with the support of Jade? I wasn't sure. But one thing I was sure of, I couldn't go on living this way, living without the one my heart was created for.

Chapter Twenty

Callie

I made sure to text Alex as soon as I was safe inside, the act of putting my groceries away seeming like the most daunting task in the world. I was so tired I could hardly hold my eyelids open, so I shoved the cold foods in the refrigerator and left the rest of the bags, needing a nap.

Alex sent a big red heart emoji in response as I snuggled under my comforter and was almost asleep when my phone went off, the harsh vibrations jarring me awake.

"Hello?" I cleared my throat.

"He bought it! He actually bought it! I'm a genius!" Jade hooted.

"Who bought what?"

"Sorry. Dad! He's flying out literally on his birthday! This is perfect!"

"What did you tell him?" I smirked, imagining an array of excuses she came up with.

"Basically, that my entire house was flooded, and I needed him to help me."

"Oh my God," I laughed. "You pulled out the big guns."

"I had to. But get this, he said there's something he really wants to talk about in person."

I threw the blankets off, pacing back and forth. "Wait a minute. He said what?"

"And that can only mean one thing, right? What I've suspected all along! He's getting back together with my mom!"

"Jade, wait a minute. Have you even asked your mom about this?" My stomach gurgled.

"Well, not directly. But it doesn't take a rocket scientist to figure this one out, Cals. They are getting back together. Just wait. You'll see!"

"Right. Time will tell," I sighed.

"What's the matter, Callie? You sound terrible."

"I feel awful. I think I have the flu."

"Oh no! Well, feel better soon! I'll see you on March 17th at the Meadow Inn! Seven sharp! Dress up fancy and wear green!"

"You booked the Meadow Inn? How?"

"I'm a miracle worker. Last-minute cancellation and poof. We're in!"

"Wow. I'm impressed," I gagged. "Sorry, Jade. I have to go."

I barely heard her say goodbye before I was over the toilet again, puking my guts out. For the longest time, I just sat there, waiting for the next round to hit me. And when it didn't, I went back downstairs and swiped a bag off my counter, scared to death.

You need your best friend in moments like this. Potential life-altering moments when you feel like you are moving in slow motion while the earth keeps spinning. But to tell her this would be to reveal more than I was prepared for. I didn't want to lose her yet.

I opened the rectangle box and pulled out the stick, popping off the lid as I sat on the toilet. A steady stream of urine came, and I held the stick under it, sealing it back up before resting it on the sink and praying.

I flushed and washed my hands, thinking about how this was even possible. Travis and I hadn't slept together since last summer, so he was obviously out. But Alex used protection. Every single time.

I thought back to the last time we made love before Alex left, remembering how passionate and desperate we both were. When he finished, I looked down and noticed the condom had slid a little, but thought nothing of it.

No, there's no way I could be pregnant.

But the test shouted otherwise, the faint but ever so pink line lighting up the longer I leaned over the sink. For a split second, I was overcome with joy, but that happiness was soon overshadowed by the impending doom of the secrets and lies Alex and I had between us. So many in such a short period of time. There was no hiding from anything anymore. This baby would either bring us all together or tear us to shreds.

I feared the latter.

Chapter Twenty-One

Alex

The rest of the week went by at a snail's pace. Thankfully, Callie and I were still texting, but that was it. I longed to see her face. To hear her voice. More than anything to hold her in my arms.

Callie was still a little under the weather, so I didn't text too much, but ordered her some get-well items that I hope she loved.

A cozy blanket.

Instant soup.

Fuzzy socks.

And a new copy of She's Having a Baby.

Callie
> **What in the world? Alex!**

> I hope you are feeling better.

Callie
> **I am now :) You are out of this world amazing.**

> Only because of you, Callie.

Callie
> **Alex...**

> I know you've probably heard about Jade's condo flooding, right?

Callie
> **Yes. That's what she told me.**

> I'm coming to NC to help her move in a couple of days. I can't imagine being there and not seeing you, baby.

Callie
> We will see each other. That I can promise you :)

> Really?

Callie
> Yes. I miss you so much.

> I miss you too, baby. More than anything. I'll be there soon.

Callie
> I can't wait :)

Ugh. Maybe I should have told Callie everything. That I was planning on talking to Jade about our relationship. I guess I wanted to handle it all for her, to make our impossible situation better. Deep down I think a small part of me thought

Callie would beg me not to and I would surrender because let's just be real here, Callie had every part of my heart in her hands. Still, I had to do something. Living without her was absolute misery.

Callie

Maybe I should have told Alex everything. That Jade was planning to surprise him for his fiftieth birthday. That his daughter truly had convinced herself that he and Marcy were mending things and getting back together. Oh yeah. And that I was carrying his baby.

It was the morning of Alex's birthday, and while I imagined being naked with my legs spread to celebrate such a day, I preferred being under the covers while Alex explored my lady bits, not on an exam table with a plastic wand up my crotch.

"Yes indeed. You are pregnant!" The older doctor printed a little picture and showed me the tiny bean, pointing and explaining everything. "You appear to be just over five weeks," he said.

"That would be accurate." I blushed. "Valentine's Day."

The doctor laughed and continued charting, pushing the glasses up his nose. "I have a feeling I'm going to be very busy over the next few weeks."

I laughed along, still not believing it all. "Thank you for working me in so quickly. I just had to be sure. I've wanted to be a mom for so long, you know?"

"I understand." He shook my hand. "Please call if you need anything. Here is a packet for you with lots of helpful information. Go over that in your free time and we will see you back next month!"

"Thank you again. Truly."

"You're welcome."

Once the doctor left the room, I quickly changed and made sure to get my script for nausea medication. The sample had already worked wonders, so I was hopeful that over time I would feel better.

How in the hell would Alex receive this information? He was fifty with an adult child. I could only imagine starting over at his age would be frightening and exhausting.

Oh well.

For now, I had to wish him a happy birthday.

I called him instead of texting, not getting any answer. Hm. North Carolina was two hours ahead of Montana. Maybe he was sleeping still. Or better yet, flying to Asheville.

My phone rang.

"Hey!" I answered. "Happy birthday!"

"Ah. Best birthday gift I could ever ask for." He sounded a little out of breath with noise in the background. "Thank you, baby."

"Where are you?"

"The airport. My flight has been delayed. By the looks of things, I may not get to Asheville until tonight."

"Oh no." I frowned. "Well, don't stress about anything, okay? Whenever you arrive will be great."

"I needed that, Callie. You have no idea."

I smiled, wishing I could kiss him.

"Will you do me a favor?" he asked, his voice muffled.

"Sure, anything."

"I've tried calling Jade to let her know I'm running late, but she won't answer. Could you keep trying her for me? My reception is shit."

I laughed, "Leave Jade to me. I'll make sure she knows."

"Thank you, Callie. I hate to rush off, but I can barely hear you."

"No problem. I'll see you tonight."

"I love you, baby," he breathed, and my heart buzzed, about to stop.

"I love you too, Alex."

And with a click, he was gone, my heart thousands of miles away in Montana for a little longer, it seemed.

Thankfully, I was able to get ahold of Jade, and when I told her about Alex's flight, she sounded surprised that I knew. I had to come up with something. At least until the truth was out.

"He sounded really worried that he couldn't get ahold of you. I guess he had my number from when we stayed at the lodge. You know. The reservations or whatever."

"Ah, that makes sense. Well, as long as his ass lands by seven all should be well!" Jade exclaimed. "I'll see ya tonight, chick!"

"Yeah!" I tried to mask my trepidation. "See you later."

Chapter Twenty-Two

Alex

By the time the flight landed, it was dark outside, and I was beyond pissed that I had let Jade down. I hoped there was still time to help her move, but at this point, I doubted I would be of any use.

I noticed my daughter's bright red hair waiting in the airport parking lot as I made my way closer, her happy-go-lucky tone easing my mood. "You made it!"

"Barely." I hugged her. "I'm so sorry, Jade. It's not too late, is it? Or have you already made other arrangements?"

She read her watch. "Well, we're cutting it close, but I think it'll be okay. And yes, other arrangements have been made."

I cocked a brow, trying to figure her out. "Wait. What?"

"Come on, Dad."

"So, we *aren't* going to your condo?" I scratched my gray hair, confused as hell.

"No, nothing is wrong with my condo. I lied to get you here," she blurted, and I stopped in my tracks.

"Well, then where in the hell are we going?"

Jade shrugged and hopped in the driver's seat as I slipped into her vehicle, speeding off until a hair salon came into view. My daughter parked and grabbed the black garment bag behind her, urging me to hurry the hell up.

"Come on, Dad! We're going to be late!"

I jogged after her as she rushed inside the hair salon, an older woman wearing a stack of gold bracelets waving me over. I shoved my hands in both pockets and went to her chair, eyes begging my daughter to tell me what was going on.

"She's just going to freshen up those ends, Dad."

"Why do I need *freshening*?"

"No questions," Jade ordered. "Sit."

That was the fastest haircut of my life, but damn it looked good. Short on the sides with a classic fade and just enough to swoop in the front. I had already shaved, so that was covered. Now, Jade was stretching the mystery bag my way, directing me with more demands.

"Go change."

"Here?"

She nodded.

"Where exactly am I going to do that?"

"The restroom! Right over there!" Jade pointed, and the entire room full of women stared at me, smirking.

"Okay." I snatched the bag and disappeared inside the restroom, hardly able to turn around because of the size. Thankfully, there was a hook on the wall, so I hung up the bag and unzipped it, opening the flaps to reveal a stunning three-piece suit, shirt, and tie. All black.

Something was obviously going on here.

Something big.

I hoped Callie was a part of this in some way, whatever was going on. She did sound confident that we would see each other when I arrived back in North Carolina, but I had no idea. Fuck. I missed her.

"Dad! Here's your socks and shoes!"

"I was wondering about that," I teased, opening the door to find my daughter wearing a long hunter green gown, her bright hair popping against the silky fabric. "Jade. You look beautiful."

"Thanks, Dad. You look like a million bucks."

I grinned, making my way through the hairdryers and clippers, every woman in the room combing me over with their eyes. Blood singed my cheeks, and I kept my head down just as my daughter said, "He looks great for fifty, huh!?"

The salon erupted with cheers and applause, and like an idiot, I waved, not knowing what else to do. Jade soaked it all in, and while I wanted nothing more than to run out of there, I let her have this moment, not knowing if after tonight she would ever talk to me again.

Callie

I was amazed at the little bump my stomach had grown into, the most tender swell protruding beneath my belly button. I admired it before stepping into my kelly green dress, my gift from Alex, and pulled the lace over my shoulders, remembering that I couldn't zip it up alone before.

Using a long piece of ribbon, I fed it through the zipper and pulled, closing the dress without a snag. God, it was so gorgeous, hugging my curves and the baby as well. I wondered if Alex would be able to spot the little difference in my body now compared to before. I hoped he did.

My hair flowed in long, loose waves as I dusted just a little makeup on, not too much, but more than Alex had ever seen me in. Rarely did I dress up for anything, but tonight was special. For so many reasons.

I made my way into the kitchen, turning off the lights before it was time to go. Alex's birthday gift was wrapped in black paper with a green bow on the counter, butterflies swarming just imagining him opening it. I debated on bringing it to the party or just having him open it here, but ultimately stashed it in my purse, wishing for the opportunity to arise more than anything.

Traffic was a nightmare, but somehow, I made it to Meadow Inn just a few minutes before seven. The parking lot was full, of course, so I had to circle a million times until a spot opened. I could see people pouring into the building wearing fancy suits and dresses, some I recognized, others not so much.

I slid my black heels out of the car until they hit the pavement, the crisp night air so refreshing to take in. Clutching my purse, I wandered inside and veered toward the sea of black and green, wondering where the love of my life was and what he would do when he saw me.

Oh, how I wanted him to embrace me and swallow my lips, to proclaim how much he loved me in person. But that was just another fantasy of mine. We couldn't do that in a room full of people who hadn't seen Alex in God only knows how long. It wasn't their thoughts I cared about though, but Jade's. As painful as this all was, I had to remember that this night was about her and her father. Not my scorching passion for him, no matter how hot it burned.

I filtered through the crowd until I spotted a table with my name tag, warmth filling me once I realized how close it was to the entrance of the banquet room. My belly zapped with electricity, excitement filling me that I would be one of the first to see Alex walk through that door into a room full of people who all loved and wished him the happiest of birthdays.

"Callie, right?" a male voice asked behind me.

I turned to see who was speaking and had a flash of deja vu, squinting hard as the memory cleared. "Wait a minute. Forgive me. The Glassy Lounge?"

"Yes." The young man flushed and sat beside me, the name tag on his plate reading, *Brendan*.

I laughed a little, "Jade got your number, didn't she?"

"She's a persistent one. I'll have to admit I was shocked when she asked for it and later invited me to this party." He scanned the room, raking his short blonde hair. "But I don't know anyone. And I can't find her."

"Well, you're safe at this table. I barely know anyone myself," I encouraged. "She will be here, I promise. I think her father's flight was running a little late."

"I feel so stupid. I must have sent her four or five texts." Brendan pulled out his phone, swiping.

"Don't feel that way. That's just Jade. Chances are her phone is dead or she is in the middle of something."

He relaxed a bit, wearing a black suit, the look of dread still painted all over his face. "Thanks."

We sat in awkward silence as the minutes passed, the crowd suddenly going silent as several people gathered at the window, whispering that Jade was pulling into the parking lot. I took a deep breath, not being able to get enough air into the depths of my lungs, when another guest turned off the lights, anticipation digging her claws into my chest with every second the room was pitch black.

I could hear Jade's happy voice carrying down the hallway, the clicking of her heels matching Alex's cadence as they came closer and closer. God, he was almost in front of me. I could hardly wait, but was so scared of what would happen when I saw him again.

Suddenly, the lights flashed on, and the crowd shouted in unison, "Surprise!"

I gasped, trying to keep my shit together and not break in front of so many people but the sight of Alex stole the last remaining molecules of oxygen from my body, and I could only cover my lips at his beauty, his breathtaking masculinity that he carried with grace and paralyzing confidence.

He was stunned, unable to say anything, but his eyes were searching despite all of the people cheering around him, studying every face for barely a millisecond before moving on. And when those blue drops landed on mine, I crumbled quietly, swiping the tears just as fast as they came, ready to move forward with the man I loved but still stuck in the present reality of our secret.

He touched his chest and offered the most subtle sway of his gray head, eyes batting as he swiped through his lashes. I noticed his lip tremble, and he bit it hard, not taking his eyes off me until Jade hugged her father and waved to some invisible person to come forward, Marcy's bright red locks weaving from the back of the room until she was face to face with her daughter and ex, their broken family united once again.

Chapter Twenty-Three

Alex

From the moment we pulled into Meadow Inn, the dots slowly but surely connected. I recognized a few familiar vehicles in the parking lot and predicted what Jade had planned. An over-the-fucking-hill party for yours truly.

Don't get me wrong, I was grateful. Beyond grateful. But more than anything, I wanted time to speak with Jade alone. I *needed* time with Callie alone. But that would have to wait now.

I noticed Callie's vehicle parked in the front row, and my steps stuttered, a bolt of lightning shooting up both legs into my belly at the reality that she was here. Fuck. I wanted nothing more than to scoop her in my arms and bust into any vacant room to ravish her from head to toe. Dammit.

Jade clung to my arm and guided me into the hotel, rushing down the hallway toward a dark room. I cleared my throat and tugged at the tie around my neck, the tension rising at an all-time high when we entered the foreign space, the blinding lights flashing at once, illuminating so many old friends and family that had gathered to celebrate me.

But where was she?

My baby.

I swept the room as fast as I could, trying to find her, desperately searching for the one who held my heart. It felt like one of those activity books you have when you are a kid, where you strain your eyeballs with all your might to find the hidden object. Only this wasn't a book or a game. This was my fucking life. And the woman I wanted to spend the rest of it with.

At last, our eyes meshed. She was so much closer than I realized. And when I caught the full vision of her, the angelic display of the woman she was both inside and out, I silently wept, deciding that I didn't care who saw. I needed her in my arms.

Jade's hug pulled me from Callie, and I whispered a breathy *thank you* in her ear, wishing there was a private moment to speak, but seeing that was not in our favor. My daughter pulled away and stared into the crowd, waving for someone to come closer.

Every drop of blood drained from my head once I realized who was approaching, my ex-wife like a viper sucking all life from my body with one bite of her wicked smile.

"What the hell is this?" I hissed at Jade, Marcy practically in front of us now.

"Dad, what do you mean? I thought that—"

"Thought what, Jade?" I seethed, ready to turn every table in this goddamn place, the love of my life feet away, covering her lips.

"Hello to you too, Alex," Marcy raked her long nails through her mane, her pride making me fucking ill.

"Dad, I thought you would be happy," Jade scrambled, trying not to break.

"Of course, I'm happy about this party. It's one of the most thoughtful things anyone has ever done for me, Jade. But," I stammered, feeling every eye on me. "Why in the hell would you invite your mother?"

Marcy's lip fell open, and to be frank, I didn't give a damn.

"Because you said you had something important to talk about," Jade whispered harshly.

"And you thought it had to do with your mother?" I wiped my lips, sweating from head to toe. "Does this have to do with the text you got? About the flight to Asheville?"

Jade looked like I slapped her across the face and barked, "Wait a damn minute. I never told you about that."

Fuck me.

Jade glared at Callie, then me. "The only person I told that to was Callie."

Well, here we fucking go.

"Why would she tell you that?" Jade crossed her arms, the tension in the room rising as the crowd went quiet.

"Jade, *this* is what I wanted to talk to you about."

My daughter turned beet red, fiery hair shaking back and forth. "You haven't been seeing mom?"

"No, Jade." I turned to Marcy, furious that she even came. "Why would you show up anyway, Marcy? For fuck's sake."

"Because our daughter invited me. I wanted to be here." Marcy looked down and then into my eyes, not a shred of sincerity behind them. "It's true I've been talking to Jade about how things used to be. I miss you, Alex."

I laughed through the fury. "That's hysterical, Marcy. Really. If anything, you miss being taken care of. I suppose your flings haven't done a very good job of that or else you wouldn't be here."

"What?" Jade's eyes pierced mine, confusion all over her face.

"Jade," I began, but she cut me off.

"So, if you weren't here to see Mom on Valentine's Day then who!?"

I turned to find Callie again, but she wasn't at her table anymore, the young man I noticed sitting with her gone too. Their plates of uneaten salmon remained, and I searched the entire party room, the tail end of her green lace barely visible out the back door.

"Callie!" I called, a desperate plea bubbling from my soul out my lips.

It wasn't my plan to leave Jade and the rest of the party in the dust, but I couldn't stay with my heart leaving, knowing now more than ever that there was no turning back after this night.

I charged ahead, my dressy shoes clacking against the hard floor just as Callie and this mystery guy went into the women's restroom together, my breath coming out embarrassingly loud and choppy. What in the hell is she doing with him?

I pushed the heavy bathroom door open, a line of toilets staring me in the face as the sound of gagging rang in my ears. "Callie? Baby?"

"In here!" a male voice responded, and I found them in the very last stall, the love of my life on her knees puking in the toilet as this young man held her hair. Shit. Oh, Callie.

"Cal." I went to her, her cheeks pale with neck veins bulging as she got sick again.

"Alex," she coughed, spitting.

"Can I get you anything?" the young man asked, and Callie tried answering but couldn't speak.

"No, but thank you," I assured. "I've got her."

He nodded and slipped out of the stall, leaving Callie and me alone. Once the heaving subsided, she reached for me, and I helped her stand, supporting her back as she walked to the front of the bathroom and collapsed in a chair.

I swiped a few paper towels from the dispenser nearby and ran them under some cold water, gathering her hair to put them on her neck. She stared at me with the sweetest gaze, leaning into my palm as I brought the damp towel to her cheek.

"Hey." She smiled.

"Hey." I flashed a bright smile, not taking my eyes off her, and kissed the wet spot on her cheek, salty from her tears, not the towel.

"Happy birthday, Alex," she breathed, mascara running.

"You are so sick and still want to wish me a happy birthday. Baby, I don't deserve you." I pecked her forehead when my daughter flung the bathroom door open, screaming, "Baby!?"

Chapter Twenty-Four

Callie

I knew this day would come. It was inevitable. Like a house of cards that threatens to come crashing down with each move, so was every day that Alex and I kept our relationship hidden. It only brought us closer to this moment, Jade's expression of shock souring the longer she looked at me.

"It was you, wasn't it? Dad came to see *you* last month."

"Jade," I cried, vomit on my breath. "I wanted to tell you but—"

"Oh, this is epic. I can't fucking believe this. Are you both for real right now!?" she shouted, her voice ricocheting off the bathroom walls.

Alex took my hand, and that sent her into overdrive. She paced back and forth in her dark green dress and heels, hands flying. "When did this even fucking start?"

"Jade, scream at me. Not her." Alex softened his tone, hoping his daughter would match him, I gathered.

"Don't you tell me what to do! This is a goddamn circus! Callie, how could you do this!? You have made a fool out of me!"

I cried, trying to stand, but my stomach quivered with nausea. "Jade, I never planned for this to happen. I'm so sorry I didn't talk to you sooner. I didn't want to lose you."

"So you fuck my dad and just expect us to be best friends forever!?"

I hung my head, defeated and barely breathing, "I love your dad."

Jade's nostrils flared, and I heard the grinding of her teeth, stern eyes slicing me up first, then Alex. If hatred had a look, it was that one. And I knew right then I would be lucky if she ever talked to me again.

"You know who else loves my dad?" Jade pointed. "My mom. She spent all evening getting ready to celebrate with us and for the first time, I had hope of my family coming back together."

Alex stood tall, guarding me. "Jade, I hate to burst your bubble, but that was never going to happen. Not in a million fucking years."

"Why not, Dad? We were all so happy! Don't you remember?" Jade shrieked.

"I do remember! I remember your mother fucking every man she could! Every man but me!" Alex's voice rumbled like the aftershock of an earthquake.

"What the hell are you talking about?" Jade asked, disgust on her tongue.

"I meant exactly what I said. Your mother was never faithful to me, Jade. I tried for years until I was fucking lost in a marriage with a woman who wanted nothing to do with me. So I got out and I've lived alone for years. And I hate to break your heart, Jade, but Callie has changed that for me. I love her too," Alex started crying, not phasing Jade whatsoever.

Jade scowled at me in silence as Alex cried, soft huffs of his broken heart saturating the air. Finally, I was able to stand and latched on to his arm, offering a gaze of understanding in the hope that he could feel my love.

"It's about money, isn't it?" Jade spewed. "My father has finally achieved everything he's ever wanted and you want it for yourself."

"Jade! No!" I clamored.

"Well, why else would a thirty year old woman want a man who is fifty? If not for money, then what? To indulge your daddy issues?"

That fucking hurt. I could only stare at the floor and take her verbal tongue-lashing, Alex not letting go of my hand.

"Not having a father never gave you the right to take mine, bitch," Jade spat. "You can fuck yourself and this friendship."

"Don't say that, Jade," Alex begged as I wept. "Don't take this out on her. I know you're shocked and angry. Believe me. It was Callie who wanted to end it for your sake. *I* was the one who pursued Callie from the start. I wanted her more than anything. So if you are going to hate someone, hate me."

Jade gave one final word before turning on her heel and fleeing. "Trust me, Dad. I already do."

The door banged shut, and I jumped, falling to pieces into Alex's side. He rubbed my arm up and down and held my head, reaching for another paper towel and cleaning my face.

I fought the urge to run away, to hide from the world and the pain I caused my best friend. I wanted to disappear. To vanish into thin air. That was until Alex's smoky voice grounded me, an offering of hope despite the storm we were nearly drowning in.

"It will get better in time," he vowed.

I hiccupped, my body weak. "But tonight is not that night."

"No, baby. It's not." He led us forward, opening the door to a mob of people all eavesdropping. Alex gulped, muttering, "Sorry to disappoint you, folks. But the party is over."

The guests scattered like roaches as we made our way back to an empty banquet room, my lonely purse sitting by my chair with the cold fish on the table. I stopped mid-step and reached for Alex's arm, feeling another wave about to knock me over.

"Could you grab my bag for me?" I strangled another heave, feeling sweaty.

"Sure, baby." He retrieved it without question. "Was it the food, you think?"

"I didn't try it," I confessed, taking his arm and moving fast out of the hotel, sucking in the cold night air, relief setting in.

"Are your keys in your bag? I want to drive you." He wrapped an arm around me as I rummaged through the purse, giving the key and hiding his gift.

Alex opened the passenger door and helped me inside, soon turning on the car and heading toward my house, the shattered pieces of the night popping into my brain one fragment at a time. I barely got inside with Alex closing the door behind us and hovered over the kitchen sink, splashing icy water on my face to ease the panic.

I felt his strong presence next to me, its warmth just as comforting to my soul. Even in the uncertainty, Alex surrounded me with peace and safety, his arms coming around me from behind, bringing my fantasy to life.

"Oh Alex," I whispered. "What are we going to do?"

He nuzzled into my hair, inhaling. "We take it one day at a time, Cal."

I nodded, squeezing his strong arms, wrestling with losing my best friend while gaining the greatest love I had ever known. "Will you come upstairs with me, Alex?"

"Yes." He took my hand. "Let me help you."

I kicked off my heels and left them in the kitchen, sinking into Alex's firm grip as we walked up the old stairs. My purse was still hanging on my shoulder when we made it to the bedroom, the green lace on my curves next on the docket to go.

"Can I get you anything, baby?" Alex cupped my arms, still wearing his beautiful black suit.

I stroked his fresh haircut, admiring him. "No, I just need to clean up. I'll be right back."

"Take your time, baby. I'm not going anywhere." He loosened his tie and sat on the bed, removing his shiny shoes one by one.

I couldn't wait to brush my teeth, the taste in my mouth borderline foul. Taking my time, I cleaned every tooth and scraped my tongue, deciding a quick shower was also in order.

Miraculously, I was able to glide the zipper down without any trouble this time, my poor dress having been through hell and back in a matter of hours. It melted like wax off my shoulders and pooled at both feet before I folded and set it aside, catching Alex's back as he sat on the bed from my open doorway.

Quickly, I showered, feeling better already. Washing never felt so good, my muscles relaxing under the steamy stream in no time. I imagined all of the literal grime coming off me and swirling down the drain, wishing the crud around my heart would do the same. But I feared that would be there for a long time.

I dried off and slid my arms into a cozy robe, reentering the room where the man I loved sat with his jacket off and dress shirt unbuttoned, silver hairs and a gold chain drawing me like a moth to a flame. He stretched his big hand and took one of mine as I joined him, his soft vibrating sigh captivating me.

"Why don't you try to get some sleep, baby? I'll be right here if you need anything. Anything at all."

My eye fell to the little black bag on the comforter, and I swallowed, my words shaking as much as my body. "Could you grab my purse for me, please?"

He saw it next and passed it over. "Sure."

I locked eyes with Alex, wishing I could plant the news into his brain somehow without saying it out loud. I was so scared. So overwhelmed. But so unbelievably happy.

"I was hoping to give you this tonight at the party if we were ever alone but—"

"Baby, you didn't have to get me anything. Being here with you is the only present I want." Alex grazed my cheek, blue eyes pouring their love into mine.

"Please," I shook, taking out the package. "Open it."

He received the small rectangle-shaped present and stared at it a second, then at me. His fingers gently peeled the paper away, revealing the DVD he bought for my birthday, his brow raising in confusion.

"There's more." I stared at the movie case, and he cracked it open, the fuzzy black and white picture sitting on top of the disc. Alex could barely hold the paper still, an audible breath leaving him.

"Cal." He read every detail on the ultrasound photo. "Baby..."

"That's right." I trembled inside my robe, my voice lifting. "Alex I'm—"

He dove into my mouth, climbing on top of the bed as I melted under his kiss, closing my eyes as his lips gently sucked mine and found my forehead. "You're pregnant. Callie. I'm—"

"I understand if this changes things, Alex," I blurted my deepest fear, that the man I loved would leave me like my father left my mother, and I would be alone in raising our child. "Trust me, I have thought about every scenario of how this conversation would go."

"Baby, no. Never." He smoothed over my thigh.

I sat up and clutched my robe. "Jade already thinks I want your money. Once she finds out I'm pregnant, that will be a certainty in her mind."

"Callie—"

"And as thrilled as I am that this happened, I'm terrified. I don't want to do this alone, but I am prepared to. Like my mother did."

"Why would you ever think you would be doing this alone, Callie?" Alex's gruff voice warmed my spine.

"Because we were careful and—"

"It happened anyway," he finished. "And you don't know how happy I am that it did."

My head snapped up, and I saw his eyes sparkle. "What?"

He crashed his lips against mine, a soft laugh slipping through his kiss. "I love you, Callie."

"Alex," I breathed, devouring his smoky kiss, fisting his silver hair and tugging. He grunted against my mouth as my robe fell open, his hand barely grazing my waist and the delicate swell of my belly. Heat surged between my legs, and I squeezed them together, moaning, "I love you, too. So much."

I surrendered to the power of his touch, his fingers coasting along the slopes of my body, exploring every inch and pecking ever so delicately. A husky exhale ripped through my chest, needing him to fill me, and I sifted through his chest hair, tangling my fingers into the gold, silently pleading.

"Baby?" he gasped.

"Please, Alex." I unzipped him, his hard cock springing free.

"But you're sick. I don't want to make you feel worse."

"I'll feel worse if I don't have you, Alex." I chucked the robe and opened my legs to receive him, marveling at his cock, the tip glistening.

"I can't tell you how any times I thought about doing this again." His smile brushed the shell of my ear, his breath causing chills to erupt from my flesh.

"Are you really happy, Alex?" My intrusive thoughts won, fear overpowering the pleasure I was craving.

He hovered over me, carefully brushing a stray hair from my brow, the compass around his neck skimming my throat. "Thrilled, baby. Absolutely thrilled."

I breathed Alex's name as he planted kisses between my breasts and observed their fullness, asking what he suspected. "Are they sore?"

I nodded, shocked that he knew. Never had a man responded to my body this way, so in tune with things I never said out loud.

Alex continued to stamp his lips down my torso, stopping at the little bulge I was carrying now. He kissed our baby while staring at me, a jagged breath whirling into my lungs.

"I need you, Alex."

He flashed his pearly white teeth, eyes darkening in the shadowy room. "I'm here, baby. I'm right here."

I whimpered as his kisses fell even lower, my inner thigh tingling with his gentle suck. The coolness of the room prickled my skin until Alex's heated breath warmed my entrance, the hot, wet laps of his tongue stoking the fire within, my skin engulfed with desire.

"Mmm," he ate, tracing my clit with the tip of his tongue.

"Alex." My legs fell open in surrender as he lifted them to rest on his shoulders, circling the most sensitive part of me and sucking.

The build accelerated faster than I was prepared for when Alex adjusted himself the slightest bit to stay on target, licking as my cries of pleasure soared. He moaned into my sex, a primal growl that tingled my pussy with vibrations. *Just a little more*, I thought and urged by folding my legs around his neck, carefully squeezing the salt and pepper mane between them. His tongue stiffened and batted my clit slowly at first, then faster and faster, soon throwing me into a blinding orgasm, cries of unabashed pleasure capturing me, forcing all doubt about our love to cease.

Chapter Twenty-Five

Alex

Callie burrowed into my side as we cuddled in bed, our naked bodies still heated from making love. I thought after Callie finished in my mouth she would want to relax and fall asleep, but she reached for my cock and straddled me instead, giving me the most exquisite view of her, a mirage I thought would disappear if I blinked.

Even in the dimly lit room, I noticed the changes she was experiencing. Her full breasts. The beautiful roundness of her belly that was swollen just a little more. Her increase in drive. Fuck. I couldn't believe Callie was mine, the fantasy of her carrying my child now a reality.

"It was morning sickness, wasn't it? The day you went to the grocery store." I thought back, barely scratching Callie's arm as she snuggled closer.

"Yes," she breathed. "I didn't know it at the time, but yes. That's what it was."

I held her tighter. "Oh, baby, I wish I was there. I would have taken care of you."

She pecked my arm, enchanting eyes gazing up at me. "I know you would have."

I smooched her forehead, loving the way she sifted through my chest hair and laced our hands together. "Well, that makes sense why the salmon made you yak."

She laughed, her body vibrating against mine. "The waiter set it down, and I was out of there in no time, praying I wouldn't get sick in front of everyone."

"Who was the man with you?"

"That was Jade's date," she explained. "He was very kind to follow me like that."

I cleared my throat, memories of the night hitting me one at a time. "Jade deserves a kind man."

Callie sat up, her full cups staring at me until she dragged the blanket over them. "I tried texting her earlier. I think she blocked my number."

"Me too," I admitted, a defeated sigh slipping through my lips.

"She's furious." Callie looked away, and I reached for her chin, slowly bringing her back to me.

"Give her time, Callie. Don't lose heart just yet."

Callie kissed my hand and grabbed onto it, her words crushing me. "It's the hardest thing in the world, Alex."

"What, baby?"

"To be the happiest I've ever been in life and not be able to share it with her."

I nodded in absolute understanding, my heart torn as well. "You asked me if I was happy, Cal. And I have to ask you the same. Are you truly happy? With me? The baby? Is this the life you want?"

"Alex." She smiled, thick waves swaying. "Of course I'm happy. You know that, don't you?"

"I know." Insecurity reared its ugly head. "I just want you to be sure. Things happened so quickly and—"

"I know they did, Alex." She touched my cheek. "But if my relationship with Travis taught me anything, it's that time means nothing when it comes to love. You can spend years with someone and still be miserably alone. Or you can spend merely days with the right one and know that you don't want to waste another second of your life with anyone else."

A throaty gasp cracked in my throat, and I leaned in to kiss her, savoring her taste, her fire for me, her love most of all. She wrapped her dainty arms around my neck, and I held her close, fisting the back of her hair before pecking her neck.

"May I ask you a question?" she whispered, and I leaned back into the pillows, giving her all the time and attention she needed.

"Anything, baby."

She stared at my arm before looking back into my eyes, offering the sweetest half grin. "Where did you and Marcy meet?"

I swallowed, wanting nothing more than to share another page of my life story with Callie but fearful of what she would think. "I'd like to go back a little further if that's okay. To give you the whole story."

She nodded. "Of course."

Deep breath.

"My father passed away just days before my senior year started. After that, I guess you could say I was going through the motions of life. Trying to be strong for my mother. Doing the minimum to get through school. Some days breathing felt like a chore."

"Alex," she soothed. "What happened? To your father?"

I grunted, tearing up. "My father had his own demons, Callie. Demons he tried to drown with drinking. It worked temporarily. But one rainy night, he was driving home after leaving a bar and lost control of the vehicle. He died instantly."

She covered her lips and blinked away tears, listening for more in silence.

"I thank God he was alone in that accident. But," I choked on the words that wanted to come but couldn't.

"It's okay, Alex. I'm here," Callie barely breathed, rubbing my back.

I forced the words out anyway, needing to share my life with her. "My mother was never the same. I didn't know until later, but she miscarried a few months after my father died. Losing him and the baby was too much for her. She left a note, and—" I fucking broke, not planning to, and Callie cradled my head as unprompted sobs came one by one.

"I'm so...so sorry Alex," she wept with me, not letting me go.

I clung to this woman, my beacon of hope, the source of my healing. She didn't try to coddle me or sugarcoat anything I went through. She sat with me in the brokenness of it all. And that fucking meant everything.

Once I was able to speak again, I sat up and dried my face, Callie's empathetic eye giving me all the courage I needed to continue. "I dropped out of school, Callie. Soon, the bank took the house and I would have been homeless had it not been for a friend of mine who had graduated the year before. I rented a small bedroom from him and did every odd job I could to save money, wanting to carve a better life for myself in the worst way."

Callie dried her damp cheeks, letting me finish.

"Soon it was April and while my classmates were getting ready to graduate, I started working full time at this little ma and pop style grocery store as a stocker. I remember it was the Saturday before Easter and we were slammed. I met Marcy that day in the condiment aisle. She asked me where the mayo was." I smirked. "From then on, she would often come in with her family. Fuck, they hated me," I laughed.

"How could anyone hate you?" Callie kissed my cheek.

"Because I had nothing to offer their daughter. Money I mean."

"Oh."

"Marcy was persistent, though. She was always flirting and giving me her number, but dating was the last thing on my mind. Eventually, though, I started to look forward to her coming into the store. It was nice. Feeling wanted. Special."

Callie edged closer, so warm and comforting. "So you started dating?"

"We started fucking," I coughed, needing to be brutally honest. "Marcy was on her way to college, and I was going nowhere fast. As infatuated as I was with her, I truly believed we would go our separate ways once the summer was over. That was until she became pregnant with Jade."

Callie's eyes bulged, and I nodded, going on. "Her parents were livid. I mean fucking pissed. They invited me to dinner shortly after Marcy told them, and I would have been better off walking into hell. Her father chewed me up and spat me out over and over, basically threatening me to marry his daughter and provide or else."

"Oh, Alex."

I held the pendant around my neck, staring hard at it. "You know, my father always inspired me to do the right thing even though many times over he wasn't strong enough to do that. I never judged him for it, but I could hear his voice in my mind, telling me to do what was right."

"That's what the compass meant," she confirmed with a soft smile.

"Yes. He always told me we have the power to change course in life, to change our destinies. He wanted more for me." I fought tears again, savoring Callie's sweet touches.

"Alex," she trailed.

"So I married Marcy. Jade was born by the time I was nineteen. And the rest is history. Looking back, I can see now that it wasn't love that drew me to Marcy. I thought it was. But I really didn't have any experience to know for sure." My eyes flickered to Callie's, voice fading into a gruff tone. "I was so hungry for love back then though, to live for someone more than myself, to be a father and a husband. Without her, I wouldn't have Jade. I can't regret any second of our experience. But the ending, Callie. That nearly destroyed me all over again."

She clung to me, her hard nipples tickling my chest. I ravished her lips next, thanking God he saved this rarity of a woman for me, to allow me the privilege of loving and being loved this way in return.

"I wish I could sit here and tell you I know exactly how you were feeling, Alex. But that would be a lie." She wiped her tears. "But what I can say with all my heart is that you will never carry those feelings alone ever again. We share that weight now, babe."

"Babe?" My heart fluttered. "Mmm, now that is a name I could get used to."

"Well, get used to it." She pecked my lips with a bright smile and rested her head on my shoulder.

"On a more serious note, thank you, Callie, for listening. For your support. Fuck. For everything."

She raked through her beautiful waves, blue eyes stopping my heart. "Our stories are all a little broken, Alex. It's for sure mine is too."

"I want to hear all of it. Only if you wish to tell me, of course."

"Of course I do," she sighed happily, tracing my fingers. "Let's make something to eat first. Are you hungry?"

"Starved," I confessed, not having eaten before the party or during.

"Great. Come on." She playfully nudged and slid out of bed as we put on clothes and mosied down the stairs. I took in the sights of the old house, and a thought entered my brain about our living arrangements. I would have to put a pin in that and save it for later.

"Do you like chicken noodle soup?" Callie pulled out a container from the fridge and winced, expecting my answer to be less than thrilled.

"I love chicken noodle soup."

"Oh, good." She reached high into a cabinet for bowls, and I came to her side, brushing her shoulder.

"I've got this, baby. Have a seat."

"Are you sure?"

"Well, I may not be a very good cook, but I think I can manage the microwave." I winked, and she cracked up.

"I'm not the best cook either. Don't feel bad. My mom made that and brought it over this morning. I briefly mentioned I had been a little under the weather when we talked last night on the phone and it was ready by dawn."

I flashed a smile, so happy that Callie's mother was a constant support in her life. We all needed that. "Well, it smells terrific already. I can't wait to try it."

The microwave beeped, and I set each bowl before us at the table, snatching a couple of spoons and napkins along the way. Callie gathered her hair and tied it in a messy bun on top of her head and swirled her soup, staring into it like it was a crystal ball of the past.

"Mom used to always make this for me when I was little. I loved the chunky noodles and tiny carrots." She took a bite and hummed. "It takes me back every time."

"Was it always just you and your mom?" I struggled to remember. My life was so busy when Jade was younger that I wasn't nearly as involved in her life as I should have been. Sure, I was there, but always working to make her life as perfect as I could. I know now how wrong that was of me. Time is something you can never get back. Every day was a reminder of that.

The truth was, I knew very little about Jade's friends, including her best friend, the woman before me now carrying my child. It was ironic how life circled back for us. I prayed our bond would never break.

"For as long as I can remember, yes. Just mom and me," Callie answered, eating another spoonful. "My father was very much in and out of our lives while my mother was pregnant up until I was two years old. I don't remember him."

"Shit, Callie. I'm so sorry."

"It's alright. I used to hate his guts, but as an adult I just feel sorry for him now. I hope he's found his way, wherever he is."

I tried the soup and nearly died. Ah. Heaven. "Well, he missed out on knowing you, Callie. That's a pity."

"Yeah," her voice softened. "I used to envy Jade so much. Your house had so many family portraits of the three of you on the walls. So happy and smiling. I can remember wishing I had photos like that in my house. It sounds silly, I know."

"No, not silly, Cal. Not silly at all," I encouraged. "But I hope you know that behind those frozen smiles was a broken home full of pain and resentment. Pictures lie, Callie."

She continued eating. "I know that now."

We finished our soup and sat back, stuffed. I dabbed my lips and took the plates to the sink, trying not to belch. "My compliments to the chef, Miss Harper."

She giggled and helped me wash the bowls and spoons. "I will tell her. Which reminds me, Mom is really sorry she couldn't come to your party. They were understaffed at the hospital and she couldn't get out of work."

"Wow, she's still a nurse?"

"Mm-hm. The very best." Callie beamed, and I melted inside.

"Well, it's probably better that your mother didn't witness any of the drama. I feel like an asshole. So many people showed up to celebrate me and I handled it all like a damn fool."

"You were blindsided, Alex. The party was a happy surprise, but Marcy wasn't. That would have driven anyone over the edge."

"Still, I owe everyone an apology. Do you think Jade will give me access to the guest list so I can mail them letters?" I smirked, still meaning every word.

"I think you'll have to break into her house and steal it first. She made her feelings very clear."

"I know. I'm sorry." I hugged Callie, loving the way she squeezed me in return. "Although it might not be a bad idea."

"What's that?"

"Going to her house to talk in person. I mean, since she's blocked me on every digital corner."

"You might want to gear up ahead of time," Callie joked. "I haven't seen Jade this angry since...well...ever. It's hard to tell what she'll do to you if you go uninvited."

"That is true. But I have to try." I kissed Callie's lips. "For Jade. For you. For us."

"I have to talk to someone too. With all the buzz since your party, I'm afraid she may already know."

"Your mom?"

"Yes," I laughed. "I need to see her in person as well."

"Well, let's get some rest then, baby. Tomorrow we will set off on our quests and hopefully return unscathed."

"Oh, I'll be just fine." She tapped my chest. "You, however, entering Jade's territory under such delicate circumstances might land you in the hospital."

I cracked up, knowing she was right. "I'd be lying if I said I wasn't fearing for my life a little. But I have to take a chance. And as of right now, there is only one way to find out."

Callie started walking up the stairs, curling her head around with a painful smile. "Godspeed, my king."

Chapter Twenty-Six

Callie

Mom was quite surprised to see me at her door early the following morning, her smile just as bright as the pink pajamas she wore. Immediately, she welcomed me inside and started some coffee, nerves eating my guts away at how she would receive the news. Would she be happy? Upset? Or a little of both? Regardless of how she reacted, I had to keep reminding myself that it was vital she heard it all from me and not someone else.

"How was the party last night? Did you girls dance the night away?" Mom joined me at the kitchen table, completely unaware that I was about to turn her world upside down.

"Well, the party ended a little early, Mom."

"Oh no! What happened?"

I cleared my throat, praying for the words to come. "Mom, I have to talk to you about something."

She read my face, concerned. "Of course, Callie. You can tell me anything."

I started sweating, feeling lightheaded. Was it morning sickness or anxiety? Well, I couldn't tell the difference. But Mom did. She just knew.

"Callie?"

"Yes, Mom?"

"Are you pregnant?" She covered her lips, eyes popping.

I gulped with a nod as Mom squealed, clapping and hugging me in celebration. Once I bit my lip and locked gazes with her, she sat back down, her eyes straining in thought. "Oh, Callie. Is Travis the father?"

"No," I sighed, relieved that we never had children. "No, it's not Travis, Mom."

"Oh, good." Mom relaxed, grabbing her heart. "Do I know him?"

I teared up, afraid of what she would think of me. "Yes."

"You're crying. Are you alright? Were you hurt or—"

"No, Mom. This was," I sighed, smiling, struggling to explain it all.

She took my hand, studying me closer, a tender knowing exchange happening between a mother and her daughter. "You love this man."

I held back a sob, confirming, "Yes."

"So, these are happy tears?" she asked, eyes full of hope.

"Unbelievably happy," I began, frowning. "But Jade hates me."

"Why in the world would Jade hate you?" Mom shook her head, puzzled.

"Because, well," I huffed.

"This man isn't some ex of hers or something, is it?"

Fuck.

"Not an ex," I rambled, unable to look her in the eye. "Her father."

Mom squeezed my fingers harder, silence crashing between us. Not even a breath could be heard, only the pounding of blood in my ears. And when I finally gathered up enough courage to find her eyes again, she was crying, swimming in her own sea of emotions too.

"Oh, Callie." She got up and bear-hugged me, stroking the back of my hair so much like when I was little. "Oh, it's alright. Everything is going to be alright."

"I didn't plan for any of this to happen, Mom. You have to believe me. I didn't fly to Montana with some twisted scheme of seducing Alex, much less having a baby with him."

A short chuckle broke from Mom's lips, and I dried my face, laughing and crying at the same time. She watched me a moment, letting things settle, and offered a slice of wisdom as she always had in my life, the heaviness of my heart lightening.

"Rarely do we plan on love, Callie. At least not true love. It hits us out of nowhere when we least expect it."

"I fought it, Mom. But soon it was like I had no control of it anymore. I wanted him more than anything," I divulged.

She curled the side of her lip. "Oh, I know what that's like."

"God, this is so messed up. Jade hates Alex *and* me. I feel like I've ruined the little family she had left."

Mom winced. "Did something happen at the party?"

"Yes. Jade thought Alex and Marcy were getting back together. What she didn't realize was he had come to Asheville to see me, not her mom." I blew a sigh. "Jade discovered that part last night. That we've been seeing each other. But she has no idea about the baby."

"Oh my." Mom poured another cup of coffee, sipping in silence.

"Alex is on his way to talk to her in person." I sniffled. "But I have a bad feeling about it."

Mom hummed a sigh, setting her mug down. "You've told me that you love Alex. How does he feel about you?"

I rubbed my brow, smiling. "He said it first, Mom."

She touched my arm. "Well, Callie Jo, I must say that I was not expecting this news today. You've jumpstarted my heart quite a few times over the last few minutes."

I barely smiled, needing her support more than anything in the world.

"But I can see the torment you are in. And that type of pain can only come from falling in love."

I nodded, breathing a weepy, "I do love him, Mom. But I love Jade too."

"Have a little faith in that love, Callie. Things may not get better right away, but give this wound time to heal. Your friendship is worth saving, isn't it?"

"Of course it is. But Jade won't talk to me. I can't say that I blame her one bit, though."

"She's in shock. Let the dust settle." Mom stood from the table to wash her cup.

"If she's this angry now, I can't imagine how she will take the news of the baby," I fretted. "What if—"

"We can't control how others react, Callie. Let that go."

"But I've broken her heart, Mom."

She joined me one more time, eyes seared to mine. "Your heart is broken too, Callie. I can see that for myself. Surely, that means something."

I shrugged. "I hope so."

"Give it time, Callie. Give it time."

Alex

I knocked repeatedly on Jade's door, hearing a scuffle at first before it went dead silent. Shit. I waited before knocking again, pleading, "Jade? Please open the door."

Silence.

Fuck.

I was about to knock again when footsteps shuffled to the front door, the young man from the party opening the entrance, looking terrified. "Oh, hello. Mr. Harrington?"

I raked the back of my tresses, nervous as hell. "Uh, yes. Alex, please."

"Alex." He shook my hand. "I'm Brendan."

"Nice seeing you again," I cleared my throat. "Is Jade home?"

"Honestly? No. She left earlier to get some things from the store." He read his watch. "I would expect her back soon, though."

"Dammit, okay. I'll just wait out here."

Brendan paced. "I'd invite you in but—"

"No, don't do that. Jade would kill you too," I joked, my daughter's shrewd voice filling my ears seconds later.

"Well, you do have a little sense left," she scoffed. "That's encouraging."

I turned around. "Jade."

"What the hell are you doing here?" She whipped around me, about to go inside and slam the door.

"Jade, I'm begging you. Please. Talk to me."

"Why in the fuck should I, Dad? You are just as sick and twisted as Callie!"

I crossed my arms, trying to choose my words wisely. "You can judge me all you want. But at least let me explain it all first, Jade."

She sucked in a puff of air, red hair shaking back and forth. "I'm going to regret this."

Brendan tried sneaking out, but she stopped him. "Oh, you aren't going anywhere. I might need someone to call the police."

"Jade, when have I ever laid a hand on you or anyone for that matter?" I followed her inside the condo, Brendan left scratching his head.

"You sure as hell beat the fuck out of Travis." She smirked, putting a few groceries away. "Yeah. I checked that story out. You were quite busy on Valentine's Day, weren't you?"

I gulped, not knowing where to start. "Well, that fucker deserved it. You would have beat the shit out of him too if you heard what he said about Callie."

"Callie," she snickered. "Not my concern anymore."

"Dammit, Jade."

She yanked a cutting board from the cupboard and slammed it on the counter, casually strewing raw vegetables and chopping away. "How long, Dad?"

"What do you mean, Jade?"

"How fucking long!?" She pointed the knife as she spoke, quickly slicing a cucumber. "When did this start between you and Callie? Hm? When did you first see her and want her? High school? Fuck. Middle school?"

My body felt like someone had set it on fire. "Put the knife down, Jade. For fuck's sake."

"How fucking long!?" She chucked the knife into the sink with a loud clang and glared at me, fire blasting from my soul, ready to defend the atrocity she was accusing me of.

"On your getaway to Montana. Not one day before," I admitted. "The day I knocked her over, if we're talking specifics. She came into the pub alone that night. It was almost closing time. So," I went on but was cut off.

"So what...you just let her stay?"

"I wanted her to stay!" I roared. "I wanted to be around her. She was upset. And for the first time, I saw myself in someone else, Jade."

"You saw yourself? What the fuck does that even mean, Dad?"

Shit, I struggled to put it into words.

But fuck, I tried.

"Dammit," I hissed. "The pain she carried that bled down her face over a man that broke her heart. I recognized it, Jade. I felt it. I connected with it. Hell, I lived it too."

"She was vulnerable and you took advantage of that," Jade assumed. "How dare you?"

"No," I explained, praying to God she would somehow understand. "That's not true. We connected, Jade. I know that's weird for you to hear, but it's the goddamn truth!"

"The truth?" she laughed. "Now you want to tell the truth. Tell me about the house Callie lives in now."

I held my breath, ready for the next hit.

"You know, ever since I found out your little secret, I've been thinking back over it all. You renovated that house years ago, and that just so happens to be the gem Callie found supposedly on her own in a market where hardly anyone can find anything. So, what's the story, Dad? What's the *truth*, as you say?"

Well, there was no sense in hiding a damn thing anymore. "I called the owner and paid the rent through April."

"I fucking knew it!" She clapped, pacing around the room. "What is this for you, anyway? Some sugar daddy, sugar baby kink? It's so fucking gross!"

I hung my head, gathering my thoughts a moment before saying, "Callie didn't need me to pay her rent. Honestly, I've only told you that I did that. But I wanted to make sure she was okay, Jade. In a safe place that would make her happy."

"To make her happy," she seethed. "That's all you want?"

"Jade," I struggled.

"I think there's a lot more in this for you than that. You used my friend to get your rocks off just to feel better about yourself. Because you are old as fuck. And fucking her made you forget that! Didn't it!?"

"Enough!" I screamed, not planning to, panting, "Fucking hell, Jade."

"I have to wonder if Mom was the real adulterer in your marriage. Hell, if you could pull a stunt like this, what the hell else have you done over the years?"

I couldn't breathe, the weight of feeling misunderstood and judged sitting on my chest like a damn elephant. Without answering, I rushed to the balcony and slid the door open, taking in as much air as possible before returning to my daughter, her eyes softer now.

I stood before her, words stringing together with more clarity. "I know I wasn't a perfect father, Jade. I did so many things wrong that looking back, I can see where I fucked up. I hid the ugliness from you because I never wanted you to experience the childhood I did. I wanted so much more for you, Jade."

She swatted her lashes, mad as hell.

"I know I worked too much. Even more when I tried working things out with your mother. I'm sorry for not being honest with you about things as you got older. I was trying to protect you."

"And by ugliness, you're talking about Mom cheating?"

"That was just the tip of the iceberg, Jade," I took a breath. "The icing on a spoiled, rotting cake that made up my life."

"Are you talking about me too, Dad?" Jade tilted her head, confused. "Am I just another layer of disappointment in your world?"

"Fuck, no! Jade, I'm talking about my childhood. I loved my parents but God, it was awful. The things I saw. The things I experienced." I batted my wet lashes. "So, when I learned that I was going to be a father, Jade, I did everything in my power to do better. To give you more. To make sure to God that you were safe."

"Dad," she broke a little. "Of course you were an amazing father! I never thought otherwise."

"So, please, Jade. Give me a little credit here. I'm begging you," I pleaded for mercy. "Believe me when I say that Callie is not some phase or fling to me. I'm in love, hopelessly and unconditionally in love with her."

Jade ran her tongue over her teeth, scowling. "So you're in love with my best friend. Where does that leave me?"

I sighed a husky breath, feeling like I was drowning. "You're my daughter, Jade. I love you with all my heart. I can't imagine my life without you."

"I think you can," she cried. "Look at what you've been doing this whole time, Dad! Playing house with Callie like I don't even exist!"

"Playing house? Jade, everything that has happened between Callie and me has been authentic and genuine. And regardless of how much we love each other, still, more than anything, your heart has been our number one concern through it all."

"But that didn't stop you, did it, Dad? My feelings didn't stop you from sleeping with her. It sure as hell didn't stop Callie."

"We couldn't stop it, Jade."

"God, Dad." She rolled her eyes, grossed out.

"I'm being honest with you. We tried. Well, Callie tried the hardest to end things for your sake. It worked for a little while. But we were miserable."

"Well, forgive me for causing such misery." Jade went back to the kitchen, pretending to clean.

"Please talk to her, Jade," I humbly requested. "Unblock her number."

My daughter smirked. "Over my dead body."

I sighed desperately, words failing me.

"She made a choice. And so did you." Jade scrubbed the countertop. "I don't have to support it nor do I want to."

"I know that, Jade. You're right." My stomach burned. "I only wanted you to hear her side too."

"I've heard everything I need, Dad." She tossed the towel down. "That friendship is over. And you are barely hanging on by a thread."

"A thread, huh?" I tried to lighten the mood, but that did little good.

"Yes." She marched over and stared up at me. "You have to choose. It's either her or me, Dad."

"I'm not fucking doing that."

"Then you have made your choice," she cried. "Get out of my house."

"Jade—"

"Get out!" she ordered, and as much as I wanted to stay and talk more, that door was literally closing, leaving me with barely a glimmer of hope that things would ever improve in the future.

Chapter Twenty-Seven

Callie

I was curled on the sofa when my front door squeaked open, the man I loved looking like he had been through the war. I expected him to take a cab back to the house after speaking with Jade, but there was no sign of a vehicle. By the looks of things, he decided to walk, the red rings under his eyes destroying me.

"Alex." I met him at the door, falling into his firm embrace, a tender groan vibrating his chest.

"Hey baby," he sighed, pulling back to look at me.

"How did it go?" I already knew the answer.

He shook his beautiful silver head, dark flecks woven with lighter ones. A painful smile tugged the corner of his mouth, a dimple appearing. "Not good, Cal."

"Babe," I breathed.

He planted a soft kiss on my forehead, speaking into my skin. "But that's okay."

My belly jolted, wishing for a better outcome. "No, it's not."

"It will be," he promised, grasping at invisible hope. "But I'm afraid it's going to take a while."

Alex moved through the space, removing his jacket and pouring a glass of water. He gulped it down and rubbed his lips, eyeing me with the tiniest smile. "How did it go with your mom?"

"It went really well." I brushed my stomach. "Honestly, I didn't have to say much. She knew I was pregnant from the moment I sat down."

Alex's chest swelled in pride, happiness radiating his cheeks. "Fuck, I'm so relieved to hear that."

"She understands," I assured, over the moon thankful.

"Thank God, baby. It's everything to me that you have that support." Alex stretched his hand to me, my thumb tracing over the bulging veins.

"Did you tell Jade about the baby?" I winced, Alex's subtle headshake answering me first.

"No, she threw me out of the house before I could go there," he blew a deep sigh. "I'm so sorry, Cal."

"Maybe it's for the best." I scoured the situation for anything positive. "To be honest, Alex, I was hoping to talk to her too."

He scrunched his face like I had kicked him in the gut. "Baby, I want that too. More than anything. But right now, she doesn't want to talk to either of us."

My head fell, guilt hacking my heart until Alex spoke again. "But we can't stop trying."

I gazed into his baby blues, finding hope there. "No. We can't."

He pecked my lips before taking my hand and moving into the living room, eyes traveling from wall to wall, the wheels visibly turning. I watched him and waited, wondering what was running through that mind of his.

"What are you thinking about?" I asked, rubbing his arm.

He patted my knee and took one more thorough look at the house. "I sort of have a secret that I need to tell you."

The look on my face must have been God awful because Alex's eyes swelled and his shoulders relaxed, words like salve on a wound. "No, baby. Nothing bad. I'm sorry."

"I'll be the judge of that," I teased.

"Fair enough," he laughed and cleared his throat. "I may not have told you the entire story about this house."

"What do you mean?"

He blushed. "I mean, everything was true, but I left out a small detail."

"A small detail?" I cracked up. "How small?"

He squinted and bit his lip as the edges lifted. "I sort of paid the rent through April. I wanted you to have this house more than anything, and fuck, I'm sorry. I should have told you."

My heart gushed. "You paid? Alex, I can't imagine how much that costed you. You didn't have to do that."

He grabbed my hand and kissed it, eyes on fire. "Baby, I know I didn't have to. I wanted to."

"I..."

"Are you angry?"

"God, no. Alex. Surprised, maybe. Overwhelmed." I ruffled through his hair and took his mouth into mine, gently sucking his lower lip. "Why April, though?"

He sucked in more air, wrapping his arm around me. "Because that's when the lodge is officially closed for the season. I know it sounds silly, but I didn't know where we would be at that point. Deep down, I wondered if you would be staying with me in the mountains."

My belly fluttered just imagining it. "The mountains?"

"What do you say? You and me. Snuggled in the cabin by the fire. With nothing in the world to do. No place else in the world to go."

"That sounds like a dream." I quickly thought of my obligations. "You know, even though I can teach from anywhere, the school year is over for me at the end of April too."

"Really?" Alex glowed. "What are the chances?"

I laughed, "It looks like a trip to Montana could be arranged. Although..."

He squinted, waiting.

"My doctor is here. My mom. This gorgeous house." I took it all in. "With the baby coming in—"

"November." He smiled. "I know."

I swooned, stroking the side of his face. "Yes. November. I'm just wondering where the best place would be to settle. I can work from anywhere but you can't."

"Still, that doesn't mean you should have to move, baby."

"What do you mean?" I tried reading him.

"I mean, you're right. You have so much here already. People we are going to need in the worst way soon."

Jade's face popped into my brain, and I shuddered, absolutely torn about what to do. I wanted to move forward with Alex but was frozen in this awful, unfinished place with her. Was it wise to stay in the same town as her? Would space help or hurt things? I wished I had all the answers.

"This may sound pretentious, but could we have both?" I absorbed the beautiful living room, eyes landing on the bookshelf.

"Both? The lodge and this house?"

I nodded, knowing it would be expensive. "I've already imagined us living here, Alex."

He smiled, taking it all in himself.

"I want our family to live here. But some time away sounds wonderful too."

He curled his lip and leaned forward, rich musk and mint washing over me with his gentle kiss. "I will call Mr. Davidson today, baby. Let's make it happen."

"Really?"

"The worst he could say is no." He shrugged. "And while we figure out those details, what do you say we head back to Montana? Just for a little bit?"

"Yes," I agreed wholeheartedly. "I think that would be great."

"That way I'll get to wrap up some last minute things before closing, and you and I can relax and just breathe for a while." He winked. "You up for it, kid?"

"Kid?" My mouth dropped, and he lost it, swatting my thigh before hopping off the sofa.

"Okay, Pop. I see you."

"Okay, that's not allowed." He whipped around, pointing with the cheesiest grin.

"Oh really?" I followed him up the stairs as he scooped me into his arms and, like a feather, lowered me to the bed in one fluid motion.

"Really," he answered with the sweetest, velvet kiss, making me forget what we were even talking about.

"I'll try to remember," I whispered, receiving his tongue.

"Mmm," he peppered my neck with kisses, making me weak.

"Alex."

"How are you feeling?" he whispered in my ear, barely skimming my hip.

"Good. I want you." Desire fueled every cell in my body as I stripped down to nothing, hormones raging. Alex was shocked at how fast I undressed and got on all fours, pushing my ass out for him.

"Baby?"

Fuck, I was so wet, my pussy pounding, needing him. I rolled my neck to get the hair out of my face, my chocolate waves gathering over one shoulder. I heard Alex disrobing and soon felt the heat of his body hovering behind mine, urging him to keep going.

"Baby, you're soaked," Alex growled. "Fuck."

"I need you," I choked on my own drool, hardly able to wait another second.

He guided himself into me, the tip alone making me yelp. I arched my back, and he gave me a little more. Then some more. And the last of his shaft. To my pleasant surprise, his fingers came around and rubbed my clit as he carefully pumped in and out, teeth scratching my shoulder.

"Get on your back," I ordered, and he obeyed without pause, his cock glistened with my arousal, jerking.

"Callie?" He smiled with a look of terror on his face, my drive frightening even myself a little. I hovered over him and squatted down until his cock was lost inside of me, dangling a nipple over his lips until he sucked.

"Yes," I confirmed how good it felt. "Like that."

He cupped my ass, and I rolled my hips with him all the way in, closing my eyes to experience him deeper. His big hand found the side of my jaw, moving carefully to the nape of my neck as he tugged my hair.

"Holy fuck, Callie." Alex panted, brow wrinkled.

"Too much for you?" I teased, this newfound confidence coming out of nowhere.

He smirked, his free hand squeezing the flesh around my hips. "Never."

I slowed down, riding him in smooth, even strokes with my body leaning backward, exposing it all for him to see. He moaned out loud, fingertips dragging over my thighs, and I pushed him further into the pillows, softly kissing him.

"Shew, baby." Another peck. "Holy shit."

"Are you as close as I am?" I asked in a heavy, sultry tone, Alex's eyes rolling back.

"Yes," he barely breathed. "So fucking close."

I slid off and rolled over, bringing Alex along for the ride. "Then fuck me until you come."

He gripped the headboard and snatched my thigh, anchoring our brows together. "You are going to wreck me, baby."

"Don't stop," I demanded, and he pushed himself inside my slick heat, thrusting with intoxicating pressure, my soul leaving my body.

"Alex!" I cried, coming. He continued to pump until sweat glistened on his chest as his mouth fell on mine, catching my moan in between his lips.

"Cal." He struggled to breathe, swiping over my forehead to clear the stray waves.

"Yes?" I gazed above me, his luscious blue hues taking my breath away.

His mouth fell open, but nothing came out. The slightest grin curving his lips. He was speechless.

The man I loved could only roll over and gasp as I snuggled into his side, feeling his come pool between my legs. I propped up on an elbow and covered my smile, watching him unravel more and more by the second.

"Are you alright?"

His head swayed, and he bear-hugged me close. I heard the drumming of his heart under my ear and pecked his chest, savoring his full lips on my brow as he answered, "I was a little scared."

"What?" I cracked up.

"You captivate me, Callie." His serious tone stopped my heart. "Fuck, I still can't believe you're mine."

"I love you, Alex," I proclaimed, studying his strong jawline before skating my lips over it.

"I love you too, Cal." His lips fell to my belly next, voice barely above a whisper. "And you."

Chapter Twenty-Eight

Alex

I couldn't pull my gaze away from her if I wanted to, Callie's angelic body resting so peacefully as she slept. The crisp cotton sheet wrapped around her body like a Greek goddess as her breasts threatened to spill over the edge of the fabric. I grinned when I saw her little foot sticking out, admiring the dark polish on her toes, almost black.

Fuck.

She was so beautiful.

The love of my life.

The mother of my unborn child.

My lips barely touched the top of her hand before I got dressed and ventured out the balcony door to light my pipe, savoring the night as much as the flavorful smoke.

It would be good for us to get away, to enjoy the pleasure of just being together without the lying and sneaking. After my birthday party, it was safe to assume that our secret was out anyway. I didn't mind at all. But I hoped Callie didn't suffer because of it.

I set the pipe down and slipped back inside the bedroom before taking my phone off the nightstand and searching for flights. I was able to secure two same-day tickets that would have us back in Montana within twenty-four hours.

Thank God I remembered to delete Jade's number from the account. Again, not that I gave a damn. But I didn't want to add any more fuel to the fire. Callie's heart was so fragile right now. Between getting out of an abusive relationship, falling in love, and finding out we were going to be parents while losing her best friend, fuck, I wasn't sure how to make it all better for her. But I was going to try.

After piddling around for a bit, I packed the few items I had flown with to North Carolina and sent Mr. Davidson an email inquiring about the possibility of purchasing this house. It was a tall order, I know. Especially with the money he was making from rent, no doubt. But I had to ask. For Callie. For the family we were making.

I wandered down the hallway and peeked into an empty guest room, imagining a room filled with toys and a little one crawling around. Just like Callie, I could see it all too. Here. In this house. Our own little sanctuary.

Now, if you had told me I was going to be a father again last year, I would have suggested you get your head examined. A man my age? Fucking fifty with hardly any obligations or commitments? You would have to be out of your mind to think such a thing.

But I was.

Absolutely out of my fucking mind in love with her.

Maybe insanity is a requirement to love. To push logic off to the side and just go with it, to follow your heart and dive head first into an unknown sea, not knowing if you will get eaten by a shark or make it to shore.

I didn't give a fuck what anyone thought about us. This was a risk I wanted to take. To experience shameless love with a woman for the first time in my life. To give her everything she deserved. To cherish the days of this life together because let's just be honest, there aren't nearly enough of them.

God, I loved her.

I only hoped my daughter would be able to see us the way I did one day. But even if she didn't, as painful as that wound was around my heart, I would have to accept it.

Morning came, and I had barely slept a wink, so I decided to stop fighting against the insomnia and shower, the sound of

Callie hurling in the toilet only a few minutes later wrecking me.

I shut the faucet off and wrapped my lower half in a towel, stepping out to find her sitting on her rump, cradling the porcelain throne. "Shit, baby. Hang on."

She coughed and spat in the bowl, wiping her mouth with a tissue. I offered my hand and helped her stand, her chest still heaving on its own.

"I'm okay," she assured. "It always happens when I try to brush my teeth."

Marcy never experienced morning sickness with Jade. Thinking back, she really had no complications of any kind when she was pregnant. So, while I had experienced fatherhood, this was very new to me.

"What can I get you, baby?" I knelt before her as she sat on the toilet seat, taking big breaths.

"You are too sweet, Alex." She smiled. "I just need to take my medicine. But I like to eat first. Just some toast and orange juice."

"I'm on it."

She watched me remove the towel from my waist to dry my neck and arms, the slight curl of her lip making me weak in the knees. Her eyes skidded over my body as a rosy blush filled her cheeks, the sight of her biting her lip and looking away damn near paralyzing me.

I cleared my throat, getting hard already. "Butter? Jelly? Cinnamon?"

She stood up and held her stomach, walking behind me and brushing her hand against my bare ass. "Just a little butter."

Her hungry eyes trapped mine on the way out of the bathroom, a giddy grin frozen on my face as I grated the morning grime from my tongue and spit out the toothpaste. I shook my head in awe of her and quickly threw on some clothes before making her the breakfast she requested, her slippers shuffling behind me in no time.

"Thank you, babe." She crunched the toast and took a swig of juice.

"I'm so sorry you are sick. I wish I could take it from you."

"It's getting better. Really." She opened her pill bottle. "I'm still learning what triggers it the most. These really help."

"Well, if there's anything I can do, please don't hesitate to ask." I poured myself a cup of coffee, drinking it black.

"You always go above and beyond, Alex. I never knew men like you existed in this world." She finished the first piece of toast, and I watched her eat in silence, my heart breaking that she was deprived of the most basic things in a relationship.

"You haven't seen anything yet, Cal." I winked and showed her the ticket confirmation on my phone, asking one last thing on my mind before we left. "Is your mom home today?"

"Um. I think so. Let me text her. Why?"

I slid the phone into my back pocket. "It's important to me that I talk to her in person."

"Oh, can I come?" she joked and finished her drink.

I blew a long exhale, licking my lip. "If I can help it, baby. Every single time."

"Alex!" She swatted my ass and pulled her hair up, blue eyes sparkling.

"Yes, of course I want you there. I know it sounds dumb but I want your mother to see us together, to see for herself that I'm not some old ass pervert trying to steal her daughter."

"Alex." She shook her rich locks. "She doesn't think that."

I pecked her nose. "Still, I want to talk to her."

"Okay." She flashed a heart-stopping smile and reached for her phone. "Let me find out if she's home."

Callie typed away and waited, the little chime on her phone lighting up her face as much as the screen. "Yay! She's off today."

It felt like someone had jabbed a live wire into my gut, unexpected nerves hitting me with the reality that I would be chatting with Ruthanne Harper, the mother of the woman I burned for every second of the day.

God help me.

We were the same age, well roughly. To say that didn't burn a hole in my brain just as much would be a lie. It meant everything to me what Callie's mom thought. And even though she said her mother understood, I had to see for myself.

We arrived not long after eleven in the morning, the fresh scent of muffins wafting in the air. Ruthanne rushed to the door and squeezed the life out of Callie, urging her to eat whatever she wanted. I lingered in the doorway, almost afraid to come inside, when Ruthanne stepped closer to me, her warm smile easing the bees stinging my gut.

"Mr. Harrington," she greeted with her arms crossed. "My God, how long has it been?"

"Bet I'm the last fool you expected your daughter to bring home," I joked, trying to break the ice, already fearing I fucked up.

She cackled and opened her arms to me, relief washing over my frazzled state of mind. I hugged her in return, looking up to see Callie's understanding eye, and swallowed a sob, grateful as hell.

"And please...call me Alex." I pulled back, and Ruthanne nodded with eyes damp.

"Yes, you are right. We're family now."

Fuck.

Hold it together.

"Yes," my voice cracked against another wave. "I can't tell you what it means that you agreed to see me today."

"Well, why in the world wouldn't I?" Ruthanne laughed and led the way into the kitchen, setting a big fruit tray on the table.

We sat together, rehashing the last several months piece by piece. Okay, not every panty-dropping detail. But together, Callie and I painted the picture of how our relationship had developed and where we were now. Most importantly, where we wanted to go.

"I need to go to the bathroom. Be right back." Callie scooched her chair from the table.

"Are you feeling okay?" I asked as she wandered down the hall.

"Fine, Alex!" she called and shut the door, a smile on the tail end of her words.

I turned every shade of red possible, my face burning hot as Ruthanne stared at me and sipped her tea. Finally, I mustered the courage to look her in the eye as though begging for mercy or a pardon of some sort. The most extraordinary thing was she wasn't angry. Not even a little bit.

"I haven't seen Callie this happy since," she thought out loud. "Well, ever."

"Ruthanne," I choked.

"Listen to me, Alex," she insisted. "I know what you have with my daughter may be considered unconventional, but that doesn't mean it isn't love."

I dabbed my lashes with a shaky hand, overcome. "I do love your daughter, Ruthanne."

"I can see you do, Alex. Truly." She drank some more. "You don't know how long I wanted Callie away from Travis. He never loved her."

I gulped, feeling that my relationship with Marcy was quite similar. "I know what that's like."

"I know you do. More than most, Alex."

I nodded, thanking her in silence as she went on.

"It won't always be easy, but I know you can make it work." She smiled, silver strands catching the light above us. "Just ignore the haters, Alex. There will always be people who like to stir shit even when the pot is squeaky clean."

"What are they saying, Ruthanne?" I begged, making sure Callie was out of earshot. "You can tell me."

She casually waved. "Oh, I've deleted my social media since Callie told me she was pregnant. I only saw a few comments."

"Who?" I pleaded again.

She sighed, the toilet flushing in the distance. "Jade made a post, Alex. I'm sure she was just shocked and angry, but there were several comments under it. Degrading and downright hateful. I never told Callie."

"Thankfully, she never saw it. Jade's blocked us on everything."

"Good. I haven't told a soul about Callie expecting either. That's your business to share as you will," Ruthanne assured.

"Thank you." My eyes bled in gratitude as Callie returned, her smile as beautiful as ever.

"Okay, what did I miss?" She reached for a slice of watermelon and chomped, elbowing me.

I coughed, meeting her mother's wide eyes. "Well, I was just about to tell your mother that we plan to travel back to Montana for a little bit before the season closes."

"Oh! That sounds great. Although, Callie, I wouldn't do any skiing if I were you in your condition."

Callie cracked up and rubbed my arm. "No, I think I'll leave skiing to the professionals."

I raised my glass, not wanting anything to happen to the woman I loved. "Cheers to that."

We shared another round of laughter and finished brunch, the heaviness in my spirit lighter now. Being accepted and understood as a couple never felt so good. And the fact that it was Callie's mother was even sweeter. Though we didn't need anyone's permission, it was unbelievably freeing to experience her blessing, especially while so many others rejected us, Jade first and foremost.

Chapter Twenty-Nine

Callie

Montana was just as beautiful as I remembered, the snowcapped mountains creating their own winter wonderland even though the temperature was a little warmer than my last visit.

Guests were scarce compared to January, with only a few families here and there. Many were packing their things and heading out from what I could see, the season visibly winding down as March did the same.

"Home sweet home." Alex curled his lip, a dimple popping as he opened the front door of his cabin for me.

It was quaint and cozy, the wooden walls and ceiling a rich gold with dark knots speckled through the lumber. A brown leather sofa drew my gaze in the center of the living room with a plaid blanket draped on the back. I could see us sitting there already, snuggled and warm, the fire crackling around us.

"Are you hungry, baby?" Alex removed his coat and went to the kitchen, opening the door of a loaded fridge.

"How did you manage to stock that?" I cheesed, my hair snapping with static as I removed my winter hat.

"Oh, I had a little help. An employee of mine picked up the order and put it away for me." He beamed and came close, holding my waist. "I wanted to make sure you had everything you needed."

"Well, you are the most thoughtful man on the planet." I kissed his full lips, cheeks bristled with shiny gray stubble. "And yes. I'm starving."

He laughed and pecked again, rubbing my shoulders. "Me too. I'll get dinner going. Feel free to make yourself comfortable."

"Ooo, you are cooking? I'm intrigued." I followed him to the stove, watching him pull ingredients from the cabinets.

"I only hope I can do it justice."

"What's that?"

"Your mother's soup recipe. She gave it to me before we left her house."

I studied the bundle of carrots, noodles, and chicken stock, hormonal as hell and on the edge of crying. "Alex."

"Plus, it's one of the only dishes I knew that didn't make you hurl, so," he laughed, and I brushed his back, coming to his side to help.

"Well, this sounds perfect." I tied up my hair. "Here, let me wash those."

Alex passed the carrots, and I ran them under the faucet, soon rummaging through a cabinet for a cutting board and slicing them into small chunks. He filled a pot with water next to boil the noodles and grabbed a second knife, chopping right along with me.

God, this felt so good.

So natural.

For so many years, I had missed out on this—sharing the precious simplicities of life with someone. Cooking was just one of the things Travis never wanted to do together. He was far too busy. So often, he would eat out after work with clients or grab a sandwich on the way home. He couldn't be bothered, I guess.

Now, I was completely immersed in the solitude with Alex, and while nothing was verbally said between us, our bodies communicated in the sweetest exchange against the dicing of metal against wood—the soft brush of Alex's arm against mine as he scooped the orange pieces away to make room for more, his careful eye that landed on mine when I gasped, nearly cutting my finger off, the way my chest would swell when he would reach above my head into a cabinet, his blend of fruity smoke and musk about to put me in a coma.

An ember of guilt burned my chest, remembering Jade's kindness in offering my first getaway to this resort. I was willing to bet every cent to my name she regretted that decision now.

Her words of prophecy rang out loud in my head. *This is going to be the best year of your life, Callie.*

In one regard, she was absolutely right. I fell in love. But losing Jade was killing me. I wondered if that wound would ever heal. A wound that Alex and I created.

The soup was bubbling, so we covered the rumbling pot and made our way to the cushy sofa, Alex sitting first only to take me in his arms. I molded to his side, closing my eyes as his fingertips stroked my arm, shaking as chills covered me from head to toe.

I met his flickering gaze, receiving the tender kiss he offered. He tasted so warm and sweet, a flavor I never wanted to be without again. Soon, my head was resting upon his chest, and he sifted through my wavy hair, husky words liquefying my bones.

"I'm so happy you are here, Callie."

"Me too, Alex," I whispered into his cotton tee, the savory aroma of chicken and carrots filling the room.

"I know this place isn't much, but it's all I've needed as a single man." Alex's heart thumped under my ear.

I wanted to see his face, so I sat taller, drawing my knees up and tilting my head back. "It's a wonderful cabin, Alex."

He gave a half grin, raking through his two-toned hair and drinking in the space. "The bones are here for sure, but you simply walking through that door has illuminated what's been missing for so long."

"What's that?"

He bit his lip, tracing my palm. "A woman's touch."

Heat filled the apples of my cheeks, splashing them pink. More than anything, I wanted to be that for Alex, to complement his life as he had mine. But a question loomed in the dark corners of my mind, a curiosity that I desired to know while we had time to unpack it all.

"I have a question."

He rested both elbows on his knees, eyes open like a book. "Ask me anything, baby."

I nodded in awe of his humility and understanding. "Did you ever date anyone after your divorce?"

He didn't take his eyes off mine. "There were times I went on dates, yes. Off and on since Marcy and I divorced nearly a decade ago. But they never turned into anything."

It wouldn't matter to me if they did. Although, the thought of anyone touching Alex made me sick with envy. "I was just curious."

"I want you to know everything about me, Callie." He smiled. "So, yes. I did occasionally date."

"Anyone I know?" I teased, deep down dying to know.

"No, baby." He brushed my knee. "No, those dates were few and far between, anyway. Friends setting me up. Old friends reaching out. The dates rarely ended well as I was so miserable with my life. Often the ladies would cut out early. I suppose I was pretty poor company."

I stroked his cheek, watching him as he continued.

"But there were times I would indulge in the company of a woman. More often than not when the wine was flowing, and I had forgotten how hurt I was. It felt good in the moment, but left me feeling more alone than before."

"Alex," I breathed.

"That was years ago, Callie. I want you to know that."

"Even if it wasn't, Alex. That's okay too." I nodded and went on, "I know firsthand how sex can make you so hopeful for connection in the beginning but leaves you devastated when it's over."

He gulped, breathing, "Yes."

"That was my entire relationship with Travis." My belly churned, remembering. "Of course, in the beginning it seemed good, but I quickly realized that sex for him wasn't to connect or please me. Over time, I felt like something he was just using to masturbate to."

Alex squeezed my hand, breathing, "Fuck, Cal."

"I thought I could change his heart." My head swayed. "To make him see what a wonderful woman he had. But every year that passed seemed more hopeless than the one before. I was trapped in this cycle with him. Always striving to be better. And when he would initiate sex, I sadly thought, *This time will be different.* It never was."

"It wasn't you, baby."

I dabbed the corner of my salty eye. "I know. But when you catch the person you love in the act of screwing someone else, it does a number on you, regardless of how fucked up the relationship is."

A soft grumble broke through Alex's chest. "It does. I know that firsthand too. Things with Marcy had been fucked up for so many years, but I was still there, you know? Loving her the best I could. Showing up for my family every day. It wasn't enough."

"I'm so sorry that happened to you, Alex."

The corner of his mouth twitched. "It's an image that you can't get out of your head. Although for me, I try to see the humor in it."

"The humor?" I covered my smiling lips.

"Well, the shower was running and while he was spearing her from behind at about a hundred miles an hour, she was choking on the stream of water, cursing him to go faster."

"Oh, God," I laughed, not meaning to.

"Yeah, she said that too." Alex's serious face cracked, and soon we were both rumbling, my head tumbling on his shoulder.

"I love that sound. Your laugh," Alex whispered, my belly stinging.

I barely dusted his chest, feeling the hairs from the outside of his shirt. God, I wanted to bury my face in them and inhale his intoxicating scent. There was nothing in the fucking world like it.

"I haven't laughed this much in a very long time, Alex." I traced his lower lip as he kissed my finger. "Or cried."

"Your tears are my undoing, Miss Harper. They call my own out of hiding." He held the side of my face, my cheek almost disappearing inside his giant palm.

"Alex?" I leaned into his touch, cherishing it. "Do you ever wish that we were the same age?"

He studied me intently, lashes shifting left to right as his chest swelled. "No. I don't."

"But wouldn't it be easier if we were?"

"Maybe." He shrugged. "Maybe not."

"I just worry about you is all. People can be so cruel with things they don't understand. It won't take long for word to break about the baby. Maybe it already has."

Alex's eyes rounded for barely a split second, then softened. "I don't give a damn about what anyone thinks about us, baby. My concern is you and our child."

"But your other child is a few months older than me," I said in the cozy room, insecurity consuming me again. "Does that make you uncomfortable, Alex?"

He tipped my chin so I could look him in the eye, raspy words bleeding into the atmosphere. "I see you for the woman that you are, Callie Jo Harper. The only woman who has opened her heart to me."

I shivered.

"The only woman who comes so beautifully for me." His jaw rippled, nostrils flaring with air. "The *only* woman I love more than fucking life itself."

A gasp snagged in the middle of my throat as our lips collided, pitchy moans and hoarse grunts competing with one another through sealed lips. I yanked the hem of his white tee and peeled it away, running my hands over his pecs, exploring the lush terrain of silver fluff. He called my name when I licked his tight pink nipple, drawing it into my mouth as he fisted the back of my hair, diving into my mouth again.

"Fuck, Callie. God, you drive me fucking crazy." He swirled his tongue around mine, continuing to hold the back of my head with one hand and unfasten his belt with the other. I trembled at the sound of leather flying through denim loops and clacking on the floor, his zipper clawing open next.

I reached into the denim flaps, feeling his solid erection, nearly busting through his briefs. He let my lips go with a wet pop and flashed a gorgeous smile, removing my top next and unclipping my bra.

"I want to suck them, Callie. God, I want to drink from you," he begged.

"Please," I muffled, falling back on the sofa topless, the crotch of my leggings soaked.

His tongue lapped around my nipples, long, hot strokes before drawing each one into his mouth, summoning a guttural moan from my core. Once he was satisfied, Alex hooked his thumbs around the stretchy band of my pants and glided them off, my knees parting for him on their own as my pussy throbbed.

He purred as he licked my inner thigh, tasting the most delicate part of me before he found my clit and latched on, sucking and pulsing with his tongue.

"Alex!" I shrieked, grabbing a handful of his hair.

He moaned again into my sex, squeezing my thigh and increasing speed. Warm tingles spread through my chest and neck as I climbed higher with him, so close to finishing.

"I want you inside of me, Alex," I demanded.

He looked up and rubbed his dripping chin, standing to step out of his jeans, the massiveness of his cock erupting from his underwear next. "God, you're so wet for me, baby."

"I need you," I pleaded.

"I'm going to fill you, baby." He hovered above me on the sofa, keeping one leg on the ground to steady himself, my pussy screaming.

He was so careful, fully aware of his size and how tight I was. But God, I didn't care how wide he stretched me. It was an orgasmic experience alone, taking him completely.

My head went back, chin aiming toward the ceiling as his hard dick stimulated every spot, my walls contracting around him, milking him, bringing his orgasm just as close as mine.

"Cal," he growled, rubbing into my clit. "Fuck, baby."

My pussy clenched harder, and my belly tightened, my body rocking into the blissful ascension. I opened my eyes and took in his beautiful body and soul, glancing down at us pleasing one another, forcing another deep grunt out of him.

"I love you, Callie," he panted, his rock-solid chest damp. "And fuck, baby, that's enough for the rest of my life."

It was forever for Alex.

And for me too.

Like a tiny seed buried in soil, hidden from the sun, so was our love for one another, a union made on rocky ground, struggling to survive at first but thriving now as new life grew between us. Our love had bloomed from a very dark place. Not a shameful place. A place of protection.

"I love you too, Alex." I struggled to breathe. "So much, babe."

"Come with me, baby." He flashed a smile, eyes fixed on mine. "Come with me."

I screamed, unable to stop the pink frills around his cock quivering with release. Soon, I felt the rhythmic jerking inside of me, Alex's forehead falling to rest on mine, his cream smearing my inner thigh.

He kissed my forehead as I wove through his chest hair, absorbing what he said just as much as before. "It's going to be okay, baby. Everything is going to be okay."

Chapter Thirty

Alex

After dinner, Callie was sleeping away in no time, her soft snoring making me smile. Having her in my bed felt so surreal, a dream of true love brought to life that I never thought would happen for me.

Still, even underneath her peaceful countenance, I knew she had concerns with good reason. More than anything, I wished to ease them for her, but felt utterly helpless, especially after my last discussion with Jade.

I hadn't stopped thinking about what Ruthanne spoke of, a post my daughter had made. I wanted to believe she had realized the error of her ways and deleted the damn thing, but also feared that it was still up for the world to see and comment their opinions on.

Using an alternate account I had for the lodge, I logged on and typed my daughter's name, immediately seeing for myself what Ruthanne was talking about. I slid on my glasses and read every cryptic word over and over again, skimming through the comments, my head feeling light.

> *Just when you think you know someone. Think again. Never in a million years would I have imagined this happening. I'm disgusted. Hurt. And mad as hell. I'm convinced that best friends do not exist. One day sooner or later the bond will sever, leaving you more alone than you ever thought possible. I just never thought I would be losing two of the most important people in my world. Fuck them both. Karma is a sweet bitch and she will take care of them.*
>
> *Comments:*
>
> *We heard all about it, Jade. How embarrassing of your father. I always thought he was the nicest man. Never thought he was such a creep.*
>
> *Talk about a midlife crisis!*
>
> *You deserve better, Jade. Forget them both.*

Son of a fucking bitch.

I gritted my teeth as my eyes fell lower, Travis Carter's name glaring back at me, his comment the cherry on top.

> *Little Miss Perfect isn't so perfect anymore, is she? Never knew she was into geriatrics. That's news to me. Look at it this way, she'll be the one wiping his ass instead of you. LOL*

I slammed my laptop shut, thankfully not waking Callie. God, I wanted to beat that fucker all over again. Geriatric? Are you kidding me? To hell with him. But Jade. Dammit. I knew we were in a fragile place, but to blast it all over social media was an all time low.

My phone rang, and I answered right away, seeing it was coming from the lodge. "Hello?"

"Hey, boss. Nick."

I scooted out of bed, moving into the living room. "Hey man. What's up?"

"Um, I know it's late, but would you be able to come into the office?" He sounded worried. "I've got something you need to see."

"Absolutely." I held my breath. "Be there in a few."

I quickly dressed and decided not to wake Callie. She was sleeping so soundly. The last thing I wanted to do was disturb her sweet dreams, especially with all this shit going on.

I was practically jogging into the office, everyone gone for the evening except for Nick, who was sitting at the front desk, typing away. "Hey, boss."

"Hey. What's going on?"

He waved for me to come around, and I plopped into a computer chair, squinting at the screen. Dammit, I forgot my glasses. Immediately my stomach twisted on itself, countless one-star reviews for Sugar Slope Lodge filling the entire fucking webpage.

"What in the actual fuck?" I blurted.

"Yeah, that's what I said," Nick sighed, clicking to reveal another entire page of sour remarks.

Technology wasn't my strong suit by any means. Hence hiring Nick. But one thing I was completely aware of was the power of social media. It could change your life for the better or destroy you.

"Clearly, these aren't authentic reviews," Nick encouraged. "None of the emails are verified stays. I've already sent requests to get them taken down."

"Shit." I examined them harder, the accusations of my character forcing my heart into overdrive. "Who in the hell did this?"

"That may be a little harder to prove. But this is obviously personal. The tone and wording of each review mimics the one before." Nick clicked again, the letters going fuzzy.

I started to hyperventilate, feeling the need to vomit. "Fuck," I cursed.

"Is everything okay?" Nick was genuinely concerned, and rightly so. This was not only my reputation on the line, but his too. He worked for me and represented the lodge to countless guests. I had to get to the bottom of this.

"Nick, I—"

He locked gazes with me, eyes full of understanding.

"I'm dating a younger woman," I began, and he cracked up.

"Alright, alright. The pieces are coming together a little more," he chuckled. "I thought you were happier these days."

"This younger woman is Callie Harper."

His mouth clapped shut. "Callie Harper? Your daughter's friend that stayed here a couple of months ago?"

"Best friend," I corrected, and he whistled through his pursed lips, lacing his fingers behind his head.

"Woah," he blew another sigh. "So these comments about you being a womanizer and pervert are about *her*?"

I groaned, "I believe so. My daughter is furious."

"Jesus Lord." Nick covered his lips, reading more reviews. "You know, I wondered what the fuck was going on when we started getting calls about an hour ago. I hadn't checked the company email since yesterday. Of course it was filled to the fucking brim with notifications that we had received new reviews."

"Shit," I hissed, kneading my temple.

Nick finally closed the browser and sat back, his exhale audible. He watched me for a second and leaned forward, offering another slice of support. "It's going to be okay, man. We'll get them removed. This will all blow over."

"I hope so. Fuck, has anyone canceled their upcoming reservations because of this?"

"You know," Nick stammered. "Don't even worry about that, boss."

"How many, Nick?" I asked, and he pulled up the booking page, showing me.

"Goddammit!" I roared, mad as fuck.

"Hey, you know what? We've got this under control," Nick assured. "Shit like this happens all the time."

I combed through my hair, not convinced. "My relationship with Callie has been one hundred percent consensual. But these reviews make it sound like I'm some sick predator! Who the fuck comes back from that, Nick?"

He swallowed, beady eyes terrified.

"I'm sorry, Nick. Forgive me. I know you're just trying to help," I huffed.

"Hey man. It's alright. This is a lot to take in." He shut the computer off, ready to get the hell home, I'm sure. "We'll get the reviews taken down. On the upside, we've already cleaned up our social media pages."

"There's more?"

"Don't even worry about it, boss." He smiled, grabbing his coat. "You've done nothing to be ashamed of. People who know you will understand."

"But guests that don't know me will avoid this place like the plague."

Nick whipped his scarf around, consoling me all the more. "So you're with a younger woman. If that's the scandal here, who the fuck cares? People love to feast on drama. It's all bullshit, man."

"I'm sorry, Nick. You don't deserve any of this."

"Neither do you." He curled the side of his lip. "We'll get it squared away. Hang in there."

"I will try." I watched Nick leave and hung my head, feeling defeated. Clearly, someone wanted me to hurt as much as they were hurting. Was this the karma Jade was referring to? It wasn't hard to connect those dots.

Fuck.

I made it back to the cabin and into bed with Callie, shivering from the unforgiving cold. She was toasty warm underneath the covers and wanted to be close to me, even in sleep. I peeled my shirt and pants off and snuggled, fighting tears about how this would affect her. Short term and long term. What if I had to sell the lodge? I couldn't even fathom it. For the last five years, it provided more than any of my other jobs combined. I was able to give back to the ones I loved. How could I provide for Callie and our child if that went away?

"You're freezing," Callie murmured, half asleep.

"You're so warm," I burrowed, feeling her grow heavy against me.

I whispered, *I love you*, despite her falling back asleep, wrestling with the fury building against the person or persons who were targeting us. I didn't want to pin the blame on anyone for certain. But only one stuck out in my mind.

Jade would be hearing from me.

Tomorrow.

Chapter Thirty-One

Callie

The morning sun filled the bedroom with light, but oddly, that wasn't what woke me. Alex's harsh tone carried from somewhere else inside the cabin, the silent pauses in between telling me he was on the phone.

I padded down the hallway and found him pacing in the living area, unaware of my presence. His face was red as he carved a path in the wooden floor over and over again, his words just as hot.

"I called you at work because that's the only way I knew to get you to talk to me, Jade."

I wanted to curl in on myself, imagining every scenario that took place between the time I fell asleep and the time I woke up.

"This could absolutely destroy my livelihood. I'm already seeing the effects of what you've done!"

Shit.

I dissolved into the wall behind me, not wanting to interrupt, but sure as hell not leaving now.

"Leave her out of this, Jade!"

Fuck.

That would be me.

More painful silence.

"No, the truth is you want to ruin me so there's nothing left, right? You do realize you are screwing yourself out of money too."

I gulped, my back sweating.

"Why in the hell would everything go to Callie?" he laughed through fury. "Have you lost your damn mind!?"

Finally, his darkened eyes collided with mine, the soft tilt of his head and puffy exhale drawing me closer. I took one of his hands into both of mine, unable to translate the screeches blaring from the speaker against his ear.

"I know you're angry, Jade. That's a given. But attacking my business not only affects me but all of my employees and guests. You are so smart, but fuck, this is the stupidest thing you have ever done. I never would have done this to you."

I overheard her last sentence before hanging up. *"Yeah? And I would have never fucked your best friend!"*

Alex let out a disgruntled sigh and tossed the phone on the sofa, desperate blue hues tinged with embarrassment. I had no idea what had happened, but circled my arms around his tall form, the top of my head landing in the middle of his chest, his scent enveloping me.

"I'm so sorry you had to hear that, Cal."

I lifted my lashes until our eyes locked, still confused as hell. "What happened?"

Alex pecked my hand before retrieving his laptop, soon pulling up the Sugar Slope Lodge that went from a nearly five-star establishment to barely under a two. My eyes bugged as I read through each dehumanizing paragraph, accusing the owner of being inappropriate with guests. What in the mother fucking hell? Damn you, Jade.

"Alex, this makes me physically sick. I don't know what to say," I blubbered, closing the laptop.

"Nick called me last night after you went to sleep. He claims we can get them removed, but time will tell."

I shook my chunky waves, appalled. This could ruin Alex and everything he had worked so hard for. A crushing pang flared through my chest, feeling utterly responsible for the avalanche threatening to sweep it all away.

"This is all my fault." My lip wobbled as Alex's gravelly voice snapped me out of it, the truth rising above the bullshit.

"Jade did this. Not you."

I held my breath. "I know we provoked her but—"

"But this is absolutely uncalled for," Alex vented. "One of the lowest blows I can even fathom."

The tips of my fingers brushed over his chest, a new fear rising. "Do you think she found out about the baby somehow?"

"No," he answered instantly. "She would have used that detail to her advantage, I believe."

"You mean when she said that your money would be mine one day?" I winced, Alex's wealth the last damn thing on my mind.

"Yes," he whispered. "She would have mentioned the baby too if she knew."

I absorbed it all, eventually nodding in agreement. "I think you're right."

The rigidness of Alex's chest slowly softened, and he pulled me in, planting the warmest kiss on my forehead before folding his arms around me. I melted into his vibrating sigh, wishing things weren't so complicated, but knowing that life without him wasn't an option anymore.

"You know that's the last thing I care about, right?"

"Hm?" He brushed the ends of my hair off both shoulders, eyes asking what I meant.

"Your money." I curled one side of my lip, hoping he believed me. "Although I'm sure once Jade discovers we're expecting that will only seal the deal in her mind that I'm a gold digger."

"Baby," he gasped, his salt and pepper head falling until our lips met, leaving me lost in his warmth, tasting him.

"Yes?" my voice cracked.

"We know the truth. That's all that matters. Others will catch up in time." He cupped my cheeks, eyes piercing through my soul. "But I'd be lying if I said I didn't want to give you everything you ever wanted, baby."

"Alex," I breathed, running my fingers into the buzzed hair above his ears.

"Maybe a little gold too?" He winked, and I bit my lip, my belly tossing and turning.

"I just want you," I whispered in his ear, pecking his smooth cheek.

He swallowed, turning his cheek so our lips brushed. "There's no need to want for something that's already yours, baby."

Dammit, if he wasn't holding on to me, my legs would have surely given out and dropped my ass on the floor, his words turning my bones to mush. I reeled back my jagged exhale, shaking under his soft touch.

God, this man. He was otherworldly.

"I love you." I rested my head in the crook of his neck.

He bear-hugged me, tilting my face so he could look at me fully. The whitest smile formed on his lips, so big his eyes creased. "I love you. Forever, Callie."

∞

So many nights I went to sleep alone even though Travis was in bed beside me. He rarely initiated any form of touching or cuddling. Looking back, I can see now the nights he *did* want to have sex were the nights he didn't get any of his side pussy. But the way my body responded simply lying next to Alex was electrifying, our bodies crying out to one another in silent cues, urging to come together in a blissful union before having a good night's sleep.

You hear stories about men losing interest after so many years, or not having the ability to get it up anymore. But Alex proved those quite false for me, my horny hormones not phasing him whatsoever, his ability to perform every night turning me into a damn puddle by the time we were finished.

I had never had so much sex in all my life.

He knew exactly how to use that beautiful equipment of his, filling me and locking into place, erotic thrusts sending me to the fucking moon in minutes. For so many years I was just a hole for Travis to jackhammer into, my clit ignored every damn time. But Alex aimed for it, not satisfied until that tiny pink bud was pulsing on her own, tonight no different.

I rolled over, laughing like I was drunk, still riding the high he created inside of me. Milky strings oozed from my center as we struggled to catch our breath, Alex's hand cupping my belly as his chest hair tickled my back. It's for sure if I wasn't pregnant already, I would have been by the end of this trip.

"We're going to have to wash these sheets. Again." I smiled, feeling his nose drift into my scalp.

"The night's not over yet, Miss Harper." He kissed the back of my neck, chills exploding down my spine.

I laughed out loud, turning over to find Alex's two-toned hair a beautiful wispy mess. My hair was all over the place too, brown tendrils fanned in every direction but down. Alex smoothed over them, gathering the strands and twirling them in one big twist, laying it gracefully over my shoulder.

"I don't know if I can keep up with you, Mr. Harrington," I teased, wiping the dew from his brow.

"I can't get enough of you." He plunged into my open kiss, tongues caressing, tasting one another.

"Mmm," I sighed into his silver chest, choppy breaths gently slowing down.

We snuggled in the stillness of the room, basking in the peaceful quiet of the night. I felt Alex's warm hand against my stomach and looked below, the tender swell a little bigger these days.

"Fuck, you're so beautiful." He propped himself up on an elbow, eyes landing on my lips. "How are you feeling?"

"Well, if I was going to puke that round would have done it," I wheezed, and he blushed.

"God, I'm sorry. Was I too rough?"

"Of course not," I laughed. "You make me feel so good, Alex."

He blew a sigh of relief, taking me under his mossy arm. "Well, that's music to my ears."

Our laughter soon settled, and I curled on my side, eyes trailing off in thought. Alex slipped away to use the bathroom and came back wearing a pair of briefs, gulping the water on his nightstand.

"You okay?" He sat on top of the comforter, pulling my gaze back to him.

"Yeah. I was just thinking." I sat up straight, my breasts dangling. Shit, they were so heavy these days. I really needed to go bra shopping.

"Anything you want to talk about?"

I sighed happily, the emotional maturity of this man never ceasing to amaze me. "I was just imagining us. This time next year. We'll be parents, Alex."

I know pregnant women glow, but my God, this man was too. "I can't wait, Callie."

"Have you heard back from Mr. Davidson about the house yet?"

Alex reached for his phone and scrolled, tapping his email app. "Shit, baby. No. Not yet."

"It's okay. I was just curious."

More than curiosity, I was dying to buy it. It would bring another layer of security and stability to our fragile situation in my mind, having a home to call ours. Even with our slice of serenity in the mountains, it was so important for me to be able to raise our child in Asheville. Alex felt the same way.

"I'll call him tomorrow if I don't hear back," he assured. "I have a good feeling about it."

"I'm holding on to hope. I can see it all there, Alex." I daydreamed out loud. "Birthdays. Christmases. Even Halloween."

"Okay, I have to ask. Do you ever dress up and trick or treat?"

I slid out of bed, Alex's eyes pinned to my ass cheeks as I walked toward the bathroom. "I never stopped."

He let out a hearty laugh, tugging the sheets off the bed as I returned in my cozy robe. His cheeks were frozen in the sweetest grin, bright blue eyes finding mine. "What did you dress up as last year?"

"I think you mean *who*."

"Okay. *Who*?" He balled the white cotton and tossed it in the washer outside the door, brow popped in suspense.

"Freddie Mercury," I answered, and he cackled.

"Please tell me you have pictures."

"Absolutely!" I grabbed my phone and went into my photo folder, searching until a picture of me in a white tank top, tight blue jeans, black wig, and mustache stared back at me. Alex took one look and stole my phone away, screaming and clapping.

"Why is this not on your profile?"

I tilted my head with a smirk. "How would you know it's not on there?"

He clamped his mouth shut, turning redder by the second. "Oh, I may have looked a time or two."

He was so endearing. "Well, you are correct. These never made it to social media. Travis and I got into a huge fight right before this selfie was taken. He promised he would dress up as Brian May. I had the curly wig and everything. But in true Travis fashion, he backed out at the last minute. So, I went trick or treating solo."

"Jade wasn't there?" Alex looked so sad for me.

"No, she had a big event she was in charge of. The community carnival they have every year for kids."

"Ah, right." He scanned my face, swallowing. "So, I think it's safe to say that without a doubt, you are an 80s girl."

"I barely remember the 80s." I frowned, feeling like I was born a tad too late. "However, you could say I'm a little obsessed."

"Favorite song."

I nudged with a squeaky laugh, "Oh, you're going to have to narrow that down a little more for me."

"Well, I already know you're a Queen fan." Alex squinted. "So, let's start there."

I fell back on the bed, staring at the ceiling. "How can I pick just one?"

He fell next to me, watching the fan spin above our heads. "They're all pretty fucking great."

I rolled over, eyes rounded. "You like Queen too?"

"Anyone who doesn't needs their ears checked."

"Yes! Thank you!" I cheered, feeling like a fangirl. Both for Queen and Alex. "Jade didn't even know who Freddy Mercury was."

"Well, in that case...I have failed."

I cracked up some more, my belly stinging. "No, it just wasn't her thing. Still a tragedy."

Alex snorted. "I was a teen in the 80s. Ah. What a time to be alive."

"I'm so jealous of you," I whined.

"The music, the movies, the clothes," he rambled.

"The hair," I added.

Alex closed his lips with a sultry grin. "I will admit. I did have some badass hair."

"You'll have to show me sometime."

He bit his lip, gazing into my eyes with stars in his. "It was a decade like no other."

I rested my chin on a fist, wishing I had lived it all with him.

"But you know something?" he leaned close, husky tones rolling off his tongue.

"What's that?"

"As great of a time as that was, it doesn't compare being alive now, Callie. Here. With you."

Chapter Thirty-Two

Alex

3 Months Later

June was upon us, and with the recent closure on the Cedar house, Callie and I were wasting no time in making it our own. Today in particular was especially bright, the sun shining just as much as the yellow rose bushes we were planting.

I didn't think it was possible for Callie to be any more beautiful, but as I watched her stroll through our backyard in her denim overalls, baby bump on full display, my heart ached all the more in disbelief that she was mine.

"Lemonade?" Callie stretched a glass to me, my old Levi's and white tee covered in dirt.

"Ah." I received the drink. "Thank you, baby."

"The yard looks beautiful, Alex. Better than I ever imagined." She took in the sights of a newly planted tree, paver patio, and fresh flowers. The guys I used to work with recently left with their equipment, making the job much easier than if we were to tackle it alone.

"Not as beautiful as you, mama." I stood tall, using my shirt to wipe the sweat from my brow, gulping down the tart beverage. She leaned into my side even when I tried to warn her I was a stinking, sweaty mess.

"Nonsense," she cooed, her smile about to send me to my knees.

I pecked her lips, the hair on my head touching the back of my neck these days. I curled my lip and winked at the woman I loved, her cheeks flushing at the sight.

I took one last satisfying glance at our day's work, thrilled with the results. "I think I'm going to grab a quick shower."

"Just a quick one?"

I peeled the cotton from my chest, Callie's eyes hooking on every bare muscle. She met my eager stare, taking my hand without a word spoken between us, desire on both of our minds.

Callie

He made it happen. He actually made it happen. Not just the stunning landscape of the backyard, but this entire house and property was ours now. Officially ours. I had to pinch myself most days to make sure it was real.

Mr. Davidson was very reluctant to sell, but Alex wouldn't let up, offering way more than the house was worth until the savvy businessman accepted. I think he knew Alex wasn't going to take no for an answer.

The air conditioning was so refreshing as we came inside from a rather humid summer day, Alex's tanned back and arms practically dragging my eyeballs out of their sockets as he went up the steps first.

His ashy hair dangled just above his shoulders, a little shorter in the front just to stay out of his eye, and God, if I wasn't turned on all the more by it, his beautiful body and luscious locks melting under a steaming shower as he waved me to join him with a finger.

I unfastened my overalls and stepped out of them, removing my top and bra next. Soon, I was standing chest to chest with

Alex as the water beat on the top of his head, brown water swirling down the drain the more he scrubbed himself.

"Turn around, baby." He twirled his finger, and I listened, loving how he always did this for me.

I gathered my hair and soon felt the soapy circles of his fingers glide over my shoulders and back, an unpromoted moan leaking through my lips. I rolled my neck to the side, and he worked his way there, kneading into my stiff flesh with his thumbs.

"God," I purred, closing my eyes and cupping my belly.

"Feel good?"

"Yes." I turned back around, watching Alex wink and roll his neck side to side, cracking it. He finished washing his hair and rinsed, quickly stepping out of the shower before we could, well, you know.

I was disappointed for sure, his sexy smolder outside giving me the cues that he wanted to do the nasty. Oh, well. Maybe I read him wrong.

I shut off the faucet and dried myself, wrapping a towel under my arms before heading into the bedroom where Alex was sprawled out on top of the bed, one knee bent, one arm behind his head, his cock full and vertical.

My lip flopped open like a damn fish at the sight, his sunkissed skin making him look all the more exotic.

"Took you long enough." He bit his lip with a teasing smile, and I nearly tripped over my own feet to get to him, dropping my towel on the way.

I hovered over his naked body, taking his lips as he wrapped his arms around me, carefully flipping me over, slinging a thigh over his shoulder.

"I thought you didn't want to." I squeezed his damp hair.

"When have I ever *not* wanted you?" He kissed my inner thigh as my legs fell open, his tongue against my clit sending shockwaves through me.

"I guess you're—" I began, but was cut off when his tongue slipped inside of me. "Ah!"

He growled against my sex, sucking a little harder. "Fuck, Cal."

I yelped as he went a little faster, gripping his hair in both fists. He swirled and flicked his tongue in steady beats, forcing a cry out of my throat. "Alex!"

"God, I want you to come in my mouth. You're so beautiful, baby," he moaned and ate, my legs quivering as I climbed higher with him, shivering uncontrollably with my head falling back, warm tingles consuming me.

"Yes, baby," he praised. "Just like that."

I could hardly see straight by the time he released my pussy from his mouth, his gorgeous head popping up as he wiped the juices from his chin.

"Come here," I demanded, barely breathing.

Alex suspended himself over me, damp shadowy tresses falling around his face, his bicep flexing as he gripped the headboard. "I'm right here, baby."

I was soaking between my legs and reached for Alex's hard cock, gliding it in with ease, savoring how well he filled me. I pulled his beautiful face lower and kissed him, tasting myself, our bodies rocking as another surge of pleasure began, like a small firework being ignited, about to explode.

"I love you, Alex," I was chasing the high again, so close I could almost feel myself coming with him.

He flashed a gorgeous smile and lowered his brow to mine, thrusting with the side of my ass in his hand. "I love you too, baby. Fuck. So much."

Alex's cock turned to marble inside of me as he groaned out loud, moaning my name. He sat straight, his exquisite pecs and belly before me, grinding one last time before we tipped over the edge, our limbs tangling in euphoric exhaustion.

Once the sun went down, I slipped onto the back porch with my pen and paper, gazing at the beautiful yard and imagining all of the wonderful get-togethers we could have. I envisioned picnic tables with Alex manning the grill, floating balloons, and even a swimming pool. As happy as the thought made me, instantly I thought of Jade and withered inside that she wouldn't be here.

My best friend continued to ignore our calls and messages despite our efforts to reconnect. The last Alex spoke with her was back in March, the night everything went to shit in Montana. Thankfully, her poor reviews were taken down, and things at Sugar Slope were on the mend. I knew that situation weighed heavily on Alex. It was a relief to have that burden lifted.

I really didn't know if Jade had learned about my pregnancy or not. It was no secret that Alex and I were living together, and our little one was growing more every day. I loved that I could feel the baby fluttering now and wished more than ever that I could share this experience with my best friend.

As hurt as I was, however, I really couldn't blame Jade. I knew the risk going into this with Alex. More often than not, I ran imaginary scenarios of how I could have handled things better or differently. But the outcome was always the same.

To ease the void, I began writing letters to Jade. They read almost like a journal, an open book of my thoughts and feelings I wanted to share with her and couldn't. Tonight, I longed to tell her about the house and all the work we were putting into it. But more than that, how sorry I was to have lost her.

Dear Jade,

I wish we could start over, but I know that's not possible. Our friendship has been pushed to the point of no return, but I'm still holding on to hope that someday it can be saved.

Maybe your optimism is rubbing off on me.

There is so much going on in my life right now. So many happy things that I never thought would come to pass. I wish we could sit and talk about it all. I never imagined not being able to share it with you. But I understand why you don't want to talk to me. Honestly, if the shoe were on the other foot, I wouldn't want to talk to me either. I lied and betrayed your trust because selfishly I wasn't ready for our friendship to be over.

Being with your dad, though, has changed everything in my world. For the first time, I'm excited about the future. You were right when you said this was going to be the best year of my life. With him, it has been. But without you, a huge part of my heart is missing.

I hope this letter makes it to you. I hope you know how much you mean to me and how sorry I am for the way things ended. I miss you, Jade. Please know I'm always here if you ever want to talk again.

I love you,
Callie

"There you are," Alex called from the back door, joining me in the creaky porch swing under the stars.

"Hey." I closed my notebook as he sauntered closer, squinting.

"Oh, you're writing. I'm sorry, I'll leave you alone."

"No, please. Sit," I encouraged. "I just finished it."

Alex slowly sat beside me, wrapping one arm around my shoulder as the crickets chirped their night song. His open palm found my belly, and I peered up at him, the baby kicking all over the place once he did so.

"Someone's active tonight." Alex studied my bump, holding his hand still to feel the baby move.

"Yes." I covered Alex's hand, receiving his warm kiss.

Silence fell between us, a tranquil peace suspended in the air. "Were you writing another letter to Jade?"

I brushed the metal spiral, flushing. "I know it's silly."

"No, baby. It's not," he sighed, a painful grin pulling his lip. "I want to talk to her too."

"It's a fine line," I added. "She's set a boundary that we must respect. I just miss her, Alex."

"I miss her too, Cal."

I rapidly blinked into the night sky, my lids stinging. "Jade rightfully sees me as a traitor. I know I betrayed her." I curled my neck around, catching Alex's worried eyes before they fell. "But to deny my love for you, Alex, would be betraying myself."

He held me tighter, sniffling against his own budding emotion. The hot breath of his kiss warmed the top of my scalp as I sank into his side, his words mirroring mine. "I've betrayed her too, Callie. But the truth is, I couldn't stop loving you if I tried."

"Me either," I breathed.

"Things will get better," he encouraged despite not knowing what the future held.

We stared into the hazy landscape, the tips of the Carolina mountains stretching toward the sky. The view was breathtaking. So symbolic of the journey we were on.

"What drew you to Montana?" I asked, swiveling my head, mocha waves dancing in the wind.

Alex relaxed in the swing and crossed a foot over his knee, beaming. "Years ago, I stayed there for an entire summer with my grandmother before she passed. My father's mom."

"Really?"

"Mm-hm. It was actually the year before my father died. Things were really bad at home. So, I took her up on the offer and packed a bag in no time. That was my first flight."

"You flew all by yourself?"

"Sure did." He nodded. "It was so nice getting away. So peaceful. I guess you could say I was craving the same sense of comfort after I divorced Marcy. I stumbled upon the ski lodge by accident, really. I wasn't looking to own my own business or anything, but when I saw the property for sale online, it was like a sign from above. I saw my home. A way to make a living."

I held my breath, admiring Alex's strength.

"With that said, baby, it was you who gave me a life I didn't know was possible. A life with so much love that it's hard to imagine what it was like before."

I looked away, overcome. "Alex."

"You have given me purpose again, Callie. I wake up every day with so much hope. I'm so thankful for this second chance to experience love, and the love we have made together."

I brushed over my belly, taking his smooth jaw into my palm and kissing him. "It's only the beginning, Alex."

"Yes."

"I can't wait to see what's in store for us."

He smiled so big his beautiful dimples popped, something on the edge of his tongue, but he held back. "Me too, baby. Me too."

Chapter Thirty-Three

Alex

The weeks of summer were flying by, and so was Callie's pregnancy. I watched her beautiful belly swell tighter and tighter against the airy dresses she wore to keep cool in the hottest month of the year. This July was no different. The humidity was killing us as much as the high temperatures.

Callie was off for the summer and had decided to take a break from teaching with the baby coming in the fall. I was managing the lodge from home, relieved that the cabins were quickly booking up along with season passes. Pride blossomed inside of my chest like a peacock that I was able to take care of our family so Callie could focus on what she truly wanted. Our baby would be here before we knew it.

I was covered in grime from yard work, the green blades growing just as fast as Callie's baby bump. I was exhausted from the sweltering heat, my heart pounding with sweat pouring off my face. Stepping into the crisp house quickly eased the thumping in my chest. Well, until the love of my life glided toward me, making my heart race all over again.

She was talking on the phone but didn't hesitate to offer me a tall icy drink, winking as she spoke with her mother, it sounded. "Mom, if we have a baby shower, I want it to be here. At our house."

She rolled her eyes with the cutest smirk, listening to her mother.

"I know, Mom," she laughed. "I think this is more important to you than it is to me."

I could hear Ruthanne squealing on the other line as Callie cracked up.

"No, we aren't finding out what the baby is. We want to be surprised!"

I washed up at the sink, taking in Callie's rich tresses and sleeveless dress, her rounded breasts and belly making me fucking weak in the knees.

"I love you too, Mom. We will start planning very soon." Callie nodded with a smile. "Okay. Bye, Mom."

I dried my damp hands and dabbed my forehead and upper lip, Callie stepping closer and closer until her belly touched mine. God, she was so stunning. So angelic. She wore motherhood so fucking beautifully it nearly made me cry some days.

"Baby shower?" I winked, pecking her ruby lips.

"How did you guess?" She drew her lower lip under. "I'm sorry. I know it's a lot to think about."

"What?" I was utterly confused. "Why would you say that, baby?"

She rolled her lips and pressed them together. "I don't know. I guess I'm just wondering if it's rude of me to throw a big party with Jade not talking to us."

"Baby, no," I insisted. "We have every right to celebrate. Anyone who wants to join us is welcome. And those who don't...well...that's fine too."

Her gaze trailed off, a sad tone darkening her voice. "I always imagined Jade planning stuff like this for me. More than anything, I wanted to tell her about the baby in person, but that doesn't look like it's going to happen anytime soon."

Fuck.

My heart.

"Have you mailed any more letters?"

"Not since last month."

I met her disappointed stare, knowing she wished Jade would have reached out in some way. For a while now, an idea had been bouncing around the walls in my brain, a bridge, if you will, to help mend what was broken between the three of us.

"Baby, there's something I want to talk to you about." I pulled out a chair, and she followed, her smile masking concern.

"Okay."

"No, I don't want you to worry. It's nothing bad, I promise."

Her shoulders fell away from her ears, and she let out a breath. "Good."

I smiled, taking in her glowing cheeks and bright eyes, wanting nothing more on the face of the earth than to take care of her forever. "Baby, I want to offer Jade a partnership. At Sugar Slope Lodge."

Her eyes bulged and glistened, the wide grin on her face telling me she approved. "Oh, Alex. That's wonderful."

I took her hand, wanting her to hear what I was truly saying. "Everything I have, Callie, is yours. You know that, right?"

Her nervous laugh dwindled, lips tightening and eyes popping with fear. She never had to be afraid or insecure. Ever. Not with me.

I rubbed her left ring finger, recognizing it was empty. It wouldn't be for long. But I didn't want to spill all of the beans yet. "It's just a matter of time, baby. I promise you."

Callie read me, watching her hand practically disappear inside of mine. "I trust you."

Hearing her say that meant everything. Not only that she trusted me in our relationship, but the relationship I was desperately trying to mend with Jade. Not just for myself. For the woman I loved. She missed her best friend. And while things couldn't go back to the way they were, I hoped that if nothing else, they could move forward.

"I have to ask you something, though." She leaned back in the chair, touching her bump.

"Shoot," I encouraged.

"Was that your plan all along? To partner with Jade?"

There was a hint of worry in her tone, her blue eyes peeking up at me through a black fan of lashes. I sensed what she believed and wanted to ease her mind, not wanting her to carry one more burden.

"Yes, baby. That was always what I wanted to do. Once Sugar Slope was well established, I wanted to bring Jade into the business. Not just as a partner, but to expand her event planning. Weddings, birthday parties, whatever she had in mind that would flourish in Montana."

Callie gazed in awe, her body relaxing. "That makes me feel better. I would never want you do to anything out of pressure because of me."

My fingers tangled with hers across the table until I found her eyes. "I love you, baby. Everything I do is *for* you...not because of you."

Callie teared up and softly shook her head before I heard the subtle sniffle of her tears, the soft hiccupping of her breaths. Squeezing her hand a little tighter, I longed to absorb everything she was feeling, hoping that a broken heart wasn't the cause of her emotion.

"You really are amazing, Alex," she huffed. "No man has ever made me feel so appreciated and loved."

"Callie, baby," I urged, needing her eyes again. "Look at me, sweetheart."

Ah.

There she is.

"You give me the same things every single day." I curled the side of my lip. "I treasure you."

She melted when I kissed the top of her hand, soon offering the brightest smile in the world, her lashes glittering with dew. "I love you, Alex."

I rose from my chair, needing her in my arms. She stood as my arms folded around her, clinging to my body. I closed my eyes and rubbed her back, breathing into her scalp, "I love you too, Callie. Forever."

I made sure she was alright before letting her go, glancing at my watch to see what time it was. Callie moved into the living room and started dusting the bookshelf where her movies lived, my lip twitching in remembering the first time I saw it.

"Baby, I found the perfect truck," I blurted, and she twisted her head around, mouth open.

"Really?"

"I was searching online and spotted it. But I want to know what you think." I reached for my phone and scrolled. "Now it's old, you know, like me, but," I laughed.

She peered over my arm, taking in the photos. "Oh, I love it. Not old. *Vintage*."

"She's from the early 90s."

"A Dodge Ram, huh?" She curled her lip. "Well, it's for sure with that orange color I'll be able to find you anywhere."

I cracked up, clicking my phone off. "You won't ever have to go looking."

She pecked my lips and continued cleaning. "Well, I think it's amazing."

"Yeah? I just figured we needed one, you know. Nothing fancy, but it would be great to have a vehicle to haul things. The nursery furniture coming to mind first."

She agreed with a warm glint in her eye. "Yes."

"I'm supposed to meet the salesman soon to take a look at it. Then, by God's grace, of course, I wanted to try to get in touch with Jade and head to her house to talk." I held my breath, hoping for the best. "Would you want to come with me, baby?"

Callie froze, brushing over her belly before answering, "No, I think I'll stay here. I want you and Jade to have time alone to talk."

Fuck, her maturity astounded me.

"Okay. Call if you need anything, okay? Anything at all." I raked through my ashy hair, falling in love with her even more. "I won't be long, baby."

"Think about what you want for dinner." She smacked her pretty lips against mine. "Although, I'm craving pizza."

"Hey, that's perfect." I grabbed my wallet and phone, planning to take Callie's car to the used car lot to check out the truck. Worst case scenario, I would get a buddy to help bring it back if the sale went through without any snags. "Bye, baby."

"Bye!" Callie waved and continued cleaning as I slipped outside into the unforgiving heat, my skin tacky already.

"Alright, Mr. Harrington, if you would sign here and here, you've got yourself not only a fantastic deal but one hell of a truck," Josh, the salesman, cheered and handed over a pen. Shit, he looked like he was barely out of high school. Thankfully, when it came to vehicles, I knew my shit and wasn't falling for any of the bogus tactics. I think I might have intimidated him a little in the beginning, but at least things were ending on a positive note. Honestly, I think he just wanted to get me the hell out of there.

"Thanks, man." I squiggled my name, and the deal was sealed, the keys jingling in my hand all the way outside as I dialed Jade and waited for her to pick up the video call, assuming she would decline, but when her face filled the screen, I nearly dropped the damn phone.

"You just don't quit, do you?" Her lip barely curved in a smirk, green eyes creased and stuck to the screen.

"Thank you for picking up," I exhaled, thrilled. "How are you?"

She shrugged and glanced away, bright copper hair running over her shoulders. "I'm okay, I guess."

I nodded, swallowing the burning lump that wanted out. "Jade, I—"

"I'm really sorry, Dad," she rushed every word. "About the reviews. There's no excuse for it. No matter how angry I was at you and Callie."

"Jade, thank you, but I didn't call to talk about that," I assured with a smile, and she teared up.

"You didn't?"

"No. Although I did want to talk to you about the lodge."

"Is everything okay in Montana?"

I smiled. "Yes, but I think it could be better."

She flashed a white smile, meeting my eye. "Okay, Dad, you have my attention."

"Good," I sighed. "Could we talk soon? In person?"

"Of course. I'm home today if you want to drop by." She squinted. "But first, what is that giant pumpkin behind you?"

I cackled out loud, holding the phone up so she could get a better view. "That would be my truck. What do you think?"

"Oh my God. Dad. How old is it?" She wrinkled her nose.

I clicked my tongue. "Oh, a little younger than you."

She let out a *psshh* sound and rolled her eyes. "That seems to be the common theme these days."

"Jade," I began, and she cut me off with a hearty laugh.

"Kidding, Dad."

I relaxed despite the bile creeping up my throat, wanting this to go well and not blow up in my face. "I'll be right over as soon as I put some gas in the pumpkin."

"You mean they didn't fill it up for you?"

"No," I scoffed. "But I think I got the better end of the deal either way."

Jade curled her lips, walking around her house. "Alright, Dad. I'll see you soon."

"See you soon, Jade."

Callie

I succumbed to the wave of exhaustion that turned my muscles into goo, nearly two hours passing since Alex had left for the dealership. The living room was spotless, but I could barely hold my eyes open on the sofa as I waited for a call or text from Alex to hear how things were going his way. I hoped all was well. Not only about the truck, but that Jade was open to talking with him. Maybe this door would allow me to talk to her again too. I missed her more every day.

My lashes felt like weights were dangling from them, so I rolled over and curled into a blanket, allowing them to close. I felt the subtle twitching of my body as I drifted further and further to sleep, only to be startled awake by a call, Jade's name across the screen not seeming real. Was I dreaming still?

"H-Hello?" I asked with caution, not believing she was reaching out to me.

"Callie!?" her panicked voice screamed, causing me to leap off the couch.

"Jade? I'm here. What's wrong?"

She was crying so hard I couldn't understand a word of what she was saying. I felt sick, realizing something catastrophic had happened for her to be calling me in the first place.

"Jade, I can't understand you." My limbs trembled as I paced the floor.

She took several big breaths and asked, "Is Dad there?"

"No." I held my breath. "He went to look at a truck and said he was trying to meet up with you."

"Fuck," she wept, sobbing her head off.

"Jade, please talk to me! What's wrong?" I yelled, feeling like there wasn't enough oxygen in the room to keep me alive. But what she said next nearly killed me, anyway.

"Dad was supposed to come to my house over an hour ago. He won't answer my calls or texts," Jade's voice went an octave higher. "So, I started driving toward the dealership, thinking maybe something had happened. He bought that old ass truck, so," she trailed, breaking down all over again.

I gripped the phone in silence, my heart about to beat out of my chest.

"I was forced to turn around because of an accident," Jade heaved into the phone. "I saw the truck, Callie. It's completely totaled."

My legs went numb as I fell into a chair, my throat closing in. "Wh-what?"

"I got as close as I could before they made me turn around," she choked. "They were loading someone into the back of an ambulance," she wailed. "Covered in a white sheet."

The phone fell out of my limp hand as I opened my mouth to scream, but no sound would come. No. This wasn't possible.

The sound of a vehicle screeching into my driveway gave me the energy I needed to get up, the door flying open, revealing my best friend, her ivory skin covered in red blotches from crying.

Her eyes fell to my belly, and she broke down all over again, running to me at full speed and taking me in her embrace, my mind hardly processing what was happening around us.

"He can't be gone," I protested. "Please, tell me everything again."

Jade's entire body shook, and I clung to her harder, two frail trees about to fall over if even the slightest gust of wind blew. "Cals," was all she could say.

I slumped over, holding my belly as I went to the trash bin in the kitchen, puking my entire stomach dry. "Jade, I know you hate me, but don't do this. Don't fuck around!"

Jade yanked her frazzled red mop, screaming, "Does it look like I'm fucking around?"

Another round of vomit into the trashcan. Soon, her arm supported my back, and she helped me stand, the room still spinning. "Why did you ask if he was here, then?"

Jade helped me into a chair, violently trembling. "Because I didn't want to believe it was his truck."

"How do you know what the truck even looks like?" I shouted, wanting her to be wrong.

"He video called me!" Jade gawked, eyes wild with shock. "It was an old as hell Dodge. Bright fucking orange."

"No," I hissed and charged across the room, swiping my phone off the ground. I called Alex over and over as Jade became more hysterical, his voicemail greeting sending me to my knees in grief. "No."

The soft rumbling of a vehicle caught our ears, and together we went to the front window, a police cruiser inching at a snail's pace closer and closer to my house.

Jade covered her lips and slammed her lashes closed as we held each other, cries wracking our throats and splitting our mouths wide open. We fell onto the floor, hearing footsteps in the distance, neither of us having the strength to face what was coming.

"Callie," Jade's shoulders bounced, my back facing the door as the knob rattled.

I could only break into her shoulder, not believing that the only love of my life was gone, when the door creaked open, and

Jade screamed and peeled herself off me into her father's arms, the man I thought was now a ghost standing before us…very much alive.

Chapter Thirty-Four

Alex

Throughout my journey of falling in love with Callie, I often wondered if my daughter would ever hug me again. It was a painful intrusive thought I pushed away each time it invaded my brain, but the possibility always lingered in the back of my mind that my relationship with her was just a memory. But as Jade latched onto me, weeping and wailing, I cherished the fact that she wasn't detested by me anymore, the future so much brighter now with her in it.

"What the fuck? How are you here right now?" she shrieked and pulled away from me, Callie crumpled on the floor looking like she was seeing a ghost.

I brushed Jade's arm but had to get to Callie, her face wrinkling as tears poured. "Baby."

I cupped her elbow and lifted her up, Callie's body vibrating from head to toe as she huffed, "We thought you were dead."

I swallowed, my mouth feeling like I was chewing cotton as I guided her into a chair, Jade's whimpers audible behind me. I sat next to Callie, not letting go of her hand, and Jade followed, her eyes the perfect blend of relief and rage.

"I went straight to the gas station after I called you, Jade," I explained, not even believing the turn of events myself. "I filled up the truck, started it, and realized my wallet was missing."

"So, you *did* buy the truck?" Callie blotted the corners of her lids, and I felt like a dick that I hadn't had the chance to tell her anything yet.

"Yes, baby. I bought the truck, called Jade, and it all went to hell."

Jade let out a frustrated sigh, urging me to go on.

"Before filling up, I bought a drink and paid for the gas inside. I assumed I left my wallet at the counter, so I went back in. No sign of it anywhere," I explained. "By the time I went back out, someone was driving my truck away. I had no phone or any way of getting in touch with either of you because I'm an idiot and don't have any numbers memorized."

Jade shook her head, stewing. "So, you leave the damn keys in your truck, with it running I might add, and someone stole it."

"Yes," I admitted, embarrassed as hell. "I was able to call the police from the gas station, which led to a chase. The cop who brought me home told me what happened. The man swiped my wallet from the counter before taking off in my truck. He crashed and was killed instantly."

Callie squeezed my fingers as fresh tears poured, Jade speaking up on her behalf. "Oh, believe me. I saw the truck. And the fucking dead body under a sheet. I thought that was you!"

Fuck.

"Jade," I croaked, blinking tears as my gaze shifted. "Callie, baby."

"Jesus, Mary, and Joseph, Dad." My daughter scooted her chair from the table and went into the kitchen, opening cabinet doors one after another until she found a bottle of whisky, unscrewing the lid and pouring herself a shot, chugging.

Callie's rapid breathing was hardly slowing down, the permanent look of dread still painted on her alluring face. Fuck. I hated that I was the cause. "Deep breaths, baby. I'm right here."

She shook her brunette locks and rushed to the kitchen sink, splashing icy water on her face as she softly moaned. Jade didn't hesitate to rub her back and offered a glass of water, whispering in her ear.

Seeing the two of them together warmed me to the bone, though I hated that I worried either of them to the point of breaking down. I knew it wasn't intentionally my fault but still felt utterly responsible, and while I wanted to hold them in my arms to ease their hearts, I held back, letting them have their moment instead.

Callie

"Thank you, Jade," I barely breathed above a whisper, receiving the icy glass of water and sipping.

"You're welcome," she smiled, and I cried all over again, not for Alex, but for the friend I thought was lost coming back into my life again.

Jade wrapped an arm around my shoulder and turned toward her dad, not hesitating to say, "Well, now that we know you're alive, I need a moment with Callie."

Alex's dimples formed, and he nodded in understanding, stepping outside to give us space. To be honest, I was still recovering from believing he was dead to having him back, my body so heavy I could have collapsed right there.

"Will you sit with me?" Jade asked, and I smiled, moving into the living room with her and sinking into the sofa.

Her bright green eyes studied my belly, and I offered a sheepish grin, the baby kicking like crazy.

"You're pregnant." Jade met my gaze, wearing a smile instead of the scowl I expected. "When are you due?"

I cleared my throat, surprised. "November."

Jade counted on her fingers and smirked. "God, Dad really *was* busy on Valentine's Day, huh?"

I flushed, not able to look at her as I bit my lip, trying to hold back a grin.

"Callie, please look at me."

I turned my head, wrestling with guilt and shame.

"I'm so sorry for the things I said," she whispered, her tone laced with heaviness. "The things I did."

I shook my head against budding emotion, breathing, "I'm sorry too, Jade. You have no idea how I wish I could go back and do things differently. I never wanted you to find out the way you did."

"Callie, if it makes you feel any better, my reaction would have been the same, regardless." Jade winced, her brutal honesty refreshing. "There's nothing you could have said or done differently that would have changed anything."

I let out a breath, a little relieved. "As happy as I was with Alex, my heart was in agony the entire time too. I never wanted to hurt you, Jade. Or lose you."

"I shut you out, Callie."

"But I deserved it."

"Did you, though?" Jade questioned. "You fell in love, Callie. And I made you feel like shit for it."

"No, Alex didn't belong to me, Jade. He belonged to you. You had every right to hate my guts."

"I never hated you, Callie. I could never."

My shoulders softened as she went on.

"I was jealous of you."

"You were?"

She nodded, overcome. "All this time, I refused to see the good you have brought into my dad's life, not because it wasn't there, Callie. Because I chose not to see it."

"Jade," I spoke, but she continued.

"And even thinking for a second that I lost my father today destroyed me that I had robbed him of being truly happy because of my own selfishness."

"You're not selfish."

"In this I was. I behaved like a spoiled brat. He raised me better." She closed her lips and grinned, a small chuckle coming out of me.

"He's the best man I've ever known, Jade." I glanced toward the door, seeing his shadow on the porch. "I don't deserve him."

"No, you do, Cals. I see that now." Her eyes fell to my belly. "And as shocked as I was in the beginning, I can't deny that I've only ever wanted my father to find true love and happiness." She wiped her eyes, lip quivering. "And I'm so thankful he did...with you."

I covered my face, crumbling into my palm as her arms came around me. "I love you, Jade."

"Oh, Cals." She squeezed me harder. "I love you, too. And to say I've missed you would be an understatement."

I laughed through the tears. "Did you burn my letters?"

She laughed and pulled back, drying her face. "No. I read them all. And I withered like a damn worm in the sun at the monster I had become. You deserved more from me."

"You deserved more from me too."

Jade stared off, appearing so deep in thought. "You have my support from here on out. That is a promise. For you. For Dad. For my brother or sister you are carrying."

I reached for her hand and held it against my bump, wanting her to feel the kicks. "I can't tell you what that means, Jade. I've longed to share so much with you and couldn't."

"I know," she admitted. "I'm here now, Cals. I'm not going anywhere."

Alex

I stared into the pink and purple horizon over the mountain range, my girls still inside the house talking things through. Leaning against the porch railing, I lit up my pipe and puffed, closing my eyes in thanks, wishing with all my heart that after tonight, Jade would be speaking with us, on good terms, of course.

The front door squeaked and out stepped my daughter, her cheeks and eyes puffy from crying. I blew a cloud of smoke and braced for impact, her hug disarming my sudden fear that things went south between her and Callie. On the contrary. They were stronger than ever before.

"Callie just fell asleep. I didn't want to wake her." She thumbed before sliding both hands into her pant pockets, scuffing a foot.

"Yeah." I read my watch. "I'm surprised she's stayed awake this long. Seven is typically lights out for her."

Jade laughed, "I mean, she wasn't really a night owl before, you know."

A warm smile lit up my face, listening to hear more, *needing* to hear more.

Jade's happy countenance drew serious, her red strands scattering with the summer wind. I took one last hit off the pipe and set it down, studying her harder, my life in her hands.

"I'm so sorry, Dad," she began, her voice wavering. "You have no idea how sorry."

"Jade, it's okay. Please don't cry."

"No, it's not," she pressed. "The night of your party when I saw you with Callie, I knew."

"Knew what?"

She tilted her head, pausing a second before finishing, "That you loved her."

A burning ball constricted my throat, wanting to break free. "Yes. I do love her, Jade."

"And seeing Callie tonight, the way her heart shattered at the thought of losing you." Jade bit her trembling lip. "In that moment, it wasn't just Callie I was looking at. I saw a woman who had lost the love of her life."

I hung my head as teardrops fell, not able to say another word.

"I guess I thought you were ashamed of the family you had before," Jade confessed, heavy eyes staring back at me. "As I told Callie, I was blind with jealousy."

"No. Never, Jade." I stepped closer. "I may have gotten a lot of things wrong over the years, but you...*you* were the only thing I did right back then."

She breathed a happy, choppy sigh, "Really?"

I opened my arms to her, holding my child, the young woman before me now. She cried in my chest, and I held her there, not letting go until she was ready. And once she pulled back, I curled the side of my lip, wanting to bring more light into this moment.

"Jade, I have a proposition for you."

Her back straightened. "A proposition?"

I nodded, smoothing over my silver hair. "I want you to partner with me at Sugar Slope."

Her lip fell open, though her eyes didn't believe it. "Wait a minute. You want to be business partners? With me?"

"Absolutely. Yes, I do."

She popped a ruddy brow, unsure. "Is this a bribe?"

I chortled, "Would it work?"

"Dad!"

"No, it's not a bribe. I've always wanted to bring you into the business. I just had to make sure things didn't flop first."

She winced. "Shit. That's what you meant when you said I was screwing myself out of money when I left those bogus reviews, huh?"

I pointed a brow, trying not to smile.

"Dammit."

"So, what's it going to be?" I nudged. "You up for helping your old man expand or what?"

"Expand?"

"Well, I was hoping you'd bring your services to Montana. Only if you wanted to, of course."

She tucked a copper thread behind an ear, eyes glittering. "You really trust me that much?"

I swallowed that damn lump again. "I do."

"Well, in that case, yes. I would be honored."

I offered my hand to shake hers, pulling Jade in for one more hug. A soft chuckle left her lips as I hung onto her, her last request stopping my heart.

"Promise me you'll take care of her, Dad. She deserves nothing but happiness."

"On my life, Jade." I looked her in the eye. "I promise you."

She nodded and wiped her eyes, an idea hitting me that I would need Jade's assistance with. "Hey, would you be able to help me with something?"

"That depends." She smirked.

"I think it would make Callie really happy," I added, watching my daughter's smile widen.

"In that case, tell me all about it."

Chapter Thirty-Five

Callie

I dreamt of the most beautiful white feathers falling from the sky like rain, one in particular tickling the side of my cheek. Only it wasn't a feather stirring me awake, but the subtle tracing of Alex's finger along my skin, his blue eyes so bright they almost glowed in the darkness.

"Alex?" I sat up, realizing I had fallen asleep before I wanted to. "Oh, no. Did Jade leave?"

"Relax, baby. She went home a little while ago." He rubbed my arm. "I just wanted to check on you."

"I didn't mean to doze off."

"I'm happy you were able to rest. Especially after, well, everything."

My heart tightened. It was only hours ago I believed Alex was gone from my life forever. I was still recovering.

"Oh, Alex." I curled my arms around his neck, savoring the cherry smoke aroma.

"I'm here, baby," he soothed. "Fuck, I'm so sorry I frightened you."

"I thought you were gone," I breathed into his neck. "My world stopped."

He fisted the back of my hair, fire burning from his eyes into my soul. Without a beat passing between us, he dove into my mouth, taking my lips into his, tasting me with husky moans.

"I was a fucking idiot for leaving those keys in the truck, Cal." He stopped kissing only to blurt that sentence. "God, I'm so sorry."

I felt my lips start to curve, enjoying the tantalizing kiss he was giving. "Mmm, how could you ever make it up to me?"

He growled into my mouth, our teeth clashing through a ravenous kiss. "Turn on your side."

Our lips broke apart with a wet smack, and I listened, Alex's long strokes through my hair creating static pops under my scalp. I didn't realize how much tension was there until he started rubbing along the sides of my neck, gathering my chunky waves at the base and tugging.

I moaned, the stress surrendering to Alex's touch.

"Feel good?" He let my hair go and massaged some more from behind, heat pooling between my legs.

"Yes," I croaked, eyes sealed.

I pulled my shirt off as his hands traveled down my spine, tender kneading and scratches causing chills to erupt in their path. His shaft swelled against my ass, and I stifled another groan, pushing my rump against him, a silent call to fill me.

"I can't imagine what you felt today, baby." He tugged his bottoms down, peeling his shirt off last. "The thought of losing you, Callie, fuck."

I chewed my lip, melting into his hot skin and chest hair. "Please, Alex."

He skated over the elastic around my hips and dragged them to my ankles where I kicked them off, rubbing my thighs to ease the pressure. Alex's smile brushed my ear as a whimper left me, his words arousing me as much as his body.

"I'm here to serve you, baby," he whispered. "Push that ass out a little more." I did as he requested, his silky tip gliding in and stopping. He waited before giving me more of him, my hand flying behind me to grab his hair all the cues he needed.

"Fuck, you're so tight, Cal. Am I hurting you?"

"No," I mewled.

He pushed a tad more but struggled to fit, offering a suggestion. "Bend this knee for me, baby."

I did as he said, my pussy opening a little more for him with my legs spread wider. Still, I was beyond comfortable, lying on my side, his cock sliding all the way in without any trouble.

"Fuck," I hissed, clenching around his length.

"Too much this way?" He rubbed my belly, inspecting me.

"No, it's perfect," I answered.

"You're perfect." He kept his cock fully in and circled my clit, kissing the back of my neck at the same time. I could only grip the back of his head, needing something to ground me. It felt like I would have floated away otherwise.

"Alex," I breathed, tingles conjuring another moan from my core, the sensation of being completely filled euphoric on its own.

"I have to ask you something, Callie," he said through choppy huffs.

"Now?" My clit pulsed against his finger as I chased the high, damn near delirious.

"Now, baby. Are you close?"

"Yes," a chuckle broke. "What could you possibly have to ask me?"

"Look at me, baby. Look at me before you come."

I twisted my head as he continued pleasuring me, hardly able to see straight with his swollen dick inside, his fingers rubbing my clit, creating the urge to push against an impending wave of ecstasy. They all worked together to bring us closer, his white smile hypnotic.

"Callie Jo Harper," his voice quivered. "I had no idea how lonely my life was, baby, until you."

My hand slid to hold his jaw, tears tracking my cheeks.

"It's hard to imagine who I was before you, Callie. Like the sun, you have brought warmth and life to my soul." He grazed my belly, gently thrusting. "A life that only exists when we're together."

I wept, "Alex."

"You are mine and I am yours," he purred in my ear. "Everything I am is yours, Callie. To serve you. Protect you. Love you."

I shuddered, nearly coming.

"Marry me, baby." His lips barely touched my ear, subtle grunts breaking through as he climbed higher with me, his cock turning to stone. "Let me take care of you and our family for the rest of my life."

"Yes!" I cried out, answering him as my legs shook, my desire to be married matching the stars in my eyes as I finished, Alex jerking inside of me, not letting go.

"Was that a yes to me?" He smirked, swiping the loose hair from my forehead.

My body responded just as much, shivering as my pussy wept tears of his release. "That was a yes to everything. To you. To us. To the life we have made together."

Alex hummed in complete satisfaction as our lips met, carefully gliding himself out of me as his eyes danced along my face. "Don't move."

I covered my chest with the sheet, watching him scoot off the bed and rummage through his jeans. I squinted to see what he was doing, the velvet box in his hand making my eyes water.

He returned to the bed and nestled close, cracking open the lid. "Thank God I didn't leave this in the pumpkin."

I busted out laughing, admiring the round solitaire sitting in yellow gold. "Alex, it's breathtaking."

"Do you really like it, baby?" He flinched as if my answer would be anything else.

"I love it, babe."

He bit his lip, smiling, and removed the ring, the cold metal sliding over my knuckle with ease. Even in the darkness, it glittered, so much like the beginning of my relationship with Alex, a bright star guiding us out of the misery we were in.

He cupped my belly as the baby kicked and kicked, taking it all in. I ruffled through his hair and hugged him closer, planting my lips on his forehead. "Are you scared, Alex?"

"Of what, baby?"

"Of starting over. At this point in your life?"

"No," he said without pause. "The thought of not starting over with you scares me more. I would be so empty inside, baby." I melted when he kissed my stomach, gazing up at me. "I love you, Callie. You've given me a life I never thought was possible. And that is nothing short of miraculous."

I sighed, "Thank you for never giving up on us, Alex. When I was the most afraid, you stayed strong."

"You are my strength, Callie." He pecked my lips. "And that will never change. No matter how much time goes by."

"You are my strength too. Forever."

Chapter Thirty-Six

Callie

Halloween

"I can't believe you agreed to this." I dabbed a brush into a mound of blue eyeshadow and painted Jade's lids, topping it off with red lipstick, a lot of hairspray, and teasing.

"How could I say no to you?" She rubbed her teeth in the mirror, completely decked out in leg warmers, heels, and an oversized band tee. "You're the cutest pregnant 80s mom in the whole world."

I glanced in the mirror, my bump barely fitting in a thrifted pair of acid-wash jeans, hair just as big as my stomach. "I think we look pretty cute together."

"Absolutely." Jade agreed with a wink.

I turned to the side, slouching my top off one shoulder. "I can't wait to hear what the trick or treaters say!"

"Right! Will they get it, though?"

"Probably not. But this is for us not them," I teased.

"Amen to that!" Jade read her watch. "Oh no! It's almost time! Where is Dad, anyway? Wasn't he supposed to be picking up the candy?"

Before I could reply, my phone rang, Alex's concerned voice on the other end making me freeze in position.

"Callie? Hey baby."

"Hey. Are you okay?"

"Yes. I'm totally fine, but my truck isn't. I have a flat tire."

I slapped my forehead, meeting Jade's concerned stare. "What happened?"

Alex grumbled, "I must have run over a nail or something. Shit. I'm so sorry, baby. Is there any way you could pick me up?"

"Where are you?" I smirked, shaking my head with a smile at Jade. Alex rattled off a few street names that I recognized. Thankfully, he wasn't too far away. Halloween wasn't canceled after all.

"We will be right there," I assured and hung up as Jade grabbed her keys before we rushed to her vehicle, driving down the road to Alex in no time.

"Dad needs to stop buying trucks, for fuck's sake." Jade scanned left to right, searching. "He's getting a damn bike for Christmas."

I lost it, not bable to ignore the irony. "He's still grieving over the pumpkin, as you call it. This second truck is just a rebound affair."

"Oh hell," Jade chuckled. "That's it. A bike for North Carolina and a new pair of skis for Montana."

I rubbed my belly, thinking about the future. So much was on the horizon. Our baby's arrival next month, first and foremost. Sugar Slope Lodge would also be opening for its first season with Jade and Alex running things together. And our wedding, which we were still trying to figure out. Jade insisted I let her throw me the celebration of a lifetime. Still, I wanted something private and quaint.

"Wait, you just passed it." I whipped my head around and read the green street sign. "Alex said—"

Jade gave me the side eye, her half-grin speaking louder than words. I watched her zoom right past the area where Alex told me he was waiting and turn into the parking lot of Meadow Inn, shrugging. "Hm. Looks like his truck is perfectly fine to me."

I spotted Alex's new pickup in the back of the lot, butterflies swimming in my belly as much as the baby. Jade's eyes glittered as she parked the car and opened her door, soon looping her arm through mine and marching toward the entrance.

"What in the world are you up to?" I clutched her elbow as we stepped inside Meadow Inn, classic rock music tickling my ear.

She didn't utter a single thing but led me toward the banquet hall, a Journey song becoming clearer the closer we walked. I caught the faintest glimpse of pink and blue balloons as we approached the glassy door. Jade winked and cracked it wide open, a giant banner reading, *She's Having a Baby*, catching my eye first with the love of my life directly under it, dressed in a gorgeous 80s suit and sunglasses.

"You threw me a baby shower?" I squealed to Jade as Alex started walking over.

"An *80s* themed baby shower!" Jade clapped as the guests cheered, all of them wearing an array of tapered pants, shoulder pads, and neon tracksuits.

I covered my mouth, breathing the words *thank you* to my best friend as Alex gave his daughter a high-five and pulled me in for a warm hug.

"Did we get you?" he laughed, wearing a stunning hunter green blazer and matching dress pants, loose in the leg but cutting in at the waist with a tan belt. His black shirt stretched tight across his chest as his gold necklace dangled on top, my eyes rising to see his luscious hair gelled at the sides and swooped in front. My God. A makeshift mullet. Be still my heart.

"You absolutely got me!" I kissed his pouty lips, tasting fresh mint.

"You deserve it, baby. This and more."

Mom suddenly appeared and wrapped me in her arms, decked out in a black tulle skirt and lace tights looking like Madonna. "Surprise!"

"Thank you, Mom!" I squeezed her to death, soon receiving warm hugs from distant relatives I hadn't seen in years, old friends and coworkers alike. It warmed my heart to see Alex's people too, the support on his side just as strong.

"Alex, this is—" I memorized every detail of the room, his dreamy face most of all.

"I love you, baby." He took me under his arm, smooching my frizzy head as the live band started playing *Somebody to Love*, the lead singer's voice familiar.

"Congratulations to the lovely Callie Jo Harper and her radically righteous hunk, Alex. It looks like they've already found somebody to love." The young man ran his fingers along the piano, his blonde wig and big sunglasses disguising him.

The song continued playing, and I glanced at Jade. "No way. Is that Brendan!?"

She clicked her tongue. "He's a man of many talents."

I laughed out loud, taking it all in as Alex laced our fingers together, speaking softly in my ear. "I know technically this is a baby shower, but would you want to dance with me?"

I tilted my poofy head of hair, swooning more by the minute. "I thought you'd never ask. I have to warn you though, I have two left feet."

"Oh, I'm not worried." Alex twirled me under his arm, pulling me close as our bodies swayed. Thankfully, I had Converse sneakers on, but was still nervous about stepping on his toes.

Others surprisingly joined in as Brendan's band belted the remainder of the Queen song. Alex held me tighter, the slight lift of his lip stealing the air in my chest, especially when he said, "You are stunning."

"Yeah? Think I can rock this look on the daily?"

"Hell yeah," he laughed. "You could rock any look and be gorgeous."

"Well, I can say the same for you. I have never seen a more handsome man in my life."

He blushed. "I was hoping you'd like it."

"I love it!" I brushed the lapel of his jacket. "Was this your suit from prom or something?"

He cracked up. "No, baby. I never went to the prom."

"Oh. Well, if it makes you feel any better, my prom sucked. You didn't miss much."

His dimples popped. "This is better."

"Much better." I received his sweet kiss as the band ended on a crescendo, the guests moving to their tables with dinner being served. No fish this time. Soup, salad, and a giant cake.

After dinner, I mingled at every table, delighted in the happy atmosphere. Everyone was so uplifting and encouraging, even people I didn't know. It was beyond refreshing to have this much support when not that long ago, I wasn't sure if we would ever have it. I was eternally grateful. For myself and Alex.

Once the plates were empty and the gifts were opened, guests began trickling out one by one until there was no one left but us, including the band, who started packing up their equipment.

Jade soon approached with Brendan at her side, a small book of some sort in her hands. And once Brendan removed his long blonde wig and glasses, he opened his arms to me, cheering, "Congratulations again, Callie!"

I hugged him and slowly let go. "You guys were phenomenal. How have I not heard of you!?"

"Ah, we don't get out like this much. I hope you enjoyed it."

"Every minute. Thank you so much for coming!"

"My pleasure." He shook Alex's hand next. "Congrats, man."

"Thank you, Brendan. For everything."

Jade passed the book into my hands, wearing the cheesiest grin. "Dad said you wanted to see him in the 80s. Well, here you go, sis."

I clutched the old leather album, surprised yet again. "This is the greatest gift you could have ever given me."

Alex rubbed this side of his jaw, turning red. "Eh, you haven't seen them yet."

"Thank you," I addressed Jade. "Truly."

My best friend hugged me tight, pecking my cheek. "I love you, Cals. I'm so happy for you."

"Thank you, Jade," I whispered back. "I can't tell you what that means."

"You don't have to. I know," she breathed with a smile, pulling back to look at me. "We'll talk soon, yeah? That baby will be here before we know it."

I touched my belly, meeting her warm gaze. "Before we know it."

Alex and I waved goodbye as Jade and Brendan left, the band slipping out the back door too. We were the only ones left in the party room and wandered to an empty table to take a glimpse of the past, Alex's permed hair and cutoff denim shorts on the first page.

"Oh my God. This is amazing." I flipped through the pictures, admiring the man Alex used to be just as much as the man he was now. "Wait. Is that your—"

"Dad? Yes." Alex pointed, his fragrant cologne filling my senses as he leaned closer. My heart surged. It was a photo of Alex and his father sitting on an old brown sofa, shaggy carpet under their feet.

I noticed the necklace around Alex's throat and realized this was likely one of the last photos of his father. Our eyes crashed in recognition, the ball in Alex's throat hopping. "Ah, I was annoying the hell out of him this night. One of the few evenings I remember having fun with my parents. Mom took the picture."

I sank inside, watching the memory flood Alex's blue eyes. His mouth rested comfortably on a fist as he drank in the photo, lashes batting against welling tears.

"Oh, Alex. I'm so sorry. We don't have to—"

He touched my hand that started closing the album, kissing it next. "No, baby. I want to share this with you. All of me."

A single tear broke through and rolled over his cheek, crossing his lip. I kissed the wet spot and brushed it dry, gazing at another page with him. "Your mother was gorgeous, Alex."

"Yes. She was."

I studied the old photo, yellowed with age, then stared at the man I loved a moment. "You have her eyes. But your beautiful smile, babe, belongs to your dad."

A choppy breath vibrated his chest, his giant hand taking one of mine. He captured me with both—his enchanting irises and that pouty lip that stopped me in my tracks every time.

"Oh, I wish they were here to meet you. To meet our baby. Poor Jade never had the opportunity, either. They would have loved you all so much."

My thumb skidded over the top of his hand as I waited for his eyes to find mine. And when they did, I whispered, "They *are* here, Alex. You sharing their photos with me, giving me a peek into the lives they had, it keeps them with us."

Alex's chest inflated with a huge breath, blue flecks not leaving mine. He held it, pecs puffed until he wrapped an arm around me, not letting the air go until I was against him. "Ahhhh," was all he could say, breathing out.

"Are you alright?"

He pressed his lips to mine, a gentle moan bleeding into my mouth. "You leave me speechless so often, baby. Fuck, how are you mine?"

"I ask myself that all the time about you." The edge of my lip curved, my cheeks filling with blood. "I'm so happy it was you in that bright yellow coat who whizzed by and knocked me on my butt."

A deep laugh brewed and bubbled out of his belly, his forehead resting on mine. "I fell not long after, baby. I fall harder every day."

Chapter Thirty-Seven

Callie

Our daughter's arrival less than a week later gave us all the shock of our lives, a 911 call and home delivery not at all what we were prepared for. I had the most energy since the start of my pregnancy and spent the day shopping for Thanksgiving dinner and some last-minute items for the baby. I went to bed as usual with Alex, only to be wakened by the most excruciating pain of my life, the baby's head nearly out of me.

Alex couldn't have been more supportive through his own fear, having to put his worries aside and deliver the baby himself until help arrived. Now, as we celebrated Thanksgiving at home with Mom, Jade, and Brendan, they could see for themselves the effect our baby had on him.

"Dad, why don't you let me hold her so you can eat?" Jade waited to sit down, Alex moving around the kitchen carrying Sunny in one arm.

"No, you guys go on. I've got her."

Jade elbowed me at the table, laughing under her breath. "I think you broke Dad."

I giggled, watching Alex talk to our daughter, gently bouncing her. "He's been on edge ever since, well—"

"He had to play catcher?" Jade bit her lip, trying not to laugh.

"I'm surprised his hair hasn't turned completely white," I teased. "It's been three weeks. And he's hardly put her down."

"Well, you're keeping him young, mama." Jade took a bite of turkey. "Or I should say, little Sunny is."

Alex appeared behind me, setting a plate filled rim to rim with turkey ham and every side dish prepared. His fragrant arm crossed my vision once more as he set a large glass of water before me, the baby practically snoozing in the crook of his elbow.

"Alex?" I whispered. "Babe, let me take her."

"No," he whispered back with a wink, sitting down with his own plate and eating with one hand.

Mom smiled as she ate across from me, Brendan's lashes creasing as he did the same. God, he was so kind. So attentive. More than I ever imagined possible.

"So, I know this might sound a little crazy, but I've been thinking about your wedding." Jade gestured with her fork. "Now, I know you want something small, even though I highly disagree. But what about the lodge around Christmas? Most of the guests will be gone. We could have the coziest ceremony in one of the new reception halls. What do you think?"

I met Alex's warm stare, his knowing smile matching mine. Jade read the tender expression between her father and me, squinting with suspicion. "Okay, what's going on here?"

Alex cradled Sunny, swallowing a bite of sweet potato. "Well, it's just that we sort of already found a place to have the wedding."

"And it's not Sugar Slope?" Jade furrowed her brow, red wisps decorating her cheeks.

"No, it's actually a lot closer." I reached for my phone. "We're waiting to hear back from them about possible dates."

Jade took the phone from me, silently scrolling through the pictures. She released a pleasant sign and stared at me with tearful eyes, the smile on her face telling me she approved.

"This is you, Cals." Her lip quivered a little. "This is perfect."

Chapter Thirty-Eight

Callie

I would have married Alex any day of the year, but the fact that we were about to take our vows as husband and wife on New Year's Eve with our immediate family watching was the absolute perfect ending to an already perfect year, not to mention we were surrounded by six stories of books in one of the most stunning historic libraries in the country.

Alex's hands swallowed mine, rattling with nerves as we took in the atmosphere, a skylight above our heads surrounded by breathtaking archways and columns that caged around countless books like a ladder toward the ceiling.

Round lights were strung on every story, illuminating the library in the warmest, softest glow. My eyes could hardly take in everything, the marbled floors, fresh flowers, and golden tables barely skimming the surface of the fairy tale I was experiencing, a dream wedding only meant for a princess.

I shook my head against brimming tears, the pride in Alex's chest blooming across his face. When I was happy, he was happy. But we were beyond that fleeting emotion that so often comes and goes. Wedding or not, we walked in pure joy together, any fear of the future nonexistent as long as we were there to face it all together.

"You're beautiful, baby," Alex's choppy voice spoke as we stood on the white podium, fingers locked and shaking.

"So are you," I echoed, watching a tear glide over his cheek.

Mom held a sleeping Sunny in her arms with Jade and Brendan next to her, our guest list including only them. We loved the intimacy of it all, not wanting it any other way.

Alex let one of my hands go only to reach inside his jacket for his glasses and a slip of paper, reading the vows he had written, the huskiness of his tone like a warm blanket around me.

"Love came unexpectedly for me," Alex began. "On one particular snowy afternoon, on a mountain I had traveled countless times over. She was there. And I whizzed right by her."

We quietly laughed as his dimples formed, his blue eyes glazed as he continued. "Thank God that wasn't the end of our story, but just the beginning. A start to something so rare and precious, I still can't believe it's real."

I breathed his name as he smiled through weepy eyes, squeezing my hand. "Love waits for no one. It comes when we least expect it, in the most unlikely and untimely ways. We have to snatch it while it's before us, hold onto it, cherish it, protect it. Otherwise, like an ember dying in the cold, it will be gone."

Our eyes locked, fresh confidence sweeping over Alex's gaze as he finished. "You have brought life back into my world, Callie. Through the light that you carry within yourself, the warmth of your nurturing spirit, the fire of your love and honesty, the hope in your smile and laughter. With you, there is no doubt or fear. Without you, though, my love, I would carry both."

He clutched my long white sleeve, rubbing the silk. "For so long, I believed it was my destiny to live alone. You changed that for me, Callie. You took this lonely heart and held it in your hands, healing the broken parts without ever realizing it."

I swallowed a sob that wanted to break out, listening harder as tears streamed.

"No amount of time could ever change my love for you. It grows every single day." He stared at our baby and crumbled a little more. "Because of you, there will always be a piece of us on this earth long after we're gone. How could I ask for anything more in this life? To love and be loved in return."

"Alex," I sighed, completely overcome.

"I'm yours for eternity, Callie. In this life, the next, wherever our souls go, I promise to be there with you always. I love you."

Alex

As mesmerizing as the scenery was inside the historic masterpiece that surrounded us from every angle, nothing held a candle to the woman before me, an angelic vision of heavenly white latching onto my hands for dear life as I concluded my vows to her.

Her cheeks were glassy from crying, rich brunette waves decorating them on either side. I reached into my pocket for a small cloth tissue and barely blotted the wetness from her skin, the fabric as light as a butterfly's wings caressing her face.

She smiled despite her overwhelming emotion, hiding her hands inside of mine. I curled the side of my lip, holding her with my gaze just as much, and winked, telling her, *I've got you, baby*, without having to breathe a syllable.

"For so long, I thought I knew what love was," Callie began, speaking from her heart. "I truly thought that *this*, what I've experienced with you, only happened inside of books. Not in real life. Surely, something this beautiful can only be born from a fantasy put to paper to give us something to dream about when we need to escape from real life. That was me, Alex. My heart wanted to believe there was more, but I didn't think it was possible or even that a man like you existed. You destroyed both of those walls, letting me see and experience for myself that I was worthy of love like that."

I nodded, wishing I could hold her in my arms.

"I cherish the man you are. The strength you carry inside of yourself that calls me to follow you, to be protected and loved by you."

I blew a quivering sigh, head swaying against budding emotion.

"You are more than anything I could have dreamed for myself. The love you have not only for me, but your daughters floods my heart with so much peace and joy. I'm honored to be by your side, Alex. To experience life with you."

I scarcely uttered her name, choking up.

"Thank you more than anything for giving me your heart. I promise to protect it, to hide it inside of mine when you need comfort, to guard it as much as you guard mine." She flashed a heart-stopping smile, ruby lips begging to be kissed. "I will love you forever, Alex. You and only you."

I hardly pushed the gold over her knuckle and wrapped Callie in my arms, her full lips crashing into mine before we could wait another second. While everyone clapped and cheered, everything seemed to fall silent. It was just us in that moment, the whooshing of my heart pounding in both ears as I held my wife, knowing there would never be another on earth for me.

Callie

Jade and I finished our slices of wedding cake, watching Alex cradle Sunny in his arms as he spoke with Mom and Brendan across the reception area. I smiled watching his upper body gently sway back and forth, the baby's eyes falling shut again already.

"So, Mrs. Harrington, does this mean you are my stepmom now?" Jade set her fork down and sipped champagne, green eyes creasing in humor.

I coughed, inhaling buttercream frosting. "No. We have to come up with another title because that one isn't going to work."

Jade laughed, swirling her glass around in thought. "Well, technically you *are* my stepmother, however," her voice tapered.

I gulped, trying to read her.

"You are so much more than that." She touched my hand, glancing at her dad for a second.

"Jade," I struggled, meeting her approving eye.

"You're my best friend, Cals. That trumps everything."

I opened my arms and clung to Jade, releasing a soft cry over her shoulder. Flashes of us as kids popped into my brain, a lifelong friendship growing into something stronger than I ever thought possible. She was more than my friend. She was family. Regardless if we shared the same last name. "I love you, Jade."

"I love you too, Cals. Always."

Alex

Sunny squirmed in my arms as I watched my wife and daughter embrace at their little table, the sight of their hug warming my heart so much I was grinning ear to ear. The baby squealed, rooting to nurse, and Callie shot up in seconds, rushing toward me to take our daughter.

"Hey, baby girl," Callie whispered, and Sunny cooed. "Oh no. Where should I take her?"

"Already taken care of, baby. Follow me." I grazed the small of her back and guided us to a private room just down the hall, complete with a rocking chair and pillows.

"Alex," she breathed, eyes swelling in gratitude.

"Hang on, Cal. Let me help you." I lifted her hair to unzip the back of her dress as the top fell forward, the breast pads in Callie's bra full. I rummaged through Sunny's diaper bag and opened a couple more, taking the soiled ones and tossing them for my wife as the baby latched on, milk drunk already.

"What would I do without you?" Callie stared at me like I was the king of the world, the look in her eye turning my insides to mush.

"I ask myself that question all the time too," I answered, wanting her to know she was just as precious to me.

She bit her lip, drawing it between her teeth, cheeks flushing. "I can't believe we're married now."

"It's amazing, isn't it?"

"I don't think my heart has slowed down since you read your vows." She blotted her eye, head softly shaking. "I'm still speechless."

I took the empty chair next to her and sat down, raking through my short salt and pepper undercut, not able to resist kissing her again.

She tasted so sweet with a hint of salt, a blend of wedding cake and a day's worth of emotion collected in her open hollow. Her lipstick smeared a little on me, but I didn't mind. I wanted more than that on me, if I'm being honest.

"I'm glad I went first because I wouldn't have been able to say a thing after your vows, baby," I professed, the anthem of her love for me still ringing in my ears.

She looked down at our child, her breasts engorged with milk as Sunny drifted to sleep. I reached into the diaper bag again and offered Callie the wipes that she liked as she took one with a smile, thanking me.

Sunny popped off a nipple, and I chuckled under my breath, stretching my big hands to take my little girl so Callie could clean up.

Callie passed me the pink bundle that held my heart and carefully wiped her chest, adjusting the pads and fastening the nursing bra back into place. I watched my wife, the elegant creature as she was, and lost every thought in my head at the reality that she was mine and I was hers.

"Are you alright?" Callie asked, pulling her dress back over both shoulders.

"Oh, yeah." I blinked rapidly, nostrils flaring and eyes watering. "You're just...so beautiful, baby. I'm taking you all in. The beautiful wife and mother you are."

She stroked the black sleeve of my jacket, eyes on fire. "I'm only a wife and a mother because of you, Alex. Never forget that."

Callie rested her cheek against mine, and I broke, holding our baby in one arm and my wife in the other. For as long as I lived, I wanted nothing more than to give her the world, the woman who brought my dead heart back to life. The woman who healed every fiber of my wounded spirit. She had to be from a heavenly place to reach into my soul the way she did and mend the old and broken wounds. That I was sure of.

"I would go through it all over again, Alex. To be here with you now."

"Yes," I wept, kissing her soft lips. "Everything."

Epilogue

5 Years Later

Alex

The frigid air whipped against my cheeks as I coasted along the frosty mountain, my muscles nice and warm despite the winter chill. Gliding toward the end of the slope, my skis gradually slowed until I was completely stopped, a bright green blur suddenly zipping by, the unexpected gust causing my body to topple over straight into the snow.

"Babe!" Callie called, soon standing over me, stretching the cutest red mitten from her kelly green sleeve. "I'm so sorry!"

I took her hand, laughing, "My life flashed before my eyes."

"It did?" She squeezed my fingers a little more, out of breath.

"Yes." I tugged her toward me until our chests brushed, kissing her. "You."

"Alex," she whispered, breathless.

I kissed her again and sat up straight, offering my gloved hand and standing with my wife. "Let's head back, huh? It'll be dark soon, and we have to get these kids to bed before Santa can come."

Callie cracked up with a seductive grin. "Well, in that case, *Santa,* we better hurry."

"Mmm. Dirty girl," I growled and pecked the side of her freezing cheek as our little slice of heaven came into view, an upgraded cabin to spend Christmas together at Sugar Slope.

We removed our skis and stomped off the snow before slipping inside, our babies running toward us, Christmas Eve giving them all the zoomies.

"Daddy!" Sunny ran the fastest, dark brown hair like her mother in braided pigtails bouncing with every step. She crashed into my chest and wrapped her little arms around my neck, her nose covered in flour.

"Look at you." I lifted her up. "I think someone has been baking."

Jade called from the kitchen, licking icing off a thumb. "She's a pro! You should see these sugar cookies!"

I laughed as our twin sons rushed to their mommy, barely two with lighter hair like mine. Well, before it turned gray.

"Boys!" Callie scooped one in each arm, eyeing their sticky fingers. "You have been baking too, I see."

Brendan winced from the kitchen, raising his hands in surrender. "I tried supervising but—"

We cracked up, not needing any sort of explanation. Max and Miles without a doubt kept us on our toes, but we wouldn't have had it any other way.

"Let's get a bubble bath and wash up. It's almost Christmas!" Callie pecked each of their cheeks and leaned over to smooch Sunny's. God, she loved our kids so much. She was the most empathetic mother I had ever seen.

"Can I finish decorating the cookies, Daddy?" Sunny's sweet voice asked. My heart.

"Absolutely. I want to help too." I set her down, and she trotted off to Jade and Brendan, who were at the table piping red and green icing on baked snowmen.

"Take a look!" Jade held up a blue snowflake covered in blue sugar crystals.

"You made this?" I cooed, in awe. "Sunny, that's beautiful!"

"Thanks, Daddy." She plopped into a chair and began the next cookie, Jade and Brendan smiling ear to ear.

I stood next to Jade, watching Sunny continue her work. "Thank you both for watching the kids for a bit. We appreciate it."

"You and Callie were gone, what, less than an hour? We had a great time!" Jade assured.

"The best time," Brendan chimed in. "Kids make the holidays so fun."

"They sure do." I kept an eye on Sunny, then turned to Jade. "They *still* do."

"Dad." Jade curled her lip and leaned her head into me.

I smiled, my heart so full. "I love you both. And you, Brendan. You're my kid now too, you know."

"He's pretty great, isn't he?" Jade winked, her new wedding band shining.

"The feeling is mutual, Alex." Brendan finished the last cookie and went to the sink to wash his hands.

"Thank you so much again for the Christmas gift, Dad. We cannot wait to go to Europe for our honeymoon." Jade beamed, my chest swelling with pride that I was able to do this for them.

"You are so welcome." I reached for a mug and filled it with cider. "You deserve a break with all the events you've been doing. Sugar Slope has never been busier...or better."

Max and Miles screeched down the hallway into the kitchen, wearing elf pajamas and slippers. I knelt, and they charged me as I pretended to play dead, Callie soon approaching, belly laughing.

"Who let these dinosaurs in here, huh?" I blew on their cheeks until the air in their lungs ran out from laughing so hard, my wife dabbing her lashes and going to Sunny, hugging her from behind.

"Well, good luck getting those little T-rexes to bed, Dad." Jade smirked, grabbing her coat. "I think they've got a case of the Christmas jitters."

"Oh, I'm not worried." I swooped one in each arm, holding them on my hips. "They'll be out in no time."

Callie hugged her best friend, still giggling. "Thank you so much for watching them for us."

"It was my pleasure. I love kids, you know. Especially when I can give them back!" Jade laughed and took Brendan's hand, guiding him to the door. Their cabin was just around the corner.

"Merry Christmas! We'll see you bright and early for breakfast!" Callie cheered with a wave.

"Not too early," Jade teased and slipped outside with her husband. I watched to make sure they made it safely inside their cabin from the window, returning my attention to the little ones who were counting down the seconds until Christmas morning.

"Alright, kiddos. Pick out a book!" I exclaimed, and they scurried like little mice down the hallway. Callie fell into my side with the biggest smile on her face, eyes drinking me in, her sweet kiss making my belly jump.

"Daddy! Where are you!?" Sunny demanded and I raced with my wife into the kids' room, our three little bears all gathered at the bookshelf.

"Twas the Night Before Christmas? Ah. A classic, Sunny girl." I received the hardback my daughter held in the air. Soon, the kids were crawling into the giant bed, burrowing under the covers as I started the story.

Callie was wedged in between them, curling them under her arms like a mother hen protecting her chicks, taking my breath away. God, I loved them more than life.

I lowered my voice and gently read each word on the page as their little eyes grew heavy, all three snoring by the end of the story.

My wife pecked their heads and slithered out of bed as quietly as she could, turning off the light and standing close to me. I couldn't leave without tucking them in a little more. Once we made sure they were truly sound asleep, we tiptoed out of the room, placed their gifts under the Christmas tree, and snuck into our bedroom.

Callie turned on the jetted tub at once, each of us stripping down and climbing into the steamy bath. Fuck, her body. Her curves. She didn't hesitate to straddle me, her full breasts dunking in and out of the water.

"Another perfect Christmas for the books, Santa," she whispered, grazing my cheeks.

"Mmm," I cupped her luscious ass, hard as hell already. "We pulled off another one, Mrs. Claus."

"You're such a good father," she breathed, kissing my neck. "I love you so much."

"Cal," I moaned through a throaty swallow. "I've never seen a more beautiful mother in my entire life. You bring me to my knees every day, baby. Every time I see you with them."

She raised herself up just enough to take me, crashing down on my cock as it disappeared inside of her. I gripped her hips, moving with her, losing myself with every stroke, every enthralling yelp that broke through her ruby mouth.

I stared at my wife, her beautiful head rolling back in bliss, and remembered how it all began. Here in the mountains, two lonely hearts colliding in the most extraordinary but unexpected way. Tears filled my eyes as she rode me, flashes of the past scrolling through my mind one precious snapshot at a time, forcing a broken huff out of my chest, my wife's eyes slowly cracking open to look at me.

Her glittery smile illuminated my heart just as much as the white Christmas lights draped around the cabin. And with another soft kiss, she kept rocking into me, clinging to my skin, fingers weaving through my salt and pepper wisps. I growled as she pumped harder, squeezing her locks with both fists, feeling as though I couldn't get close enough to her.

Callie's open lips hit the top of my shoulder as her body shivered under my touch, a weak cry falling into my skin not long after. I wrinkled my brow and held her tighter, unable to hold back another second, firing into her body, the come of my release, the passion of my love.

Choppy pants filled the space between us, steam curling around our faces as we gasped for air. The water sloshed as our limbs erupted from the brim, heat overpowering our bodies, forcing us out of the bath.

I reached for a towel and wrapped it around my wife, lifting her in my arms, needing her close to me. She bit her sweet lip and locked her baby blues on mine, her soul crying for me as much as her voice.

"Alex?" She paused, watching a couple of tears spill from my lashes. "Babe, what is it?"

I closed my wobbly lip, locking eyes with my wife. "I'm just grateful, baby. So fucking grateful."

She folded her arms around my neck and sighed, long brown waves painting her shoulders. "We've made a beautiful life together, haven't we?"

I fucking choked, my heart exploding in thankfulness for the years we had spent together and the years that were to come. "Yes, baby. We certainly have."

Thank You

As an author, more than anything else, my dream is to write a story that others will connect with. It is true that writing comes with a slew of ups and downs, but when the story is complete and finds the reader it was created for, well, that is nothing short of magic.

Thank you to every reader who has taken a chance on my work. It is appreciated more than you know.

Reviews are critical, especially for indie authors like me! If you enjoyed My Best Friend's Dad, please consider hopping over to Amazon and leaving a review or simply a rating. You are not only helping more readers discover this series but also supporting me as I continue pursuing this dream of mine.

Much love to all of you!

~Courtney

About the Author

Courtney Roberts is a contemporary romance and children's book author on Amazon's growing platforms, Kindle Unlimited and Kindle Vella. She has recently branched into the fantasy genre as well and enjoys going where the characters take her. Regardless of the genre, Courtney loves sharing her heart, from her heart to your library, one story at a time.

Aside from writing, Courtney loves spending time with her husband, Kevin, a United States Air Force veteran, homeschooling her two boys, Grant and Lincoln, and enjoying the simple things in life, like a cup of dark roast in the morning.

To see all of Courtney's work in one place, check out her link tree!

https://linktr.ee/courtneyroberts_writes

TikTok: @courtney_roberts_writes

Instagram: @courtneyroberts_writes

Facebook Group: @Romance Books by Courtney

Email: courtneyrobertsauthor@gmail.com

Printed in Great Britain
by Amazon